The Miscreant

In his new book, a collection of fiction entitled *The Miscreant, Selected Stories 1949-2016*, Victor Rangel-Ribeiro returns to his fictional Tivolem, giving us fresh glimpses into the inner life of this unique corner of the world. What makes Tivolem distinctive is that the village is deeply rooted in its own soil while also being extremely consmopolitan: many of its inhabitants have lived in other countries and continents, often in far corners of the Portuguese Empire. Victor himself partakes fully of this cosmopolitanism having spent much of his life in New York. This aspect of his life is also well-represented in *The Miscreant*, which has several insightful and observant stories set in Mumbai and New York.

Once again Victor proves himself to be an accomplished prose stylist and storyteller.

—from the blog of Amitav Ghosh
amitavghosh.com/blog

Author of *The Glass Palace, Sea of Poppies, River of Smoke*

The Miscreant

Selected Stories
1949-2016

Victor Rangel-Ribeiro

Serving House Books

The Miscreant: Selected Stories, 1949-2016

ISBN: 978-0-9977797-1-4

Art by Mario de Miranda

Author photo by Joel D'Souza

Serving House Books logo by Barry Lereng Wilmont

Published by Serving House Books, LLC
Copenhagen, Denmark and Florham Park, NJ

www.servinghousebooks.com

Member of the Independent Book Publishers Association

Friends of Poets & Writers

First Serving House Books Edition 2017

To my grandmother, Julia Vaz e Pinto,
the first storyteller in my life,
and to all the wondrous storytellers who have enchanted me since then,
from Boccaccio through Narayan to Bharati Mukherjee

Contents

1 Other Climes, Other Times

Goa

Bombay/Mumbai

2 The Immigrant Experience

New York

Bonus Story

1

Other Climes, Other Times

Goa

The Miscreant

Lazar, the entire village of Tivolem knew, was a bad lot. Not just ordinary bad, like Lallu, the cobbler's son, who had taken to drinking coconut-palm toddy and to general shiftlessness, but bad bad. Even when they used the diminutive and referred to him as Lazarinh', dropping the final 'o', the villagers did not use the tender tone of voice that so closely ties in with the diminutives of first names; instead, it came out with the kind of rasp that generally precedes the act of expectoration. Indeed, Kashinath the barber, when Lazarinh's name came up at all, always took care to avert his face, hawking and spitting sharply into the dust.

Although there were some who held that Lazarinh' had been bad from birth, others swore he did not run afoul of the law until he was fifteen. Now that needs some explaining—not the discrepancy in recollection, which after all is only natural, but the bit about the law. In India as everywhere the mills of justice grind slowly, and our people too wonder that felons go free while lawyers grow fat. The police? There's the rub. With not much serious crime around, and perhaps one murder in sixteen years or so—well, fourteen, if you must insist—police stations are few and far between. The nearest one is in Mapusa, eight kilometers away! By the time we get a messenger out there, on foot, and the police arrive over here, do you think—?! So our people have their own way of discouraging petty crime, and it is this law that Lazarinh' ran afoul of, beginning when he was about fifteen.

Indeed, those were trivial incidents he was involved in, the first two at least—a thirty-pound jackfruit stolen from Dona Elena's garden in the middle of the night, a basket of mouth-watering mangoes lifted from Senhor Eusebio's front steps in broad daylight (the angry *bhatkar* mistakenly beat his servant boy for that one)—and the villagers let them pass while making mental note. But a brood of fledg-

ling chickens being terrorized and scattered, while the anguished
mother hen fluttered and squawked about in futile rage—ah, that
was something else again. There, in that one incident, one could
see the incipient seeds of badness, because one cannot grow up in
a place such as Tivolem without knowing that on the care and love
bestowed on helpless creatures depends the life and wellbeing of the
village. The scattering of tiny helpless baby chicks, so they could be
swooped down on and carried off by crows and shrieking kites, was
a no-no, and Kashinath, passing by, took note of it, and smacked
Lazarinh' soundly about the ears. "I cuffed him, I cuffed him really
hard," Kashinath, still shaking with anger, had later reported to his
cronies assembled in the darkness of Forttu's tavern, and Forttu and
the regulars had approved. "Perhaps he wasn't slapped hard enough,"
Forttu said more than once, as time passed and Lazarinh' went from
bad to worse. "I would have slapped him so hard, it would have
broken both his eardrums."

Mind you, the chicken incident was five years ago, maybe six,
and Lazarinh' had indeed gone on to bigger things. Just last year
hadn't Lazarinh', the people of Tivolem asked rhetorically, hadn't
Lazarinh'—shamefully, on the anniversary of Goa's emergence as
India's twenty-fifth state—hadn't the rascal Lazar stolen Govind the
carpenter's prize possession? Govind's wife Amita, returning from a
trip into a neighboring village, had been treated to a most astonish-
ing sight—their sturdy piebald bull calf, that she had raised almost
from birth along with her goats and her five children, was being
driven up the lane that led over the north hill to Goregaon, and who
was doing the driving but a man in white shirt and ragged shorts,
and even at that distance she knew: who could it be but Lazarinh'?

She tried to chase after the thief and the frightened animal, but
they were too far ahead anyway; besides, she had a child at the hip
and by the time Govind himself had been found in Forttu's tavern
and had started up the lane with a friend for company and protection, the sun's shadow had lengthened a full meter to the east. The
two men had followed the same lane over the hill a good four kilometers into Goregaon, using what short cuts they could, scrambling

14

over rocks while keeping the path in sight; and they had been told that yes, Lazarinh' had been there, had been seen spending money in the village market, and in the tavern, but that he had entered Goregaon alone, sans calf. Sans calf, mind you, but certainly with money—three, four hundred rupees, more or less, in a wad of purplish ten-rupee notes.

All this Govind recounted to his wife upon his return, asking rather wistfully, for he was the kind of man who does not lightly think ill of another, whether she might not have been mistaken? Was it really Lazarinh' she saw rustling their calf, and not some no-good migrant worker heading home to the jungle-covered Ghats?

"Wouldn't I know a *Ghanti* if I saw one?" she retorted. "And since when do you doubt my word, the mother of your five children?" And she threatened to feed his rice portion to the pariah dog who slept outside in the lane if he persisted in his questioning.

"So where is our calf?" she had shrieked at Lazarinh' when she saw him come limping home later that night. "What have you done with it, son of the devil?"

"What about your calf, woman?"

"I saw you driving it over the hill this afternoon!"

"You saw me? Then you also saw the dog?"

"What dog, liar? There was no dog!"

"Is this the thanks I get," said Lazarinh', "to be called a liar, just because your eyesight is weak, and you saw no dog? Here I was coming home tired from work this afternoon, really tired, what can I tell you, and I see a calf running up the lane with a strange dog barking after it and nipping at its heels, and I've never seen that dog before but I know that calf, I see at once that it is your calf, that is like a sixth child to you; and I shout out as loud as I can, 'Ho, Govind! Ho, Govind's wife!' but you are nowhere to be seen, not you and not your husband, so I chase after the dog and the calf, over the hill, halfway to Goregaon, and the dog turns away when I finally get to throw a stone at it, and rushes at me to bite me, and it's a big dog, so I jump on top of a wall for safety, and fall over on the other side, which is a good thing or else the dog would have bitten me and it would all have been over your no-good calf, but when the dog is gone and I climb on the wall again your calf is nowhere to be seen. Now here it is night, and I return limping as you can see, my toes bleeding from stubbing them on rocks, my ankles swollen from falling off the wall, and you ask me where is your calf as though I, Lazarinh', whom the entire village knows from childhood as an honest man, as though I had stolen it?"

"The whole world knows you for a thief," she shrilled, but he stood his ground.

"Where is your proof, woman?"

Govind's wife was rendered temporarily speechless, as a result of which Govind got very little to eat that night. "You should have been there with me, to give him a beating, instead of wasting time and money in Forttu's tavern," she said. And she slapped his hand away as he tried to reach for a second helping of okrah curry, a spicy and flavorful dish she knew he loved and thus had prepared especially to punish him with.

"I will tear him apart when I see him," Govind boasted, as much to his wife as to the four watchful children and the gurgling baby. "Limb by limb I will tear him apart, and feed his carcass to the jackals." He stood up and belched and lurched towards the door.

"If you go there now he'll half kill you," Amita said. "And if you wait till you're sober in the morning you'll be paralyzed by fear. Either way, we lose."

The theft of Govind's calf, and the problem of what to do about it, was the topic of profound discussion at Forttu's tavern for days and nights on end, even on the night of the full moon the following week when Mottu the village postman, Annabel's husband, having finished his rounds, went in there for only a second or two, he swears, and merely to inquire whether Forttu was expecting any important mail or packages in the next day or so, and having emerged fortified by only a single complimentary snort of Johnny Walker—just one, mind you, and not the four that certain slanderous tongues proclaimed was his daily quota, God forgive them, Mottu said, or they

will surely fry in hell—he had emerged he said to find his bicycle, his sole source of income, gone, missing, stolen, and a figure much like Lazarinh' pedalling erratically far down the road, shirttails flapping in the wind.

Well, the bicycle, besides being Mottu's means of livelihood, was also government property, so Mottu straight off went to the police in Mapusa, who sent a constable who placed himself on a barstool in Forttu's tavern, which like the forts and castles of old commanded the main entrance to the village. Alas, alas for Lazarinh' when he staggered up that road at eleven that night, or at 23.05 hours as the official records would soon show. The preserver of law and order showed no compassion even though Lazarinh' was carrying no loot and singing a raucous love song.

"What kind of miscreant do you take me for?" asked Lazarinh', as the handcuffs snapped around his wrists right in the middle of the heartrending finale to "Mariquinh', my Love." And turning to Mottu, he said: "Do I look like the kind of heartless evildoer who would steal the bicycle of a well-loved, much-honored public office-bearer like you?"

"You look like the kind of evildoer who would sell his own sister," interjected the policeman. "Luckily for your sister, you have no sister."

"My sister, if I had one, would have been deeply hurt to hear you speak of me in such intemperate terms, o unbemedalled great one," said Lazarinh'. "You are the one who's truly lucky that I really have no sister, for if I had had one, and you had hurt her feelings by speaking ill of me in or out of her presence, I would have had to hurt your feelings in turn, possibly by kicking your noble posterior in public."

This metaphysical exchange might have lasted much longer had not, by an unfortunate accident, the policeman's truncheon at that very moment become disengaged from his belt, and his hasty lunge to retrieve it only caused the stick to bounce rapidly off Lazarinh's shins and buttocks, rat-tat-tat thud-thud-thump, tha-thump, not once but several times. Fortunately the stick itself suffered no dents or bruises, no irreparable damage. The policeman therefore returned it smoothly to his belt, but not before carefully testing it twice again against Lazarinh's buttocks— thwack! thunck!—to make sure it had lost none of its resilience.

The above version was pure speculation, you understand, mere scuttlebutt. A far clearer light on what happened is shed by the official chronicle, the police log, which reveals that on the night and at the time in question, one Lazar, aka Lazarinh', member of the public and palpable miscreant, while in a drunken state did enter into a loud, vehement, and prolonged argument on civics with a wandering water buffalo, and after refusing to yield the right of way, and further becoming verbally and physically abusive, the said member of the public and known miscreant Lazar alias Lazarinh' got behind the said beast of burden and twice endeavoured to push it off the road, whereupon the said evildoer i.e. Lazar was soundly and repeatedly kicked by that otherwise docile and even-tempered animal, giver of milk, plower of fields, friend to all mankind. The log does not note the policeman's reactions when next morning the magistrate dismissed the complaint against Lazarinh' for lack of evidence, ignoring the affable buffalo that had been brought into court to buttress the story, and now stood to one side placidly chewing the cud.

But Mottu's wife was not one to give up. "We must tie up our statue of Saint Cornelius," she said to her husband.

Mottu winced. "For heaven's sake! Tie up a saint?"

"He's the patron saint of our village," she persisted, "and he's also the patron saint of reformed criminals, and he's not called Saint Cornelius the Contrite for nothing. I've heard my grandmother say, bless her long-departed soul, that each time one ties up the statue of Saint Cornelius, stolen goods are mysteriously returned. In fact, the one time we had a robbery at our house, when I was a child, the good saint remained tied up for days, until everything that had been taken was returned."

Mottu looked dubious.

"Bad things happen to thieves who do not return their loot

when Saint Cornelius wants them to," his wife said. "The longer the saint remains tied up, the greater his anger, the more his wrath is to be feared. Tell the baker we have tied up the saint, and swear him to secrecy; then he's bound to tell the entire village. And spread the word yourself as you make your rounds with the mail."

At midnight on the third day of Saint Cornelius's bondage in the Mottu household, Annabel awoke with a start. She had heard a dull thump, and her first thought was that the statue of Saint Cornelius had fallen off its little altar. But on striking a match she found it was not so—the saint stood where she had left him, bound with strong twine, his head tilted forward and to the left in the same attitude of sorrow and resignation. "God forgive me," she muttered, bending and holding the match closer for a better look into his glazed, reproachful eyes, until the flame licked at her fingers and she hastily dropped it. It seemed to her then that the saint had given her a taste of hellfire for having tied him up, and she was about to untie him when she heard the thump again, more clearly, and it was not anything in the house.

"Mottu!" she whispered, "Mottu!" vigorously shaking her still sleeping husband. "Wake up! The thief is at the gate!" And when he grunted and turned over she hissed again: "The thief! Wake up! The thief's outside! Go get him!"

Mottu, now wide awake, heard a scraping on the gravel path outside his door, and rushed out cudgel in hand to where he caught the faint glint of metal by starlight. The bicycle fell with a clatter to the ground, and it was then that Mottu caught sight of the black-clothed figure turning to flee. With a blow of the club he brought the man down. Thwack! Thwack! Thwack-thonck! went the club again as the figure scrambled desperately about on hands and knees.

"Mottu-u-u!" screamed the returner of stolen goods. "Stop! Don't you recognize me? I'm your neighbor, Lazarinh'!"

"You lie!" cried Mottu, who knew exactly where the truth lay, but was not giving up a heaven-sent advantage. "Take that for lying (thwack)! Lazarinh' does not dress in black (sswish)! Lazarinh' does not steal—he has told me so himself (thump)! Take that (double-thwack) for smearing the name of an innocent man!"

"O Mottu, Mottu," cried the figure, "thank you for believing in my innocence! Look closely! It is indeed me, it's Lazarinh'!"

"Aha!" cried Mottu. "So it's really you, is it? It's Lazarinh', come like a thief in the middle of the night, with my stolen bicycle, and dressed all in black like the devil himself!" and he raised the cudgel again.

"It's not what you think," said Lazarinh', leaping nimbly out of harm's way. "I was returning a few minutes ago from the funeral of a cousin in Assonorá, you know how far it is to that village, and having missed the last bus had to walk all the way home. You know how long that takes! By the time I passed Forttu's tavern it was pitch dark. Right outside the post office, in the middle of the road, would you believe it, I found your bike. In fact, in the dark I tripped right over it. If there were some light here you'd see the bruise where the pedal caught my shin. But when I tripped over it I didn't think of the pain—in fact, I felt no pain at all. And why? Because my first thought was—'Heavens be praised! This must be Mottu's missing bike! The thief has brought it back!' That's what I thought. Lucky for him he got to leave it there before I arrived, or he would have caught it from me, I tell you! And how lucky is Mottu, I said to myself, that I was the first person to stumble across it, and not some half-drunken stranger with larcenous fingers! Indeed, I said to myself, Mottu is doubly lucky that the bike was returned after the last bus passed this way or the no-good driver would certainly have driven right over it, accidentally on purpose! I must take it right away to Mottu, I said, without waiting to change out of my funeral clothes, because this bike is definitely Mottu's, no doubt about it, and what's Mottu's must go back to Mottu as fast as possible, because that's the way Mottu delivers our mail. Those were my very words, that I said aloud to myself, and too bad there was no one else there to hear me, or they too would have told you that that is exactly what I said!"

"Hit the miscreant!" screamed Annabel, appearing suddenly in the doorway. Her left hand held aloft a hurricane lamp; in her right she wielded a heavy frying pan. "Hit the misbegotten one!" she cried again. "Hold him till I can lay my hands on him!"

Seeing the enemy thus powerfully reinforced, Lazarinh' dived headfirst into some bushes, and though Mottu flailed about with vigor, his cudgel became entangled in brambles, and his quarry escaped into the night.

A week later Atmaram the shopkeeper thought he had better luck. His younger daughter, the buxom one, had heard three coconuts fall almost simultaneously to the ground an hour after sunset. Alerted by that thud-tha-thump, she heard them roll towards their front door, and rushed out to retrieve them because by local custom any coconuts that fall and roll to your door are yours to keep, especially if you have helped in the rolling. But then the thought came to her—three coconuts rarely fall to earth all at the same time, least of all on a calm and windless night, unless somebody is up there fooling with Mother Nature. Looking upwards, she saw silhouetted against the moonlight the figure of a man clinging as motionless to the tree as a squirrel that's spotted a cobra.

"Bapu! O father!" she screamed at the top of her lungs, bringing the man shinnying down the tree even as her father came rushing into the yard.

"*Badmash!* Whoremaster!" cried Atmaram, for he had recently returned from a visit to Bombay, and in that great city had learned the right words to use in times such as these. Besides, he had rushed out thinking from his daughter's cry that some stranger was about to stain the family's honor, and finding instead that it was only Lazarinh'—for he had recognized him in an instant—out to steal the landlord's coconuts, he switched in relief from alarm to uncontrolled fury.

"Thief! Steal our *bhatkar's* coconuts, will you? Take that!" and he raised a coconut-frond club while Lazar was still some six feet off the ground. Before he could strike, however, Lazarinh' bounced a coconut off his head and sent him reeling, and once on the ground

22

flung another at Atmaram's onrushing wife, who escaped injury only because she ducked under a clothesline on her way to battle.

"Ay-ee-eee!" cried Atmaram's wife, not missing a step.

Faced with this onrushing fury, now coming at him with eyes of fire and arm upraised, Lazarinh' darted nimbly past Atmaram, who found himself hampered by his unwieldy club. Hither and thither darted Lazarinh', dodging and weaving around the coconut trees, confounding the best efforts of Atmaram, his wife, and both daughters to catch him; he might even have gotten clean away had not their pi dogs joined in the chase, and one of them grabbing him by the ankle, Lazarinh' found he could not shake himself free.

The screaming, cursing, and yelping brought a host of neighbors to the scene. But as they got in each other's way trying to pummel Lazarinh', he, reeling and crying out, worked his way ever closer to the village creek, into which he gave one mighty leap and once again fled into the night. Next morning he was back, defiant as ever, confident that the previous night's punishment would ensure his safety.

While with each such episode Lazarinh's fame as a petty thief and hoodlum began to spread beyond Tivolem, it still did not compare with that of older and better-known hooligans in the surrounding areas. People wondered which of these, then, was the brazen son-of-Shaitan who, on the third Sunday in May, broke into the Church of Saint Benedict the Beneficent, in the hamlet of Aiconá, two weeks before Saint Benedict's famous annual feast? It was an hour yet to cockcrow when Apolinar', their aged sacristan, preparing the darkened church for early morning mass, shuffled to the main altar with lighted taper in hand, genuflected, then raised his light to find—nothing. Thinking that perhaps the vicar had moved the golden candlesticks, he turned to the side altars, only to see something that brought the cold hand of fear to his heart: no trace of gold candlesticks there, either, but candles strewn and trampled on the floor, vases knocked down, and Saint Benedict himself—Saint Benedict, pride and patron of the village—missing!

"Father Vicar! O Father Vicar!" Apolinar' called out in a choking voice, and rushing to the belfry sent the great bell spinning into a clangor that shook the village awake.

Hushed were the faithful as they moved through the church, counting up the missing items. The gold candlesticks, the giant candelabra, the finely wrought censer that the vicar said came from the time of Vasco da Gama, the loss of these grieved them greatly; but the loss of the statue of Saint Benedict—Saint Benedict of the heavenly blue robe and the upturned visage and the mystical rapturous eyes—that loss left them truly orphaned.

Outside, the hubbub was immense. How could they hold their feast, the village women said, when their husbands would not be able to carry the statue in procession seven times around the churchyard, as had been done for centuries? Ah, but their saint would not forsake them, Apolinar' the sacristan said, he would surely break free of the thieves and come back to his church and his people! And he had just begun to speak of the saint's great powers, of his many miracles, when his wife, who had heard those same stories too many times already, suddenly began reciting the Rosary, and all joined in the responses.

With prayers, vigils, and a novena the distraught parishioners laid siege to Heaven, and the vicar declared he was going to keep the church doors open around the clock, so his people could take turns praying day and night, and Saint Benedict himself, God willing, could find his way back into his church.

No one knows how the rumor started, but by the third night of the novena it was widely believed, even here in Forttu's tavern in Tivolem, that the statue of Saint Benedict would miraculously reappear in its usual niche on the altar at Aiconá. Some said this would happen on the eve of his feast; others held it would be on the morning of the feast day itself.

The day before, crowds began converging on the church to witness the expected miracle, many coming from far-off villages, and not a few walking there from Tivolem. It was a pilgrimage of the devout and the curious! In the church a thousand candles flickered and sank to Pater Nosters and Aves and *mea culpas*, while evening turned to night, and night gave way to morning. Yet they waited, and prayed, and waited. Not till the Mass of the Feast itself had been celebrated, not till it was quite over and the acrid smell and smoke of a thousand firecrackers displaced the heady scent of incense, did the now disheartened faithful begin to drift out of the church, leaving the niche on the altar still gapingly unfilled.

In the bright sunshine the fair awaited them, but they had no eyes for it. Still the vendors hawked and cajoled, and boldly thrust bargains in their despondent faces. So some hand-carved toys were sold, and a black lace mantilla or two, and *laddus* and other crumbly sweets that the young ones clamored for, and sugar shaped to look like churches and daubed bright red and green; but there was not much else doing anywhere, not even at the booth off to one side where the statues of saints, and other religious objects, stood arrayed on a cloth-draped table. Nothing much, at least, until the dark, full-mustachioed vendor began loudly hawking ointments, beeswax candles, and rosary beads he vowed had all been blessed in Rome by the Holy Father himself.

But the white-cowled women who gathered around at his call had another concern in mind, and having looked over those saints he had on display, and not finding the one they were after, one finally thought to ask—did he perhaps know where they could find a statue of Saint Benedict?

"Indeed, I have one," said the man, after some hesitation. "But it's not for sale."

"Could we at least see it," she persisted, "if you have it near at hand, and it's no trouble? It would mean a lot to us, since ours was stolen just two weeks ago."

"Very well, then," he said, and reaching beneath the table-cloth carefully brought out a statue with upturned visage and rapture-filled eyes, one so delicately carved that it could have been mistaken for the stolen statue itself, had not this Saint Benedict been clothed in a robe of the richest crimson instead of heavenly blue.

Oh, the rush of people to see it!

"I'll give you a hundred and fifty rupees for it," said a voice.

"It's not for sale!" said the vendor.

"Three hundred!" cried another devotee. And the women clamored: "It's for the church! Our church! A statue so beautiful must surely be in our church!"

"You have truly touched my heart," said the seller. "It's my very favorite statue, and I've had it for many years, and as my favorite it goes with me wherever I go. Of all the saints' statues I like this the best, and I would not sell it to anybody, not even to the Holy Father himself, and not for all the money in the world; but since you say it's for your church, and this after all is the Church of Saint Benedict, it is right and proper that this statue should be placed in your church, so I will let you have it for a mere thousand."

"That's much too much, but let me see it up close," said Apolinar', reaching forward.

"Leave it right there," cried the vendor sharply. "Nobody touches it until I see your money!"

But the sacristan had already laid hold of the statue, and the two grappled for possession until Apolinar' let go with a cry, holding up his crimson-stained hands for all to see.

"Ayee! Has this man cut you, Apolinar' my brother?" cried a woman. And turning to the vendor, she screamed: "What have you done to him, *shaitan*?"

But the sacristan, eyes bulging, could only point to the statue, where traces of a sky-blue robe could be seen beneath the smeared crimson paint.

Oh, the struggle that followed, with the vendor trying to hold on to the statue and run, and the crowd trying to pull it away from him! Then, all of a sudden, they had wrenched the statue away, and—surprise—the mustache was on Saint Benedict, and no longer on the thief.

"Why, it's Lazarinh'!" cried a voice.

Forgetting completely that the focus of their novenas and prayers and all-night vigils had been the simple return of the statue; forgetting that a miraculous return had been forecast for that very day; ignoring the fact that Lazarinh' had been the chief and only instrument of that return, and thus might have been fulfilling God's will, the crowd seized on him and pummelled him, shoved and knocked him about, and would have very nearly beaten him senseless had not the police, who had been watching with intense curiosity from just a short distance away, now decided that further punishment should only be legally administered. They therefore rescued Lazarinh' from the undisciplined mob, and buffeted him soundly themselves as they took him first to police headquarters in Mapusa, and then to the district hospital.

Although news of Lazarinh's beating, arrest, and hospitalization did not make the local papers, noteworthy though it was, it did reach Tivolem the way important local news always did—with the early morning thump-clank of tiny cymbals in the village baker's wooden staff as he let his still sleepy customers know he was bringing them not only fresh-baked bread but also the latest gossip.

The villagers split immediately into two dissenting groups. "He got exactly what he deserved," said Mangu the coppersmith, and all who agreed with him. But others, led by Kashinath the barber, took the opposite view, insisting that what he got was less than what he deserved—he should have been beaten half to death.

"Crime must be controlled," Kashinath said, blowing the froth off a glass of coconut-palm liquor in Forttu's tavern. "What use are the police, what use are the judges, what use is the law of our fathers itself, if criminals are routinely freed and roam about our streets? Since earlier thrashings have not taught Lazarinh' a lesson, the time has surely come to feed him much stronger medicine."

"The stronger the better," Forttu agreed.

Next morning the baker, returning from Mapusa, brought sobering news: Lazarinh's condition had worsened. He was dying. Dying!

"Oh my God!" said Mottu the postman, but Kashinath scoffed. "Lazarinh', dying? He has more lives than a cat."

Mottu, laughing nervously, agreed, then went off to Forttu's tavern for a touch of consolation.

"Have no fear, our Lazarinh' always comes back," Forttu told him over and over again, as he filled and refilled Mottu's glass with scotch and soda.

And the regulars there repeated: "Always, always. That's our Lazarinh'."

Yet, next morning, there once again was the baker, thumping his staff with shrill urgency, and telling everyone that Lazarinh' had died in the night: he'd heard it himself at the bakery in Mapusa, from a man who had just returned from the hospital.

Still unbelieving, they stopped the first bus passing through.

"What news of Lazarinh'?" they asked.

"Lazarinh' is dead!" said the driver.

And the baker added, rather maliciously, that since Lazarinh' probably had died without benefit of clergy, his soul would surely fry in hell, and how did they feel about that now?

The village was devastated. Gloom blotted out the sun, and people on their way to the fields or to market gathered in knots to discuss the tragedy.

"That beautiful lad," said Mottu, "to die so young, and in such a state!" And he shook his head in shock and disbelief that such things should be.

"A tragic fate!" mourned Atmaram. "A fate I would not wish upon my worst enemy. And Lazarinh'—he was no enemy, he was a neighbor, a—yes!—a friend! Always ready to do you a favor, when one was needed! And what a climber of trees! Even the tallest coconut trees! How many times, seeing him up there gathering coconuts for our bhatkar, I was concerned, fearing he might fall. And now—" and in a well-timed gesture he wiped an unborn tear against his sleeve.

"As a child he was always at my house," recalled Govind's wife, stretching recollection to its limits. "And he would say: 'Govind's wife,' for he spoke like no other child, he was old and solemn for his years, 'Govind's wife, are you going to give me a *laddu?*' And if I had no *laddus* to give, as sometimes happened, then I gave him some other sweet. Or some roasted gram, or a slice of ripe papaya, or even a piece of brown jaggery. He was like our own son—Govind and I could refuse him nothing."

Ah, the praise that was lavished on the well-beloved newly deceased! The happy memories that were evoked, the eulogies that were rehearsed, the tears that were shed! In the context of death, so final, so terrible, so utterly irrevocable, even the incidents of the calf, the bicycle, and the coconuts were treated as harmless escapades, greatly misunderstood at the time. The people of Aiconá were roundly and properly condemned for their heartlessness, their savagery, their inhuman cruelty in killing—in fact, in murdering (why have we been pussyfooting around that word?)—in murdering poor defenseless Lazarinh', standing proud and defiant, far from home and from those who would have protected him, quite alone against a treacherous mob. And the points were raised: hadn't he taken the statue back? Hadn't he refused to sell it? And wasn't it true that he was seized upon and beaten, before he could get it safely into the church? Strong contrasts were drawn between the ethos of the two villages; events such as this lynching, it was agreed, could never happen in Tivolem.

"Not in a thousand years," Forttu said.

It was Josephine Aunty, the local spinster, who brought the discussion back to reality.

"When," asked she, "should we have the funeral?"

"Of course," said Forttu, clapping a hand to his forehead. "We forgot about the funeral!"

"I have a little money set aside," she said. "I could at least pay for the funeral band."

"I'll pay for the band," said Forttu, "and for the casket, candles, whatever is needed. Josephine Aunty, you're all alone. Save your money—you may need it for yourself some day."

In the midst of all this, Mottu's wife Annabel, who had been listening intently to all the to-and-fros, uttered a muffled "Lord forgive me!" and, making the sign of the cross three times in quick succession, whispered hoarsely, "Look!"

"It's a ghost!" cried Josephine Aunty, and they all crossed themselves, all except Govind and Atmaram, who being Hindus could scarcely invoke the same protection. Lazarinh' alive was one thing, but Lazarinh' the ghost appearing in Tivolem, bandaged head, swollen lip and all, not waiting for night but facing them down in broad daylight—this was a type of haunting beyond all reason and experience.

"Mottu, get the vicar quick, with incense and holy water," said his wife. But Mottu saw the ghost standing between them and the path to the church, and Mottu did not move.

They fell back a step, then, and would have turned and scattered had not the ghost also stopped.

"What's that thing now squirming and shrieking in the bag he has in his hand?" asked Josephine Aunty. "Look at it move! What fiend has he brought us from Hell?"

With a piercing squeal the Thing burst out of the bag, and raced towards them as if chased by the devil.

"Merciful God!" cried Mottu's wife, and fell in a faint.

They flung themselves against the sides of the lane, and the Thing flashed by, leaping over Annabel where she lay, and they saw it first as a blur of white and gray, that's how fast it was moving, but as it sped down the lane Atmaram recovered his wits.

"Forttu, isn't that the pigling you've been fattening up for Easter, and that was feeding by the creek?"

"By heaven, you're right!" said Forttu, "and now Lazarinh's ghost has touched and defiled it."

"What ghost?" asked Mottu. "Ghosts disappear—pouf! But look! This ghost is alive and is running away!"

"That's Lazarinh'!" shouted Atmaram. "Get him! Get the motherlover! Get the stealer of our pigs and cattle, the defiler of sacred places!"

Lazarinh' heard their shouts as they surged behind him, and gaining the main road as the express Mapusa-Panjim bus came groaning up the slope, he caught it on the run, barely ahead of their clawing hands; and the last they saw of him he was leaning out the rear door, gesturing obscenely and spitting in the wind.

That Saturday afternoon the vicar of Tivolem sat, pen poised in hand, thinking long and hard of the possibilities open to him for the evening's homily, and the sermon to be preached at Mass the next morning. Should he draw parallels between Lazarinh's reappearance after reported death, and the miracle of Lazarus called forth from his tomb? Could it possibly have come about to serve some higher unseen purpose, or was it perhaps due even to the intercession of Saint Cornelius the Contrite, who after all as patron saint of Tivolem looked after the spiritual needs of all local sinners? But if so, why did Lazarinh' then steal the pig? Or could it be that these two incidents coming so soon one after the other—the statue in Aiconá, the piglet here—could they be taken to mean that Lazarinh', the known and hitherto unrepentant thief, in his inmost heart and unknown to himself really wanted to make restitution? These were the questions that plagued the good vicar's mind, and that he wished his parishioners to ponder.

But his curate Father Francisco Xavier Pires, younger by far and more worldly in his outlook, gently said no: whatever the judgment of posterity might be, at that moment Tivolem's five hundred inhabitants, whether Catholic or Hindu, would not be inclined to look on Lazarinh's reappearance as one of Saint Cornelius's more laudable achievements. Not unless, the curate said, they had first been meditating long and hard in the depths of Forttu's tavern.

With a sigh the vicar agreed, and preached instead on the general subject of minor mischief in youth, citing the case of the young man who in the sixteenth century asked Saint Ignatius to make him a priest, and when the saint took him into his own home for prolonged tutelage, the young man turned out to be an inveterate prankster. But, with strict restrictions on the number of pranks that could be played each day—Saint Ignatius limited them to seven, the good vicar said—the youngster finally made it into the priesthood. And one of his first deeds on being anointed was to write a Life of the Saint. So it is all right to indulge in youthful mischief, the old vicar said, provided it is of the inoffensive kind, and that ultimately you dedicate your life to God.

31

And that, Mottu the postman told Annabel his wife in a whispered aside, is exactly where Lazarinh' had failed, and for that he would come to a no-good end.

"Amen!" said Forttu the tavern-keeper, sitting three pews to the rear.

But Mottu, keeping his eyes up front, said nothing more, and the Mass proceeded.

Angel Wings

It was that predawn hour of peace that comes when half the world has finally fallen into a profound sleep and the other half has not yet begun to stir. Into that time of suspended awareness the revving of the distant motor first insinuated itself into dreams and then turned them into nightmares. Like an ill wind the car sped through the sleeping village, its pistons grinding as it bounced up the rutted road that wound over the hills towards the capital city of Panaji. A car at that hour was a rarity; but even more than the straining engine the startled villagers remembered that other sound—the high-pitched crying out and yowling that sounded somewhere between a long-drawnout "Mam-maa" and the panicked bleating of a goat. Who was it keening in that car, and why?

It was a child from Goregaon, the baker on his rounds told them next morning, a child who had been boarded at a school in that neighboring village, a child who the previous evening had climbed a distant jambool tree to pluck the luscious purple fruit, had filled his pockets and climbed higher still to the swaying topmost branches, where one had snapped, sending him crashing to the ground. They had only found him late at night, semiconscious, and it was his moans and screams the villagers had heard as he was being rushed to hospital.

"The Angel of Death passed over our village," the vicar of Tivolem said from the pulpit that Sunday, "and we heard the flapping of his wings. The boy died, and we are left wondering why God allows such things. One might as well ask, why did he not create trees with unbreakable limbs? Why did He put in boys the quickness to climb tall trees, in men the urge to scale the highest peaks from which to fall? We cannot begin to understand His ways, and must trust in His infinite mercy. Other than that, I have no answers. All I know is, when a dear one is struck down, whether young or old, infant or grandparent, it is always too soon. Much too soon."

Carefully, he adjusted his vestments, knowing that all eyes, following the movement of his hands, would be reminded from whence he derived his authority.

"*De mortuis*—," the vicar said and paused, finger upraised, leaving the half-finished phrase hanging in air. "They say the child was good, and we know he was good. But of others, who are older and not quite so innocent, do we not also say the same thing? When we hear a man is dead, do we not praise him to the skies? And if that person turns up alive, do we not sometimes wish him dead? The same man, to be judged good or evil—is death then the deciding factor?!"

The vicar's hands were white as they clasped the pulpit's marble rim. "Many good things will be said about us, too, when we are gone," he continued, "but only we and God will know whether we deserve such praise or not. And if we don't, by then it will be too late. Much, much too late."

Of all the people attending Mass at that hour, it seemed to Pedro Saldanha, standing with gray head bowed just inside the crowded church, as though the vicar had singled him out for that sermon and that admonition. Others in the congregation felt the same way; the vicar's eyes, when he turned their way, bore deep into their souls. But Pedro Saldanha was overwhelmed. A humble and deeply religious man, he was known for kneeling during long stretches of the Mass, his knees burning through the cool stone floor, his arms outstretched in a symbolic crucifixion until he felt them no longer, feeling only pain. That Sunday, following the sermon, he knelt down in prayer and remained kneeling, self-absorbed and self-crucified, long after all others had gone their separate ways.

In their modest home his sister Geraldine waited lunch for him, anxiety replacing irritation as the hours passed and still he did not appear. She took the large wooden ladle from the pot and gave the curry another stir, feeding a bit of it to the scrawny tortoiseshell cat that turned and purred and rubbed herself insistently against her shins.

"Yes, yes," she said, when the cat turned away from the food. "So you'll wait for him, too. That's the way it is with the three of us, all growing old together, he perhaps fastest of all. But we too, cat; yes, even you, you with your nine lives."

She moved to the window.

"Sometimes you'd think I'm his mother," she said. "Perhaps our mother would have wanted that—that I should look after him so. But what if I should go first, cat, what then? So I pray that God should take us both at the same time, but you know how rarely I get what I ask for... We're stuck, unmarried—last of the family. No one after us, to mourn our passing, pray in our memory. No one, but you."

The cat leaped on to the sill and looked down the lane, its tail swishing. "All right, so you can tell he's coming," said the woman. "Now I see him too." She went to the hearth, and blew on the ashed-over wood to bring the flame back to life, feeling the heat flare up against her face even as she drew back from the sparks and flying cinders.

"Hellfire," she muttered, remembering the vicar's sermon at the early Mass she too had attended. Not that he had mentioned Hell itself—he seldom did; instead, he had spoken of the hereafter, which was close enough. But the priest who had been vicar long before him, that old priest had been able to work Hell and hellfire into every sermon he preached, no matter what the text for the day. She had been a young woman then, terrified with the vastness of the afterlife, sleepless at the thought both of eternal bliss and eternal damnation. When the present vicar arrived, what she had liked best about him was he kept Hell in its place. Somewhere over there, but out of sight.

The garden gate creaked, and as she pushed the one chair back to the kitchen table her brother entered the room. Silently she placed the pan and the clay pot on the table, and he sat and helped himself. He glanced approvingly at the curry, his favorite—yesterday's fish sauce, cooked in a blend of spices, ripe tamarind, dried red chillies, and coconut milk, had been simmered down to a rich, paste-like consistency; a little would go a long way. He ladled three heaping spoonfuls of rice onto his platter, then slowly put some back.

She turned to face him. "It got to you that bad? Are we going to have fasting and abstinence now, in addition to prayer?"

"That vicar's got me thinking," Pedro Saldanha said. "You heard him at the Mass we attended. Most priests would be happy to preach just one sermon a week, but not he. And what he said today is true! What will they say about me when I'm gone, Geraldine—and how little of it will be true? I never thought of it that way, not ever, and I've thought a lot lately about passing on."

"So? You're a good man; you've led a good and decent life."

"You think so? And is that enough? Not harming anyone, is that enough? And praying for hours—is that enough? No! I've got to go through the whole thing. I've got to see myself dead. Not really dead, but in my mind. Yes, dead in my mind. And I've got to hear in my mind what they—what you and they—are saying about me, now that I—I'm gone. Then I've got to match the two—see if I've deserved the praise. Change my life, if I have to. Change it, even now."

"Shall I heat the food again," she asked.

"No, it's fine as it is; yesterday's curry tastes so much better cold."

But in a moment he pushed the platter away and rose from the table.

"I must go to the city," he said. "I'll be gone a while."

He began changing his clothes.

"You're wearing black? All black? Even the shirt?"

"It fits my mood." He did not look at her.

"If you're walking you'll be gone a good four hours," she said.

"It may be five," he said. "I have much to do. But I'll be back before sundown."

But it was not quite three hours later that she heard the throbbing of an approaching engine and the unaccustomed crunch of tires in the gravel-strewn lane. The cat leaped on to the sill, and Geraldine looked out the window in time to see a hearse stop by their garden gate. They must have lost their way, she thought, but then she saw the driver reach in and begin to pull a coffin out. "Mary Mother of God," she cried in a panic. "No, no, not him!" and raced down the steps into the garden. But her brother was one of the two men who were jockeying to get the casket through the narrow gate.

"Who's dead?" she asked, her heart still pounding.

"It's empty. Hold the gate!" he commanded, and with careful shuffling steps the two men carried the coffin up the stone steps and into the house. Into the sitting room they went, and set it on the two available chairs, right in the middle.

"Pedro Saldanha, are you mad?" she cried, following her brother as he walked slowly around the narrow casket, his hand following its plush-lined contours, "are you mad, inviting bad luck and death on us like this, no one dead and this awful thing here in the house?"

"I want to see myself in my own coffin," he said. "I want to get the feeling, now, while I can do something about it." He paid off the driver of the hearse.

Outside, they heard a woman's voice at the gate, and their neighbor, Josephine Aunty, rushed in, breathless.

"I didn't hear the church bells toll," the gossip said. "Who would have thought Geral—" and then she stopped, surprised. "You both—thank God! Safe! Then who?"

"Nobody," Pedro Saldanha said.

"Nobody's died?"

"Nobody."

"But—"

"Nobody's dead. I've told you twice."

"Is anybody sick?"

"No!"

"Then why?"

"For your funeral," Pedro Saldanha said, exasperated, and Josephine Aunty fled, hysterical, the gate clanging after her as it swung repeatedly on its hinges.

He closed the shutters against the fading twilight. "I'm going to lie in it," he said. "When I do, walk softly. There are candles wrapped in that paper. Light four and place them at the corners."

"I won't do it," his sister said. "You've never been quite like this before." And she asked again, leaning into his face: "Have you gone stark raving mad?"

"You may have to do it for me some day," he said. "Might as well practice now." He had trouble getting in. "Give me a push."

The candles lit, she left the room.

"Geraldine!"

She reappeared in the doorway.

"I miss the flowers."

"This room will be filled with flowers."

"Remember, I like roses."

"I will remember. But if you keep this up, I may need them long before you do."

He was silent awhile.

"It's no good," he said. "I can't see myself, not like this. Hand me a mirror."

She stood by as he watched himself intently for long minutes.

"It's no good," he said again. "It's not the same. Holding the mirror, looking at myself, it's not the same."

He climbed out.

"Are we done, then?" she asked. "Can this thing go back?"

He was looking at her with eyes of fire. Frightened, she backed away.

"Get in there," he ordered. The wall behind her, there was nowhere for her to go. But when, trembling, she finally tried to climb in, he shouted: "No! Not like that! Put these on!" and began to strip.

"God forgive me!" She wept, covering her eyes.

"What's the matter, woman? Never seen a man strip before? Wear this!" And he tossed her his clothes, standing there near-naked.

Her dress bunched up as she pulled on the trousers; his shirt and coat hung grotesquely from her gaunt shoulders. Heedless, he helped her climb in, and as she lay in the casket, clothed now all in black, he handed her a crucifix. "Clasp your hands!" And he wrapped a rosary around them. "Now close your eyes, and keep them closed!"

Through half-closed lids she watched him pace around the room, muttering to himself. Time and again he turned to look down at her, peering at her ashen face, but not seeing her trembling lips, nor the spasmodic shiver that shook her frame, nor the tears that rolled from her eyes, tears she did not dare unclasp her hands to wipe away.

"Not a word!" he admonished her, again and again, rapping on the side of the coffin. "Not a sound out of you! Not a peep! Not even a peep!"

Around midnight, when the tall candle had burned low and he had fallen asleep slumped on the floor exhausted, she climbed out of the coffin and carefully led him to his bed.

As she turned to leave he suddenly sat bolt upright.

"We must build a chapel on the hill," he said, "so high that it will be seen by those who pass by our village, whether by road or in the ships that ply along the coast. I want my chapel to remind them that after they are done with the journey they are on, they will face another that has a beginning but no end---it's Heaven or hell for all eternity. I want them to make their choice, long before they sense the angel coming their way, long before it is too late."

He sank back on to his pillow and turned and closed his eyes.

Geraldine waited until his breathing returned to normal, then went out into the coolness of the starlit garden. She stood there transfixed, looking up and beyond the constellations for answers to the questions once again swirling through her mind. Somewhere up there, beyond the shimmering stars, lay the Gates of Heaven, and beyond them God on His throne, with the hosts of angels and saints singing His praises. How would her faint voice be heard above the Alleluias? In that one moment it seemed to her that the world had suddenly gone silent; even the stars had stopped their blinking; it was as if all Creation had fallen silent, so her prayer could be heard. In her awe she found she could not pray; instead, a single thought floated from her mind straight into the sky: Please help him. Help him, please. She waited long minutes for an answer, but heard nothing. Then off to the right, she felt a single star blink. Taking that for a sign, Geraldine went back into the house, where the cat greeted her, warm against her shins.

A Single Object of
Singular Desire

When Annabel told her husband Mottu that Marie-Santana had at last returned to her grandmother's house next door, after a prolonged absence in Mozambique, his thoughts flew back to the time he had seen her last, all of twenty years ago. They had spent the evening with other children playing on the nearby hilltop, he already thirteen and she a year younger. As a fresh breeze blew in from the west and they watched the sun dip molten gold into a shimmering Arabian Sea, she had told him her parents were taking her to Mozambique; he had taken her hand in his and told her, teary eyed and anguished, that he did not want her to leave, to go so far away; he had told her that he loved her. He had felt that she loved him too, and had leaned forward to kiss her, as he had seen grown-ups do in American movies or when they thought no one was watching, but instead she had turned and run down the hillside, slithering and sliding on the grass as she went, leaving him to follow slowly after, kicking at stones all the way.

Having heard a year or so ago through Josephine Aunty, the village gossip, that Marie-Santana had become engaged in Africa to a fair-skinned *mestiço*, Mottu now asked his wife what the husband was like, and Annabel told him that Marie-Santana had broken off the engagement and returned by ship alone, that she had never married.

The news bothered him. He remembered that he himself had hesitated when the marriage broker had first approached him with the proposal from Annabel's family, wondering whether or not he should wait for Marie-Santana, for whom he still had feelings. Could it be that in breaking off her own engagement to the *mestiço*, Marie-Santana had decided to wait for him? He found the prospect disturbing. "We must find her a husband soon," he told Annabel. "She'll never find a husband on her own; people here will think she's an old maid already." He suggested the name of a bachelor he knew, as a prospective husband.

Mottu's concern became more acute when Annabel reported a week later that Marie-Santana had refused to meet the suitor he had recommended. The man was a cousin of his, a clerk in a government office, and therefore assured of a steady if not overly lucrative employment for life. Being parsimonious, he had even saved up a tidy sum of money. Yet Marie-Santana had refused to consider him.

"What does she have against him?" Mottu asked. "That he's a little deaf in one ear? People get that way in their fifties. That he's bald? That happens, too."

"It's not him," Annabel said. "She won't consider anybody. No matter who."

To Mottu, this was bad news. It proved to him that his instincts had been right—Marie-Santana had remained single because, even though she had run away as a child from that aborted kiss, she had been in love with him, and was still so much in love with him now that she would not consider any other man, would accept no substitute. It would not have mattered too much if she had lived in another part of the village, but having moved in with Angelinh' Granny, in the house just across the lane, they were bound to run into each other day after day after day. Would she be able to handle the situation?

He was still worrying about Marie-Santana's state of mind when the true significance of the problem suddenly came to him—he had gone through life underrating himself. Here was proof, if proof were needed, that he was desirable. Not just his own wife, but another woman—a woman who had been overseas, and no doubt had had her pick of suitors—another woman loved him. He looked in the mirror again, as he had done when first Annabel had told him that Marie-Santana had returned unwed. He stuck out his chin and moved his jaw from side to side and narrowed his eyes. Once again the mirror did not lie: he was truly handsome. He decided he would look even better if he grew a mustache.

That night, when Annabel joined him in bed, she was surprised by the urgency of his lovemaking. When they had finished he did not fall asleep as he usually did. Instead, he caressed her, and she snuggled up against him. In the warmth of their closeness he began to think of that other being who lived directly across the lane, just a few paces away, yet was no doubt tossing forlornly on her bed. He contrasted his own situation with hers. Annabel and he were comfortable with each other; no fireworks in their lovemaking, but deep comfort. At any hour of the night, if he turned, she turned. And if she turned, he turned as well; it was a spontaneous response. Who could Marie-Santana turn to? A pillow? He wondered what it would feel like to make love to her, who had been so long alone. On the one hand, she might be all afire; on the other, she might be like ice.

Between fire and ice, Motto now decided that Marie-Santana was a combination of the two—a volcano, gone cold. That could explain why, in all the days since her return, she had not pursued him, as he had feared she would. Either way, he might have to teach her to let go, to love. He thought again of how she had wasted all those years, saving herself for him. A tragedy! And now, even with a proposal from a good man, a man of means though bald and a little deaf, she was still waiting—for what? For him, Mottu, to leave Annabel? For Annabel to die? Lying as he now was beside his sleeping wife, he realized—although theirs was an arranged marriage—that he did not want Annabel to die. That aside, Marie-Santana would be in for an extremely long wait, for Annabel was as healthy as a—as a—but whatever animal he thought of as being healthy, whether cow, water buffalo or tiger, or even female Indian elephant, he immediately saw that animal wasting away and dying, sometimes from unnatural causes.

The possibility of Annabel's death now became more real; he remembered a cousin who had been widowed in his twenties. Why should his own marriage be immune? Shuddering, he began to imagine a life without Annabel, a desolate life, a barren life, filled with loneliness. Mottu's face contorted, his eyes filled with tears even as he pictured himself weeping. He saw himself being comforted by caring neighbors, but most of all by Marie-Santana, ministering to him day and night. Although she did this willingly and untiringly, her face was a mask, and he saw at once that he had been right, she would have to be taught the art of love, step by step. He lingered over each step, deliciously, until she, now an expert, was providing him with endless hours of connubial bliss.

"Day and night," he said, half-aloud. "Isn't that amazing!"

"Isn't what amazing?" Annabel asked, stirring sleepily by his side.

"That's amazing," he said hastily, not knowing what else to say. "I was dreaming."

She threw a comforting arm around him and once again drifted off to sleep.

Mottu, however, found sleep evading him. His wife's trusting touch had shamed and humbled him; he became aware that he had committed a grievous sin against her, if only in his mind. Now that he thought about it, he had committed a whole series of sins in his mind, he a married man, against her and against God and the sacrament of marriage, in the lustful way he had pictured himself and Marie-Santana tumbling about. Tumbling and rolling. All that wild moaning! And in recollecting it he was sinning yet once again. This was March, this was Lent, the middle of Lent, when the vicar in all his sermons was calling attention to sin and the need for contrition and repentance. And he, Mottu, had committed adultery, had even killed off his wife. In his mind, true, but had the vicar not said, impure and sinful thoughts were often worse than deeds? With Easter around the corner, he would be expected to go to Communion. To receive Communion, he would have to go to confession. That meant having to confess to the vicar or to the curate, and though a carved wooden screen would shield him from being wholly seen by the priests, either of them would recognize his voice. They always did, he knew, even though they gave not a hint of it when assigning penance: three Our Fathers and three Hail Marys, and three Glory be to the Father, the Son, and the Holy Ghost. This was the penance imposed on him most often in the past, because all his sins had been venial. What would they assign him now, loaded down as he was with mortal sin?

At last the solution came to him: he would simply receive Communion without going to confession; each priest would think he had confessed to the other. "Thank you, Lord," he cried inwardly, ecstatic. But then he felt, not God's grace, but God's frown: Instantly the thought of receiving Communion while not in a state of grace appalled him; he would be adding a far more grievous sin to those he had already committed, so grievous that for that alone he could fry in Hell. Had the Devil gotten him already? He crossed himself as well as he could with his left hand, because his right was pinned under Annabel.

No sooner had he crossed himself than a far better solution suggested itself—he did not need to go to the vicar at all, nor even to the curate. All he had to do was walk over the north hill to Goregaon, a very long and tiring walk up its steep and unforgiving slopes, but there at the end of it he would find a most welcome sight—the centuries-old Church of Saint Martha of the Miracles, where the vicar was so new, and so old, and so troubled by cataracts that he could not recognize his own parishioners, let alone a stranger making the long trek from Tivolem.

The vicar of St Martha's gave Mottu not just absolution, but some very sage advice: to avoid sin, all Mottu had to do was avoid the source of his temptation. And in doing this Mottu indeed found some mental peace. But it also caused some concern. "Is Mottu all right?" Marie-Santana asked Annabel one Friday, when she ran into her at the weekly Mapusa bazaar. "I haven't seen him in the longest time."

"His work keeps him busy," Annabel replied. "I'll tell him you asked."

A week later Marie-Santana, setting out as usual for her trip to the Friday bazaar, had walked halfway down the long and palm-fringed road to Mapusa when she spied a cyclist riding somewhat erratically towards her. Seeing it was Mottu, she waved; he let go of the handlebars and waved back enthusiastically. As the bike veered to one side, she held her breath, fearing he would fall.

"You've still got a long way to walk, Mar'-Santan'," he said, stopping alongside and planting one foot on the ground to steady himself. "I'll give you a ride. Come, climb on to the crossbar."

"Thank you, Mottu, but it's pleasant and I'd rather walk," she said. "Besides, I see you've already been to Mapusa. Why should you go back again?" Her suspicions were confirmed; she could smell liquor on his breath.

He made a face. "I've not been to Mapusa yet," he said. "I was almost there, when I remembered that you too have shopping to do, so I turned back. I've been riding back and forth here, waiting for you to show up."

"Waiting for me?" she said, surprised. "Did Annabel send you, with a message?"

"Yes," he said, then added, somewhat sheepishly, "that is, no. Yes. She said you had told her you missed seeing me. I missed seeing you too, and I felt that this way we'd not only get to see each other but I'd also spare you a tiring walk."

"Mottu," she cried, "what's come over you? You're a married man. What are you thinking? And what would people say?"

He had stopped in the middle of the narrow road; now, with a bus approaching, they moved to one side.

"And what would people say?" he asked, as the bus whooshed by.

She put a hand to nose and mouth and waited for the dust to settle, then resumed her walk, anxious to get away from him; he turned his bike around and rode unsteadily beside her.

"I'll tell them the truth," he said.

"The truth!" Her uneasiness increased. "And what would that be?"

"That you love me," he said.

"Mottu, are you crazy?"

"Don't call me crazy," he said. "A little drunk, maybe. But crazy, not me! You love me, but are afraid to admit it." He leaned a hand on her shoulder.

"Take your hand off me," she snapped.

He leaned even harder. "Mar'-Santan', I'm going to do what I should have done the day you came back. I'm going to kiss you."

She backed away and he lost his balance, and had to struggle to right the bike again.

"For shame," she said. "Think of Annabel."

"I don't want to think of Annabel," he said. "I want to think of you." His face puckered.

She watched him warily.

"Come closer, Mar'-Santan', love," he pleaded. "Annabel's not here to see us. Come, just one little hug and a kiss."

A rage seized her. As he leaned into her again, she grabbed hold of the back of the saddle and pushed with all her might. The bike went off at an angle; she watched him teeter at the edge of the road, and the next moment he and the bike had fallen into the field below. It was a four-foot drop and Marie-Santana became concerned. She ran to the spot to find him sitting, shaken but unharmed, on the soft and sandy ground.

"Are you all right?" she called.

He picked himself up without answering.

"We've been friends since childhood," she said. "You are a married man, and your wife is my friend. Must you spoil everything now, for all of us?"

"I'm ashamed," he said. "And sorry." He was weeping now. "If you tell Annabel, I'll die. She's a good woman, Mar'-Santan; don't hurt her, please!"

"This madness has to stop," she said curtly. "Go home, Mottu!" And she set off briskly towards town.

"Don't tell, please don't tell, Mar'-Santan'!" He was back on the deserted road, his voice carrying on the wind. "Annabel, my wife, forgive me! Forgive me, my Annabel!"

By the middle of June the monsoon had struck Goa in all its demonic fury, and by June 23 the water in Angelinh' Granny's well had risen to within six feet of the brim. "Here's a bottle of cashew *feni* I've kept ready, Mar'-Santan'," her grandmother said to her. "Tomorrow is St. John the Baptist's feast day, remember what that means? To honour the Baptist, menfolk go from house to house and jump in each well. You'll have to give them a peg each before they jump in ours; they're baptizing themselves, and getting liquored up as well."

They came in a small but boisterous group, with Mottu bringing Annabel and their child Little Arnold along; the six-year-old, who could not swim, had two dried coconuts tied to his back to keep him afloat. By the time the bottle was half-empty Forttu the tavern-keeper had jumped on to the parapet, pinched his nose shut, and leapt into the water, followed by Govind and Kashinath and Braganza the postmaster, with Mottu the last to jump. The square well had sides of rough-hewn stone, and was barely fifteen feet across, but Mottu was a weak swimmer, and the water was forty feet deep; having dared to jump in, he had panicked on surfacing, and immediately made his way to the side, spewing water out of both sides of his mouth like a tugboat steaming into Panaji harbor. He found a crevice between stones and clung to it, content to watch others jump in one after the other.

Standing on the well's wet parapet and about to jump in as well, Little Arnold had watched his father thrashing about in the water, seen the panic in his eyes, and found the sight less than reassuring. If his father was having so much trouble down there, even after all those years of holding his nose and jumping in feet first, what was the point of jumping in when one did not know to swim at all, and needed to have two dried coconuts tied to one's back to keep from drowning?

"I'll hold your hand," Marie-Santana said, climbing up beside him, and Josephine Aunty the gossip drew in a sharp breath of disapproval because Marie-Santana should not be jumping into that well at all, not with all those married men down there just waiting to see her skirt go ballooning over her head. But Little Arnold backed off, even though Marie-Santana told him he'd be safe with her.

Forttu was climbing out when Marie-Santana bent over and

dove in. Mottu was chagrined; he had avoided her since the incident on the Mapusa road; yet here she was, in the same well with him, to escape he would have to climb out in a hurry, drawing attention and losing face. The other swimmers stayed to the side until she surfaced; seeing Forttu preparing to jump in again, she too got out of the way, quietly treading water. Though she was facing away from Mottu, he was sure she had seen him in the shadows.

Forttu stood right next to Little Arnold. "Come on, let's both jump," he said, and Little Arnold wanted to right then; his heart said jump but his knees said no, and his feet pulled him back from the brink.

"Pinch your nose shut!" Forttu said, and the child did, and the next thing he knew Forttu had picked him up with a hand beneath each armpit and tossed him right in the center of the well. Little Arnold saw the water rush up, and closed his eyes as the well swallowed him, but the next second he opened them to see bubbles sprouting in front of him, bubbles flashing by him, bright bubbles, brighter by far than water. Two hands he could see, pumping furiously up and down in front of his eyes. Two feet he could feel hard at work, kicking as fast as they could. At his back an irregular thumping, a tugging at his waist—the coconuts a pair of hands yanking him back to the surface, with the water getting brighter and lighter in color. He had not known water so blue could so quickly turn so clear.

Mottu by the wall watched his son break the surface and flounder around in a circle, the yellow coconuts at his back bobbing along with him. Little Arnold sputtered, but seeing the sheltering wall and friendly faces at hand, he paddled their way, making more noise than progress.

"Over here, Little Arnold," Marie-Santana said. "Come over to this side." She was treading water right next to his father. Mottu and she exchanged glances; she gave him a cool smile. "It's easy," she said to the child. "The coconuts will hold you up. And I'll catch you. I'm right here!"

Marie-Santana stretched out her hands to him and smiled, and once again the agitated wavelets rippled out in all directions as he struggled to reach her.

"Move your feet, Little Arnold. Kick! Kick!"

Annabel and Josephine Aunty, watching up above, clapped their hands as he inched forward. Little Arnold looked up at his mother and laughed, forgot to keep up his puppy stroke, and promptly sank beneath the surface. When he came up he found not only Mar'-Santan' Aunty there ready to help him, but also his father, concerned for him and no longer afraid for himself.

Little Arnold felt good. "You'll swim like a fish," Marie-Santana said, backpedalling till she was again just out of his reach. "Come on, let's see if you can catch me."

Mottu was unusually preoccupied at dinner that night. His thoughts were on what had happened in the well that morning—he jumping in, Forttu in the well, Little Arnold on the parapet, and Marie-Santana appearing out of nowhere. Forttu could have taught his son to swim; Forttu was always teaching others how to swim; but no, Marie-Santana had to climb up beside the child and hold his hand and try to get him to jump. Even when the child had refused, and she had jumped in by herself, and he, Mottu, had turned his face half away so she would not think he was there gaping at her, hoping to see whatever there was of her to see, Mar'-Santan' had swum round and round sleek as a dolphin within inches of where he was clinging to the wet stone, and when her face came out of the water for air and her mouth was open, so were her eyes, and she was looking straight at him. Then, when Forttu had tossed Little Arnold in and the boy was dog-paddling as any novice would, she had swum to where he, Mottu, was and called the child to her. Or was she calling *him?* Now he was sure she was. All that jumping in, those fancy strokes, showing off for whom, if not for him? And when she treaded water, bobbing up and down in her tight wet dress, tempting him with her ripe mango breasts—a mating dance, that's what it was. And that smile—how brazen, with his wife standing right there on the parapet. The changeable minx! He should have given her a sign, perhaps a secret sign that he was on to her game, even with Annabel there at the mouth of the well, peering down at them both.

Mottu had had his share of feni that day, before going into the well and after coming out of it, and also before sitting down to dinner, but now that he was done eating and the cashew liquor was a warm glow in his stomach, he leaned over and poured himself another shot. He felt masterful; let Annabel object if she dared.

"You've not said a word during dinner," Annabel said to him. She had been watching him throughout the meal and he had as carefully avoided meeting her gaze. "Didn't you like my cooking?"

He seemed not to hear; he had decided to ignore her. Her womanly intuition working at peak level, his wife sent Little Arnold off to do his homework, then came straight to the point.

"If you so much as look at her sideways, I'll kill you," she said.

"Me, look at her?" Mottu said, startled that she had read his thoughts. Had Marie-Santana complained to Annabel about the incident on the road, in spite of all his pleas? He decided to brazen it out. "Look at whom? At her? Mar'-Santan'?" He laughed hollowly. "She looks at me," he said, drumming his right forefinger on his chest.

He saw at once that she did not believe him.

"In the well," Annabel said. "I'll drown you in the well. Either in our well, or in hers."

"Can't see how," he said, "since you're afraid of water, and can't swim a stroke."

"That'll make it that much easier," she said.

He puzzled over that, but made no reply. He could not see how it could be done, without her being down in the well with him, something he knew she would never do, and he took a last large swallow of feni to clear his mind. But of this he was sure—if she were even half-way serious, she'd find a way.

Later that night, after he had drifted off to sleep even though Annabel had busied herself banging pots and pans about in the kitchen, Mottu found he had acquired miraculous powers. With a single arching step he was able to cover as much ground as if he had done the running broad jump; he was gliding through the air in slow motion. Not quite believing what he had just accomplished, he stepped forward lightly again. Starting from the top step of his own front porch, he felt three easy leaps would place him squarely where he wanted to be; and so it was. The first took him to within inches of his own garden gate. Landing lightly on his left foot, he bounced off it high enough to clear the gate and land on the other side of the lane. A slight kick off the toes of his right foot and he had cleared Marie-Santana's garden wall and was skimming along inches above her steps. Now, standing by her front door, his own home seemed very far away and below him. Nevertheless, he regained his own porch with just one upward leap and a graceful swoop. He felt so good about having done all this that he turned and looked about to see if there were any witnesses.

He found one. Marie-Santana was standing where he himself had been just seconds earlier; she was looking directly at him and smiling, and as she waved he could see that her dress was wet and tight from swimming and it clung to her figure like onion skin. She put her hand to the side of her mouth so her whispered words would carry more clearly: "Move your feet, Mottu! Come on, move! Quick! Let's see if you can catch me!"

He saw then, as Marie-Santana swayed seductively to and fro, that to reach her he would have to leap over his own well, where Annabel, now grown much larger than life, was standing squarely on the parapet, daring him, arms akimbo.

Moon Dance

They were silent, the both of them, as they rode back in the old wooden carriage at dusk from the annual pre-Christmas fair in Mapusa, Barnabé tired from long hours of supervising the setting up of his booth of antiques and bric-a-brac and dealing with customers under the hot Indian sun, Rosa holding on to the restless four-year-old now straddling her knee. The child swayed as the carriage lumbered along the deserted road, and his mother braced her elbow against her side to steady him. Up front on his perch, Ramu the old coachman crooned gently to the two bullocks that pulled the carriage smartly along, and the bulls responded, nodding and shaking their heads at each cadence, the tiny bells in their collars adding counter-rhythms to the plaintive melody. From time to time a cyclist overtook them, ringing sharply at his bell to alert Ramu and the bulls, calling out "God give you a good night!" to whoever rode within; "God grant you grace," they answered in chorus into the fitful wind.

"Grandmama's carriage," little Angelo called the weather-beaten coach, but it had been built for Dona Esmeralda's father, back in 1853, by the coachbuilder who lived on their property. That was the year in which, vast oceans to the west, Dom Pedro V ascended the imperial throne of Portugal; the year in which, in forests and mountains a few miles east of where the carriage was now clumsily rolling, Goa's warlike Rané clans had stubbornly maintained their rebellion against the Portuguese crown; also the year in which Dona Esmeralda's own father—Barnabé's grandfather—had finally chosen sides, defining himself as a loyalist and boldly but mistakenly declaring, "This parcel of India has been and will forever remain Portuguese." Fortunately for him, he had picked the winning side. He was duly rewarded with land, and though he now could ride on horseback to oversee his farthest and newest estates, the bullock-drawn carriage still came in useful.

Dona Esmeralda herself, ten years old at the time, had used the carriage ever since, but only recently, with the birth of the grandchild Angelo, had she felt the need to make any significant changes. The large panel directly behind Ramu, the all-wooden windows on either side, and the entry door at the rear had all been altered to admit glass panes.

"We can't afford it," Barnabé had protested when he first learned of his mother's plans.

"The child should be able to look out," his mother had answered firmly. She did not add, though she could have, that he rarely counted cost as a factor when it came to fulfilling his own desires, no matter how much it set back the rest of the family. Now, having survived some eighty monsoons, the carriage still made a sturdy and reliable conveyance, once one got used to the spine-wrenching jolts that came each time the wheels hit a large stone embedded in the road, or moved in or out of a rain-caused rut. Occasionally Ramu had to ask one of Dona Esmeralda's other rent-free tenants, the village blacksmith, to replace one or other of the metal hoops that, like tires, protected the two large wooden wheels from the hazards of the road. The man gladly obliged. The old retainer thus kept the carriage in good repair, tending also to the two lively bulls who strained at their yoke so willingly.

The Mapusa fairgrounds lay at the southern edge of the town, and once the travelers had left the last house behind, Ramu turned the carriage on to a narrow road that cut through miles of paddy fields. From time to time they passed people on foot; there were no other vehicles in sight. The empty road stretched before them like an avenue, with coconut trees standing tall on either side, their crowns barely stirring in the soft salt-laden breezes now wafting in from the ocean.

The darkness deepened. "It's time to light the lamps, little master," said Ramu, leaping off his perch and guiding the bulls to the side of the deeply rutted road. This was the part the child loved especially, being held aloft by those strong bony brown arms so he could strike a match and light the stubby candles in turn, one on each side of the carriage, and then slam the lantern doors shut; the flame sputtered and flickered violently each time he did so, and sometimes he managed to put it out entirely. Then, of course, he'd clap his hands and get to light it once again. Ramu, laughing, indulged him.

The moon had not risen yet, but with the Great Bear well above the horizon and a thousand stars overhead, the twin lamps added enough of a glow on the familiar country road for the bulls to pick their way. A half-mile ahead, sharp beams of light swept around a curve, approaching rapidly, yet slowing and dipping each time a wheel met a depression in the road. Soon the roar of a motor filled the air. With a soft oath Ramu once again leaped to the ground, talking soothingly to the bulls as for the second time he pulled them to the shoulder.

"It's that crazy neighbor back from the Persian Gulf and his insolent driver, master," the coachman said, as the lights drew near and slowed to a crawl, "back with a car and three rupees in oil money in his pocket, and now both he and his lackey have forgotten how to respect their betters."

"It's all right, Ramu, just let the man go," Barnabé said evenly. So the world was passing him by; it had done so all of his life. Why should 1933 be any different? Rosa pulled her son to her, holding a kerchief to the child's nose as, with a clattering of pistons and much tooting of the horn, the Model T churned past them, smothering them in dust.

"Look at the *shaitan* go," grumbled the coachman. "The world has turned upside down. It is he who should have pulled over, to let us pass."

But Barnabé would not comment further; the annoyance was momentary. As a brightness filled the sky, Ramu resumed his singing to the straining bulls: "O Patteh! O Vinnoo! See how the moon comes dancing above the tree-robed hills. Let your feet dance, too, merrily—we're going home!"

The evening had started out balmy but now an invisible fall of dew added crispness to the breeze. To shield wife and child, Barnabé rose to shut the glass windows on either side and latch them in place. A large wooden box containing imported musical instruments, knick-knacks, and other merchandise had been placed on the seat facing him; some smaller boxes lay at their feet. He had hoped there would be fewer on the way home.

Rosa had barely spoken since they had started the journey back, and Barnabé now sought for ways to break the oppressive silence. It rang in his ears above the crisp thudding of the hooves and the grinding of the wheels in the ruts, above the jangling of the bells and Ramu's voice inventing songs with which to amuse himself and the bulls.

"We should be home in half an hour," he said at last, lamely, for lack of anything better to say. "That is, if the bulls can keep up this pace."

Rosa barely stirred. He wondered whether she was asleep, and glanced at her askance. Her eyes were wide open, staring straight ahead. He saw at once there would be trouble; her mood had blackened. Once again he began searching for things to say, words that would touch her through the wall he felt rising between them. But she spoke first, abruptly.

"How much did you sell?" she asked, speaking low, and in English. It was a question he had been dreading, and he took his time replying.

"Well?" she prompted.

"Not enough," he said. "I am sorry."

"I should have known," she said, her voice still low but now tinged with bitterness.

"Nothing worked out right," he said.

"Nothing?!"

He fell silent, his mind awash with thoughts to ward off a greater confrontation; in this confining carriage from which there was no escape, each shallow excuse he proffered could be picked apart and shown for what he really knew it to be, a sham. He had started the day badly, he now realized; had he insisted the child stay home with his mother, instead of taking him to the fair, Rosa would not have ridden out in the carriage to bring the two of them home. Then, riding alone, he could have asked Ramu to take a detour through Sangoldá, where he had cousins who were rolling in money; he realized, however, before even completing the thought, that that miserly branch of the family would not have lent him anything, not a fraction of a rupee, not even an anna, to save his marriage, not even to save his life.

"You pawned my jewels," she said. "You know they were my mother's, and they mean a lot to me. You said we'd get them back tomorrow. You promised!"

"I thought we would," Barnabé said. "But the fair was a disaster. There's no way I could have foreseen that! Not enough people showed up, and those who did were not spending the way they used to, Rosa. It's all over the world; it's the Depression. Look at America!"

"We're not in America," she said. "We have assets. And you told me you'd saved up most of what we needed, that anything we made today would just put us over the top. Now you are telling me we have—nothing? If you were not lying then, what happened?"

"Something unexpected came up," he said.

"Such as what? Another mistress, maybe?"

"Rosa, you know that's not true!"

"Then what?"

"Money I was counting on didn't come through," he said. "Ten stands of bamboo I had earmarked for sale—they were cut down and rustled this week. And the coconut crop, too, in the outlying properties—the trees have been stripped bare by thieves. Even the cashews up on the south hill—gone. There were bills we had to pay, pressing bills. I transferred money."

"And told me nothing, as usual! What about the bills?"

Yes, his mind said to him; what about the bills? What can you possibly say to her about the bills?

"I should have listened to my father," she said.

At times like these, he wished she had. He thought, glumly, he could have been rich if only he could have had a rupee for each time she had told him what her father had said, 'Never shall a rose of mine marry a scion of that crumbling old house.' He had thought of an answer: 'But you did, and I've felt the thorns ever since.' The words had died on his tongue; he had no wish to provoke a harsher anger. And now she was about to taunt him again. But she didn't.

"You mentioned bills," she said instead. "What bills?"

He jerked his head silently towards Ramu.

"Don't tell me we're not alone," Rosa said. "He's up there on his box, busy with the bulls and his singing, and he doesn't understand English, anyway."

"We also have company," the father said.

"We have company, Papa?" the child said, turning from the window. "Will they be staying for dinner?"

"What did I tell you?" Barnabé said, looking sharply at her, then turning his face away as quickly.

"Your father was mistaken, dear. No one's coming to dinner."

"The moon's rocking," the child said. "Oooh, look, Mama! It's making me dizzy, to see it rocking so." Excitedly, he knocked on the front of the carriage, crying out, "Ramu! Look up! Look up! The moon is really dancing."

"So it is!" said Ramu, laughing. And leaning forward he urged on the bulls again with a longer song: "O Patteh! O Vinnoo! The moon goddess is dancing for our little master. You dance too, merrily—come, my children, shake your feet, like the wind swirling through the paddy fields—we're going home."

The bulls picked up their pace, the bells around their necks jingling louder as the carriage moved briskly forward.

The boy clapped his hands. "I love the moon."

His mother reached out and pulled him tenderly to her, kissing him on the cheek. The child broke her hold and ran to the far window.

"There's a bull's black shadow running on this side of the road, Papa," he said. "It's right under my window. There's no shadow on that side." He stopped, questioningly, then turned to the window again. "It's a very black shadow, and it's running and tossing its head, like a real bull. Oh oh! Now it's gone."

Thank God for the child, he thought; he comes to the rescue when I need it most. Never fails.

"We've got to get this out in the open," the mother said. "We've got to talk this thing through, and seriously, before it destroys the both of us."

"The shadow's gone, Papa! Where did it go?"

"We can talk in the morning," the father said, keeping his voice even. "You may find it on that side, son."

The child ran to look. "I see it! I see it! Why did it move?"

"Would you like to go sit next to Ramu, love?" Rosa asked.

He looked from one to the other, warily.

"I'd rather be with you."

"You usually like it up there," she said. "And you'll be able to see the moon and the shadows far more clearly. Ramu will even tell you stories about the stars."

He pouted. "I want to be here with you."

"It's the moon," said his father. "When the moon's here on my side, the shadow falls over there, and when the moon's on Mama's side, the shadow falls over here."

"Is the moon playing games with us, Papa? Is it going from side to side to make the shadows move?"

"I see I've misled you," said Barnabé laughing. "It's the carriage that's moving on a winding road, son, not the moon in the sky!"

"But I see it moving, Papa. I see it running always ahead of us, running, jumping over hills, hiding behind trees, just running and smiling at me."

"It seems that way, son, doesn't it?"

"Man-in-the-moon!" the child called, waving and pointing. "You're funny!"

"Did you like the fair, Angelo, my angel?" his mother asked.

"Lots. The balloons, and all those toys, and the sweets! And I made new friends. I liked looking at the little sugar houses with red roofs and green walls and little red doors and windows. And there was a sugar church with a bi-i-ig steeple. One day when I'm rich I'll build myself a big sugar house and live in it and eat it all up! Bit by bit."

His parents laughed.

"You got yourself some very pretty balloons," his mother said. "Take good care of them; they must last you a while."

"I wanted something else, too," he said, wistfully.

"Now, son, we've gone into that already," his father said. He wished the moment had never come. "We've talked about that enough. The balloons were all your mother and I could afford."

Her eyes were on her husband, hot with anger.

"But Papa, three of my new friends each bought a mouth organ from you," the child said. "Why can't I get one, too? I didn't ask for toys, though everyone there had lots of big toys to sell, and my friends bought plenty."

Barnabé looked at her then, throwing up his hands in frustration.

"It's only four annas!" wailed the child. "Grandmama said she'll give me four annas for my birthday next month. I want it, please, Papa!"

"Oh, give it to the child," she cried. "For heaven's sake, it's only four miserable annas!"

He fumbled with the fastenings, and at last the big box was opened. The boy took the shiny little harmonica from its case and struggled with the cellophane wrapping.

"Here!" she said, undoing it for him. It was so small, it fit right into his palm.

He blew on it immediately, strongly, blowing out and then sucking his breath back in, eyes wide, blowing in and out, out and in, a cacophony that threatened to have no end.

"It wasn't just the cost, as you can see," the father said. "I hope now you're both satisfied."

"Oh darling, put that thing away for now," the mother said. "You're giving me a headache."

The child put it by, and sat back, looking out the window at a landscape gone bleak, a moon now cold and remote, dancing mockingly.

The silence dragged on.

59

"The land we have in Aiconá," she said, "that you've always told me is loaded with bamboo groves. It's not the first time the bamboo has been rustled, and it won't be the last. Why then do we hold on to it?"

"That property? It's been in the family for generations." They'd had this argument often enough before; he thought the issue had long been settled.

"We can't eat land," she said. "It's an asset, to be used as needed to sustain the family. If we can't exploit it, at least let's sell it. How long are we going to keep ourselves poor by holding on to it?"

"Not the land," he said. The very thought appalled him. "We can't sell the land. My father—his father before him—they would turn in their graves. Land is the one thing we have left. Sell that, and we will lose all status."

"Status!" she exclaimed. "My God, status! Then it's truly hopeless, isn't it? We're trapped in a backwater here, for life, and the one thing that will save us, you will not do? Until now, at least, we were held in some respect; when we went for a walk, people stepped aside to let us pass. Now even the newly rich riffraff force us off the road, making us eat their dust."

She began to cry; it angered him when she did that.

"So that's it?" he said, savagely. "That's what's bothering you? Somebody drives by us in a fancy car, and all at once we are all reduced to nothing? We know how that man got his money—away from Goa, spending year after year slaving in the Persian Gulf, surrounded by menials, working at a menial job far from his family; that's what you'd like me to do? Leave you and the boy to go work in the desert, you think that's what I was born for? So at the end of it all we would have a car? Is that what you really want out of life—material things?"

"What's wrong with that?" she cried. "What's wrong with wanting a better life for us all? With wanting food on the table? For heaven's sake, Barnabé, all I can give our son for his breakfast is a glass of milk and a slice of plain bread, and he pleads with the Virgin Mary for a blob of butter to spread on it. That is something neither I nor the Virgin Mary can give him; but you—you do not even hear him, wrapped up as you are in the morning newspaper. And have you thought about him at all lately, the dreams we once had for his future? Think ahead to when he'll be our age—while all the world drives around in motor cars, do you want him to be riding around with his family in this patched-up rattle trap still, thinking the same bitter thoughts we are thinking now?"

He turned his face again to the window.

"Sell the land," she insisted. "Talk frankly to your mother and then sell the land. As it is, it hangs around our necks like a curse. Save the house, save the grounds it sits on, so your mother can continue to live out her life there. Then perhaps we'll put the hard times behind us once and for all, and make a fresh start of it."

He put his head between his hands, shoulders heaving.

"Look me in the eye," she said, when he did not answer.

He turned to face her. But he could not speak.

"My God," she said. "You have spoken to her, haven't you. You've spoken to your mother, and she's turned you down. That's what you were counting on, wasn't it, that she'd come through for you, as she has so many times before? That's where the money was going to come from, not from the fair, to get me back my jewels?"

"Rosa!" he cried, reaching for her hand, but she drew it sharply away.

The child began whistling then, softly but with increasing intensity, anything, anything to cut through the tension.

"You're whistling out of tune, son," his father said. "You're whistling way out of tune! It's driving me crazy."

"Oh, let the child whistle!" the mother said sharply, but the boy shrank back, silent and afraid.

"Whistle, son! I'm telling you to whistle!" she said again, more vehemently.

Ramu sang, the bulls strained at their yoke, and the moon danced over the enchanted hills, but the child felt the salt tears creep between puckered lips, and no sound came.

Bombay/Mumbai

An Anna's Worth of Kindness

When Chandu came out of the late night movie at the Elite Talkies in Bombay, the first thing he saw in the semi-darkness was the brightly lit tramcar waiting on its tracks in the middle of the road, so he ran to it, unmindful of the onrushing traffic, clutching his paper fighter kite tightly by its bridle so it bucked and fluttered right by his shoulder. Even as he leaped aboard, the driver, standing at the controls, stepped on the warning bell and sent the tram lurching forward.

Chandu hurried up the aisle, leaning against the sharp thrust of the acceleration. This was the first time, in all his twelve years, that he would be riding as a fare-paying passenger; usually he traveled during rush hours, clinging to the bars outside the window while maintaining a toehold on the running board of a crowded tram or bus, jumping off only when the ticket collector got much too close. Now, finding that functionary sprawled on the very first bench, Chandu eased himself on to the second, from where he would still see the world go rushing by. All those lights, for miles and miles! What a glorious end that would be to his day.

Across the aisle from him, also enjoying the view, sat a plump, neatly dressed man, who sported the satisfied air and well-oiled mustache of a prosperous merchant.

"How fast this tram is running, uncle," Chandu said to him, addressing him with the respect due an adult, and the man, turning away from the window, was suddenly loquacious.

"*Ohé*," he said, "don't talk like that, or everyone will know you are a country bumpkin. For us, this is slow stuff. *Arre*, you should have been here a month ago, when we had seven-notch trams, then you would have seen them flying! You could go from one end of Bombay to the other in an hour. But then we had some accidents, trams not stopping in time, people getting hit, so now they have cut their speed to four-notch running. Not even five notches is the municipality allowing."

"What is a notch, uncle?" asked Chandu.

"Listen to the boy," said the man derisively to the half dozen other passengers who were scattered about the car. "He doesn't know what a notch is!" And they all laughed loudly, to hide the fact that they, too, did not know.

"You see the handle the driver keeps turning," the man said. "At its base there are many notches. The notches control the speed. The more notches a driver can use, the faster we go. Seven notches is almost twice as fast as four. Last month we would have been going much faster than we are going now. Now do you understand?"

Chandu still did not, but nodded anyway. He didn't want them all laughing at him again.

"You have a kite," the man said. "Let me see it. It's beautiful, but a little torn. Here, and here."

"I can patch it," Chandu said. "I'll fix it, and I'll fly it."

"When I was your age, I was the best kite flyer in my neighborhood," the man boasted. He ran his hand over the length of string that had still been left attached, testing its powdered glass coating for sharpness. "If any one sent his kite up to challenge me, I would send mine higher, then dive low from above, letting out my string very fast. If the other boy were foolish enough to pull on his string, that would be the end of it. His string would be cut, and he'd lose his kite. *Wah!* Always I was winning."

Chandu nodded. That was the way to do it. "Sometimes I cut five, six kites a day," he boasted as well. "But this one was cut by someone else."

"You caught it, then?"

"Near the movie house, earlier this evening. I saw boys flying their kites from rooftops, and others running to catch those that had been cut. While they were busy chasing a big one, this beauty drifted right into my hands."

"So now you are going home with it. Going far?"

"King's Circle."

"That's far enough—end of the line. I know King's Circle well," the plump man said. "I have family there. Big family. Perhaps you have a big family too?"

Chandu nodded. "Very big family." He closed his eyes and counted on his fingers. "Fourteen." He had counted the old man and the younger couple he had attached himself to, after watching for a day to see how the grown ups treated their four little ones. Then he had made himself useful, watching over the toddlers and the baby, running errands. And he had included too the half-dozen or so others, adults as well as children, who shared that same narrow stretch of sidewalk every night.

"What address?"

Chandu seemed not to hear, but looked out at the scene flashing past his window.

"What address?" the man asked again, leaning across the aisle to prod him in the ribs.

"Not far from the terminus," Chandu said, in a voice that could hardly be heard. "Not far—but I'll have to walk." He looked at his interrogator, then looked quickly away.

The man too looked away. It became obvious to him that he had been talking to a worthless street urchin, when he should have known better. He wrinkled his nose—odd that he had not noticed the unwashed street smell earlier. Perhaps the kite had distracted him. He slid away from the aisle and propped his elbow on his window sill, feigning sleep.

The tramcar rattled on as the conductor dozed. He had only one fare to collect, the raggedy urchin's, and that could wait. Occasionally a passenger got up and walked down the aisle to the front, and the driver stopped or slowed the tram to a crawl to let them off. Others walked to the rear, and when they did that he knew that they would lean back and drop expertly off the rear platform while he barely slackened speed. Still, the driver listened for the sound of their chappals slapping smartly on the asphalt before picking up speed again.

The conductor roused himself when the only ones left were the merchant, another swarthy and unkempt passenger, and Chandu. "Tickit! Tickit!" he exclaimed, leaning over the boy, holding the ticket container with his left hand while repeatedly clicking the metal punch he held in his right. He had found that he could fluster his passengers by clicking it right in front of their noses, and he liked doing that; it spiced up his day.

"Tickit-tickit-tickit! To where?"

"King's Circle," Chandu said, reaching in his pocket for the anna he had saved for the trip home; he had spent half a rupee already, on the movie and eats, and it was his last coin, but in his haste to hand it over he knocked the back of his hand against the front seat and the anna dropped to the floor.

"What is it?" asked the merchant, alerted by the clink of the coin, bending and looking when he saw Chandu bending and looking under the seats.

"My anna," Chandu said. "It fell down here, and it's gone."

They kept looking. Lalu, the swarthy man who was sitting two benches to the rear, had felt the coin come rolling against his bare feet, and now with his toes clamped tightly around it he searched as vigorously as Chandu. He made a comfortable living most days picking pockets, but even a stray anna at the end of the day was not to be ignored.

"Come, give me another!" the conductor said sourly, tugging sharply at the bell to bring the tram to an abrupt halt. "Do you want a free ride all the way home? That anna is gone! Maybe it never existed! You have already traveled far enough for free."

"Please, uncle," Chandu said to him, "that was my last anna!"

"And this is my last ticket. Come, give me an anna or get out and walk!"

The driver waited. It was a scene he was familiar with, played out each day with a different cast of characters.

"Let the tram go! Let's get going!" Lalu said to the conductor. "Don't keep us all waiting for one lousy anna!"

The conductor sneered. "If it's only one lousy anna, why don't you pay for him?"

"These young rascals," the merchant said, "always wanting to travel without paying! Cheating the tram company so it has to raise our fares! Sheesh! Come, *sala*, pay up or get out!"

"Please, uncle," Chandu begged again, but the conductor had already gone in search of a policeman. The constable came reluctantly, holding his bamboo lathi in his left hand, and when Chandu continued to plead he lost his temper.

"Get up, get up!" he shouted, seizing the boy by the arm and shaking him. "You are one useless juvenile lawbreaker!"

Lalu stirred. These meddling policemen, always pushing people around! He had felt the weight of their lathis much too often, and the tightness of their handcuffs as well.

"All right, I'll pay his fare," he announced quietly, handing over Chandu's one-anna piece that he had retrieved from between his toes.

The merchant protested. "You are encouraging a parasite!" he said. "Do you see me paying his fare? Do you think I could not pay it? These young loafers are always traveling free, relying on kind-hearted people like you and me to take care of them. Idle riffraff! It is a sin and a shame on us all."

But Lalu was unmoved. He knew that now the policeman had recognized him for what he was, knew too that at this moment he himself had the upper hand. If they crossed paths again that policeman would try to get even; now he merely dropped Chandu's arm with a muttered curse and walked out of the tram.

"Sit up straight!" the conductor shouted, punching a ticket and handing it to Chandu. "Feet in front! Don't block the aisle!"

Wordlessly, Chandu bent down to touch Lalu's feet.

But Lalu stopped him. "Sit straight," he said. "Sit straight! You heard the man." His voice sounded strange.

The merchant got off soon after, and Lalu moved up to enjoy the better view. Chandu effaced himself in his corner, holding on to his kite, and Lalu busied himself with his own thoughts. The tram was now rattling through an industrial area, and the streets were deserted. Then Lalu too rose to go. As the tram slowed to let him off, Chandu called to him.

"Uncle, would you like to take my kite?" He held it up for Lalu to see. The breeze from the tram's movement made it rear smartly in the air, and sway from side to side; Chandu had to grab at the kite's bridle to prevent it from being damaged.

"Oh, but that's a pretty kite ," Lalu exclaimed. "And you would give it to me?" He looked in the child's eyes. He himself had been a street kid once, but not quite as innocent as this one.

"Yes, uncle."

Lalu took a step towards him, then stopped abruptly. "It's too beautiful a kite," he said. "I want you to keep it. But when you fly it, be sure to send it high up in the sky, so high that I'll be able to see it here, in Parel. Here, let me look at it again; then I'll know it's yours when you send it up into the clouds." He fished a one-rupee note out of his pocket. "And so you can do that, go buy yourself some really long string."

Chandu touched the wrinkled note to his forehead and carefully put it away in his shirt pocket.

After Lalu had jumped off it seemed to Chandu that the tram had gathered additional speed. It certainly swayed a lot, almost doing a dance, much as the kite had done as it slowly drifted down into his waiting hands, and as it had done again when he had held it up for Lalu to see and admire.

He was the only passenger now and the conductor lay sprawled asleep. The man's cap had fallen off and his mouth lay open. Chandu looked past the driver to where the street lights converged in the distance. Where they met there would be a traffic circle and that's where the tram would finally stop and he would get off. He touched his pocket lightly to make sure the crumpled rupee was still there. If he were careful he could get the little ones who shared the sidewalk with him some sweets, and still have enough left over for kite string. And if he spoke to the kite man the right way he might even have an anna left over for a cup of tea for the older couple to share.

Yes, the tram was going faster. The driver was even singing to himself; perhaps he was cheating just a little and had coaxed the streetcar up to five-notch running. Surely, at this time of night, with no one on the road, no one to get hurt, the municipality would not really care.

Night Encounter

On its way through the heart of Bombay the bus had swept by the movie house that had launched him on this daring and eagerly anticipated expedition. From his seat on the upper deck he saw the long line of hopefuls at the box office window, the even longer queue of ticket holders waiting for the theater doors to open; thousands, all told, lusting to see *The Outlaw*, the movie newly arrived in town, starring the unknown starlet Jane Russell or, rather, starring her rather phenomenal bosom. Just two days earlier, his college cronies had told him about the giant poster outside the theater entrance, that showed Jane bursting out of her bodice, what there was of it. His mind inflamed, he had suggested they skip afternoon classes to go see that movie.

"We'll miss biology," one had protested.

"But we'll be studying anatomy," another had countered. Laughing, they had jumped aboard a passing streetcar and stolen a ride to the theater, arriving there, alas, too late—some sex maniac had stolen the masterpiece, the manager was even then explaining to a group of despondent would-be voyeurs. The story of the theft made the headlines the following day, and all shows were immediately sold out. They had made up for the disappointment by buying a ticket off a scalper and drawing lots to see who would use it. He had won.

The movie had not disappointed—he had indeed gotten a closer look at the Russell anatomy, seen cleavage such as no movie had ever revealed before; more, he had seen Jane Russell, sharing a railway compartment with a wounded co-star, clamber down at night from an upper berth to get into the hero's bunk and restore his will to live. A wonderful example of Practical Sex Therapy 101, he had reported back that evening; shocking but wonderful. And also mysterious, and barely hinted at, thanks no doubt to the vigilance of India's censors.

One thing leading to another, the group had discussed, animatedly, the art and science of going on the prowl, of picking up women, not in the notorious red-light district, which was filthy and disease ridden, but in that section of town where better establishments were said to prosper, and where foreign women, some reputedly as amply endowed as la Russell, walked the streets. On this trip, he was going to try his luck.

He got off the double decker at the bus terminal and started walking back, slowly. The street was poorly lit and he was not familiar with this particular section of Bombay, having only been this far downtown twice before, in the heat and glare of noon, skipping college for the day. Now, not knowing quite which way to explore, he peered down the dark and winding alleys that branched off on either side, and felt he should have brought a bag of breadcrumbs along, to scatter as he went. From time to time he let his gaze sweep fleetingly over the faces of the passersby. Sometimes, with the lights of the teashops behind the approaching figures, he could not gauge their looks till they were almost upon him; at other times the lights shone full on them, and he saw they were faces much like any other, some of them animated, others burdened with a weariness of body and spirit.

Though the night was young—just minutes earlier, the great clock on the façade of Victoria Terminus had shown it to be eight-thirty—to him the hour already seemed late. Even if he gave in to his doubts and anxieties and turned around now, before his mission was accomplished, even if he caught the very first bus back, he would still not be home by ten. But tonight he could be late, he reminded himself; he had secured his parents' permission, told them he was going to a movie. How then could he explain getting back too soon? If on the other hand he kept on, he could be on his way back—with luck on his side, that is—in something like an hour and a half. But he could not be sure just how long such an adventure would last, he hoped it would be long but not too long; he would like to be done with it and home by midnight. That's when they were expecting him back, wasn't it?

For the greater part of the long ride into town, he had rehearsed his moves, recalling what his classmates had said. They were agreed that subtle conventions prevailed; they disagreed on what the conventions were. One said you scratched the tip of your nose, and if she scratched her nose too, you had connected. Another said it wasn't the nose at all, you pulled on the lobe of your right ear; if she mimicked the gesture, that meant she was available, and willing.

The bus had once been a single decker that had had an extra deck tacked on during the shortages of World War II. That deck had no top and only vestigial sides, and as the driver had a maniacal streak in him, the entire bus creaked and groaned and swayed perilously, the upper deck threatening to career off on its own as they lurched from side to side down the long and winding thoroughfares. At each stop he had looked carefully at the women waiting in line to board. To his chagrin, they seemed eminently respectable and unapproachable; and those that seemed to be likely prospects kept their eyes on the bus; intent on not letting pushy males get ahead of them, they shoved and jostled in turn, until they were safely aboard. Only once in all that trip did a woman look up, and he caught her eye, and scratched the tip of his nose, and she did not react, and he pulled on his earlobe, but by then she had clambered aboard already and was out of his sight.

Now, on the street, the people passed him by indifferently, the young and the old; an occasional couple brushed past him, arms locked, heads close together, lips murmuring soft phrases that escaped his ear but fired his imagination. He heard muted throaty laughter.

A half hour went by, and still he walked on, his mind chaotic, headlines and lurid tales from the tabloids swirling in his head—here was the center of vice, here lay the streetwalkers' paradise. The papers said you had only to step out into the streets of an evening to be accosted by painted houris; pimps would sidle up to passersby, offering illicit pleasures. Had he somehow picked the wrong time, or the wrong day? So far, no one had come up to him. He felt cheated—this was not the way he had planned the evening. True, he would have shied away from an invitation to an orgy, of that he was certain. But a taste of private sex would be far different—an intimate yet quite anonymous experience, where he could, if he wished, be tender, even understanding. Failing that, he would like to at least have the experience of being solicited; he might turn the offer down, but it would somehow be reassuring. Or he could take the initiative himself, though that could be bruising to his ego, since he would be the one risking and enduring rejection....

From time to time he heard raucous music blaring from behind shuttered windows. Ancient handwound victrolas ground out Glen Miller's "In the Mood", or a song from Bing The Groaner, or yet another from the new singing sensation, the upstart challenger, Sinatra. Sometimes he heard the Ink Spots, or the Andrew Sisters singing "Rum and Coca cola". Mostly, however, it was Glen Miller.

By Electric House he retraced his steps, then turned once again, seeking refuge in the recessed doorway of a once elegant building. A man walked up, pulled the door open, went in. He heard vague shouting and laughter before the door creaked shut. Two other men came out, reeking of liquor. They looked at him curiously, held the door open for him a moment, and when he didn't react, shrugged, and went their way. In the light of the open door he had noticed a plaque on the wall: "À la mode française." He waited a minute and then quickly slipped into the foyer and mounted the dimly lit stairs. Music drew him up the flights; on the third landing he saw the plaque again and rang a bell and a tiny woman answered. She was an Anglo-Indian, plump for her size and dusky, her eyebrows plucked and pencilled in and her face powdered white. Blotches of rouge daubed her cheeks. Noting that she wore a dress that showed breast and thigh, he kept his eyes fixed on the hair piled high on her head. She smiled and said, "Yes?"

From within the room behind her came the sound of a piano vamping and a babble of voices and a woman singing, out of tune, ribald verses that brought forth cheers and cascading laughter.

Embarrassed, he did not know quite what to say.

"Yes?" she prompted him again, her eyebrows arching almost

into her hairline.

He said, lamely, "I saw your plaque downstairs. You know, by the door."

She smiled.

He said, "I thought perhaps—"

"Yes?"

Suddenly he was embarrassed to tell her the reason he was there. "I thought perhaps—because—the sign was in French—and it said À la mode française—I thought you might have some French fashions here, fashions I could—could look at."

"Fashions? Oh, *mode!* Carl!" she turned and called into the room, and a burly man came out immediately. "Here's a young one who'd like to see whatever French fashions we have. He's seen our sign, À la mode française." She put her hand up to primp the back of her hair-do and then hid a laugh.

He did not like the man's looks, feeling himself trapped, with no way out. "Fashions, or perhaps models," he faltered, "either." He felt totally ridiculous. "Whatever. But I see you're busy now. Got company, friends, a party going on. I'll come back another day."

"Don't go," the man said. "Fashions and models, we've got them both. Haven't we, Bertha! All the way from Paree, and that costs a lot of money. How much money you have, son?"

While he fumbled for an answer, she added: "Our models and fashions are very expensive. Very expensive." She waited for him to say something, then said slowly, "Ve - ry."

As though she felt he had not understood!

Still he stood there, fidgeting.

"This may be quite the wrong place for you," she said, not unkindly. "You could always come back, you know, when you feel more ready."

The stairs were a blur; he took them two at a time. He regretted having run down the stairs so fast, without having at least asked the woman how expensive very expensive could be. Though he might not have had enough, he would at least have been prepared for the next

77

time around. Out on the sidewalk he saw two young women come walking down the street, arm in arm, their bodies pressed possessively together. Now, with the two stepping trimly towards him, he found himself once again tongue-tied; a swish of skirts, a whiff of perfume, a sideways glance, and they were past him and gone.

He cursed himself for a fool and a coward. In his mind's eye he saw the prowlers of the night, the pimps and touts who had been avoiding him, laughing at his inexperience; but he saw once again the young women's freshness, their innocence, and he was glad he had not spoken to them, glad he had not insulted them there in the public street, at night.

From the shadow of the doorway he turned to look after them. Down the opposite sidewalk two sailors were ambling, their caps drooping over one eye, their feet finding the pavement with a thud as though they had not expected it to be where it was. He saw the men cross the street, the women turn to meet them; it was all so easy! A smile, a giggle, a whispered word, and the four of them were off together.

A crowd coming out of the Regal Theater brought him back to reality—the last movie show was over. He checked his watch: a quarter past eleven. Time to head home; he had missed his chance. Too bad! On the other hand, he had to admit to feeling a sense of relief. A bus waited at the corner across the street; it would have taken him where he was going, but he let it fill up and leave, preferring to ride alone, alone with his thoughts. When it had pulled away he crossed over to the now deserted bus stop and waited.

With the garish blue and mauve lights of the marquee behind her, a lone young woman hovered uncertainly in front of the Regal. His heart leapt even before he saw she was beautiful, then quickened as she saw him and walked across the street towards him. He noticed then a police inspector coming up behind her, and hearing the footsteps she turned her head and saw the man too. But she kept walking right up to where he stood by the bus stop and said in a loud, clear voice, "I have to get back to Breach Candy. Do you know where I can catch my bus?"

He was glad she had come to him, glad he could help. "Over there," he said, pointing past the advancing inspector to where he had seen a double decker stop minutes earlier. "You just missed one." He liked the clean soft look of her, and felt suddenly protective. "You shouldn't be out this late," he said, "not in this area, alone like this."

The inspector passed them, humming softly. "Goodnight, Adeline," he said, and sauntered on.

Abruptly she started across the road to where he had pointed, but halfway there she veered back across the street, back towards the Regal, desperate haste in her steps.

"Hey!" he called. "You're going the wrong way! The bus stop's over there!"

She turned on him in a flash.

"You blame fool," she called softly, "don't you even know when to keep your damn trap shut?"

The boy heard the inspector stop, and he suddenly felt small and mean in the night, watching her skirts go swaying into the half shadows, feeling the derisive eyes of the policeman burning twin holes in the back of his neck.

I hold thee by too many bands:
Thou sayest farewell, and lo!
I have thee by the hands,
And will not let thee go.

Robert Bridges

Loving Ayesha

Before I met Ayesha I met her older sister Moira. Moira was the one I fell in love with, back in the summer of 1941, when she was a second-year student at the college we both went to in Dharghat, and I was a year behind. Though not beautiful, she had a lively personality; her happy, healthy laugh, her wit and charm, commanded attention. One was drawn to her, as moth to candle.

So I got singed. But I got singed later than I expected and for an unforeseen reason. I thought I might have a hard time even getting close to Moira, let alone getting her to love me; after all, though she dressed plainly and modestly, she came from a wealthy family and I was embarrassingly poor. The difference was obvious; I was also embarrassingly gauche. Despite this, she accepted my friendship and returned it warmly. So it grew, and I was happy. I felt that love, from her side, could wait. Look, we were a bunch of teenagers then, she and I and the rest of our group, which was not to be wondered at; in those days in India you went through just eight years of school, and shazaam! at fifteen you were in college.

There's not much else I knew about Moira in those first days, except that she, like the rest of her family, was a devout Catholic. I'd see her in the college chapel, her head bowed, her dark hair and features hidden by a black lace mantilla. She'd be kneeling in the front row to the left of the aisle, and I'd be kneeling on the right, two rows to the rear, from where I could catch a glimpse of her without its becoming too obvious. In between those sidelong glances, I prayed—for her, for my parents, my siblings, for her family, for the two of us. She had, I was told, a large number of brothers and sisters, which helped explain the gregariousness of her ways. Anyway, I was glad enough to become part of her in-group at Saint Ignatius; there were some sixteen of us in it, all sharing the same interests, and whenever we could get together we swirled around the campus like a spinning planetary system that had Moira at its center. Ayesha at that time was still in high school; I saw her just once, from afar, a gawky shadow trailing Moira to the train station.

Clarence was the one who had the nearest orbit. A senior, he was taller than the rest of us, five foot eight at least, but he walked with a stoop, as though anxious not to stand out. Joe's trajectory was more elliptical; also a senior, bright and bubbly, at times he worked feverishly to get close to Moira, and then a word from her directed at one of us, a mere look, even a gesture, would arouse his jealousy, plunge him in despair, and send him rocketing to the far edges of our universe. But he always came back, Joe did, and then he was morose. Joe was a constant; he was also constantly contrite. I liked him, as I liked Clarence, but it did not take me long to see that, as far as Moira was concerned, Joe was a nonstarter.

Clarence baffled me. A chap of moods, there were times when he was with us and not with us. "What's bothering Clarence?" I asked Moira one day. "Why is he such a snoot? I tried talking to him this morning and he snubbed me."

"What did he say that upset you?"

"That's just the point," I said. "He said absolutely nothing. It's as though I'd been talking in a vacuum; to him I didn't exist."

"Oh, that!" she said, and laughed. "You'll get used to that. He has things on his mind, and to deal with them he goes off into another world. He's not just distracted, he's really off somewhere else, in the labyrinth of his mind."

"And what does he look at and think about, in this labyrinth of his?"

"Oh, the meaning of the universe, our purpose in life, his own place in the scheme of things, that sort of thing. Clarence is a thinker and a dreamer, and I admire him for it. Shall I tell him you felt hurt? He'll be sure to apologize."

"Oh no, let's let it go. After what you've told me, I feel better already." And I decided I'd get to know Clarence better, to become as close to him as he was to Moira.

Our group had other traits in common, besides our shared admiration for Moira. Classes took up the morning, but afternoons were reserved for extracurricular activities, and we threw ourselves into these with abandon. Yet, despite our frenetic schedule, we excelled at our studies. Most of us had won competitive scholarships; we needed them, I more than others, and whether from need or from temperament we never stopped competing. Intellectually inclined as we were, we found ourselves dazzled by the extraordinary and magnetic brilliance of our Jesuit professors. They in turn, perhaps seeing in us some faint reflection of what they themselves had been like in their youth, willingly took on the role of mentors.

The College of Saint Ignatius lay in the heart of Dharghat, which spread flatly around for miles. My mother, my four siblings, and I—my father had passed away when I was twelve—lived in a four-bedroom apartment some miles away, just off the main road that ran in an almost straight line from the southernmost tip of Kholawada into the northernmost suburbs. My sisters and brother all worked; their combined salaries helped pay the rent, and paid for the food on the table, and also for the services of the live-in cook and maid. We knew no luxuries. I, as a student, was the only non-wage earner. We were a close-knit family, but despite the forced intimacy of shared bedrooms we managed to maintain some element of privacy in our lives; for instance, though at dinner we shared our day's experiences, I kept my romantic fantasies from my sisters, fearing their sharp teasing. Since, however, my older brother was already in his mid-twenties, I assumed perhaps wrongly that he was a man with a rich fund of experiences, and consulted him as need arose.

The campus at St. Ignatius was small, catering to fewer than two thousand students, but once one walked past the squat, fan-leaved Arabian palms that screened the Gothic entrance, the giant city that enfolded it ceased to exist. Within its walls we created our own magical environment. About a quarter of the student body were Christians, that is to say, Catholic; of the rest, most were Hindu or Parsi or Muslim, with a sprinkling of Buddhists and Jains and Bene-Israelites, these last not a lost tribe of Israel, but a found and welcome tribe as far as we were concerned, and, after all these centuries, now thoroughly Indian. All told, it was a lively and exciting campus, but at the same time a disciplined campus; we knew we were there to study. Still, the growing political ferment in the country impacted on us, as did the war that, phony no longer, was now raging all over Europe and had spilled over into North Africa; the newspapers, and the mandatory British newsreels that preceded every movie in every movie house, reminded us of its dismal progress—more Allied defeats than victories, every day.

Naively, we turned bad news into good. We believed that France having fallen to the German blitzkrieg, the British would need the Indian Army more than ever, and to ensure our loyalty they would surely agree to grant us our freedom. But the Mahatma, who had first propounded this view, soon became disillusioned, and his call for a nonviolent struggle to oust the British touched our hearts. So amongst us students the pro-war movement quickly fizzled. Only a handful, Joe among them, were convinced that to help Britain would eventually help India; they joined the all-volunteer University Officer Training Corps. While we watched from the sidelines, they drilled thrice each week on the college quadrangle; the hoarse shouts of the British sergeant, unintelligible to the rest of us—"Tennn SHUNN! Zennn TAHMS!" —produced instant responses from his tiny troop. We wondered whether anything we saw them do would help them at all on the battlefield.

The student Communist cell also favored the war, for a different reason; though equally few in number, with Russia reeling under German attack they were the most vocal of all. But their attitude was really that of "Let's you and him fight"; not one of them put on the King Emperor's khaki uniforms to help save the Soviet Union, their new spiritual motherland.

Such was Mahatma Gandhi's pull that by far the greatest number of us joined the All-India Students Congress. Many of the Hindu students who did so gave up Western dress altogether and took to wearing clothes of homespun cloth to proclaim their nationalism. Few Parsis or Catholics went that far, but our devotion to the cause of independence was seldom in question.

Through all this growing unrest our principal, Father Burgoyne, and the other Jesuits saw to it that academically we maintained our seriousness of purpose; they encouraged us, cajoled us, inspired us, Christian and non-Christian alike, and if we were Catholic and so desired it, they also counseled us. It was our choice. Three of Moira's older brothers, who had preceded her at Saint Ignatius, had so chosen, had been so counseled, had joined the Jesuit order, and moved away from home.

I asked Moira about that. Didn't she miss them?

"Of course," she said.

"And your parents, how did they react?"

"Well, they didn't fight it when Edward, the eldest, went."

"But they fought for the second?"

"They were reluctant to let him go at first, but Alan convinced them that his vocation, too, was genuine."

"The third, then?"

"That was rough; my mother cried for days. Also, my younger sister Ayesha was very upset; she felt that our deep religious faith, which for so long had bound us closely together, was now tearing our family apart. But my brothers are happy, and we know it. That's a great comfort to us all, as you can imagine."

"And who's the 'us all', may I ask?"

"There's me, and after Ayesha there's little Philomena, and two younger brothers still and a baby sister; we're nine in all."

"Three down and six to go. You'd better be careful," I teased. "The priests are on a roll; you could be next on their list."

Smiling, she turned her head away; I dropped the subject.

I myself found the counseling to be quite stimulating; it made me feel special to be singled out from the amorphous mass of students. My counselor, or rather spiritual adviser, was Father Burgoyne himself, an austere, short, and square-jawed individual who exuded authority and dignity. Moira's counselor was Father Campana. The two men made a sharp contrast, for Father Burgoyne's intense blue eyes and serious mien gave him a profoundly intellectual look, which some of the younger students found greatly unsettling, while they reacted warmly to Father Campana's jolly manner and approachable style. They reacted favorably, too, to the taller priest's foot-long grizzled beard that waggled when he laughed; and they learned quickly that when Campana tugged at that beard, his mood was going to change to earnest, to more than earnest, and that they had best listen carefully.

My first impulse was to choose Campana for my counselor; however, I had little choice in the matter—Burgoyne chose me.

One of Father Campana's idiosyncrasies was that he was forever reciting Thompson's "The Hound of Heaven", tugging at his beard as he did so, as if each strand of hair he pulled on refreshed his recollection and released a further batch of lines:

> *I fled Him, down the nights and down the days;* (tug)
> *I fled Him, down the arches of the years;*
> *I fled Him, down the labyrinthine ways*
> *Of my own mind,* (tug) *and in the midst of tears*
> *I hid from Him, and under running laughter.*

Naturally, I dubbed Campana himself the Hound of Heaven, and our group gleefully seized on the name. "No, no, no!" he protested vigorously when he got wind of it. His beard beat lightly upon his chest as he shook with laughter. "You've got it wrong. Thompson had it right—Christ is the Hound. I'm merely His accomplice. Change that," he added hastily. "An accomplice is involved in wrongdoing. Consider me then not an accomplice, but a humble acolyte."

Father Campana celebrated Mass in the tiny college chapel at eight o'clock each morning, well before classes began. Our group attended without fail; girls sat to the left of the central aisle, boys sat on the right. Still, when the time for Communion came, most times I managed to maneuver so Moira and I knelt side by side at the center of the Communion rail. If Father Campana, chalice in hand, placing the host on our tongues, saw this as more than mere coincidence, he said nothing. He knew I did not go to Mass daily just to be next to Moira, to be kneeling by her for the ten or fifteen seconds it would take until it was our turn to receive. I went because I *believed*, as she did, intensely.

As the Mass went through its stages we felt at once humbled and exalted. The thrice-repeated "Lord, I am not worthy" was heartfelt, as was the belief that my soul, that very instant, would be healed. And at the moment of Communion itself, that most mystical of moments, the anticipation of it brought a trembling to the heart, and the placing of the host on the tongue a spiritual glow, a warmth and an inner peace beyond description.

Moira got along so well with Campana that at first I resented my sessions with the dour Burgoyne. The principal met me each week in his office, which was simply and sparsely furnished for its size; his plain mahogany desk and chair stood at the far end; bookcases lined the walls. Off to one side and nearer the door, an old but comfortable leather chaise and three cane chairs were grouped around a coffee table. Father Burgoyne moved from his desk to the coffee table as wisdom and intuition dictated; the desk was for those occasions when visitors came to consult or to ask for favors, or for when he was dealing with faculty or students on official matters; the coffee table served for less formal social occasions.

For our first session on Tuesday afternoons Burgoyne sat at his desk but angled his chair to the side; when I pulled up one of the cane chairs to face him, I found him silhouetted against the window; catching me squinting, he graciously suggested we move.

Burgoyne invariably began with a review of my progress; it amazed me that he knew what was happening in each and every one of my classes. He would then follow up with a wealth of practical advice on techniques of studying, or on how to achieve greater mental concentration, on the need to integrate a spiritual into a material life, on the management of time.

"How are your sessions going?" Moira asked me one day.

"Helpful, on all counts," I told her. "But why do you ask? Are you thinking of switching?"

"Oh, no! I'm thinking of Ayesha, who'll be here next year. I love being counselled by Campana, and yet, he is so— "

"Steamrollerish? Juggernautian?"

She laughed. "Intense. I'll suggest Burgoyne."

Our concern with the war grew more personal as 1941 drew to a close, and crack Indian Army divisions became locked in seesaw battles with German and Italian troops in North Africa. Then, on December 7, came the tremendous shock of Pearl Harbor, and the tidal wave of Japan's entry into the war. "The Yanks'll still beat the pants off them," we told each other confidently, welcoming America's sudden involvement, even though much of her Pacific fleet now lay at the bottom of the ocean.

But the tidal wave was headed not towards America but our way. Day by day we followed the ominous headlines: on December 8, the Japanese bombed the Philippines, while gaining a toehold in Malaya; the following day they seized Bangkok; on December 10, the same day their armed forces invaded the Philippines, their planes sank the two British battleships that were supposed to bar the way into the Indian Ocean; six days later they were in Burma. Hong Kong fell at Christmas; Manila, on January 2; all of Malaya at the end of that month; Singapore on February 15.

"The British lion, that mauler of nations, is itself being mauled," Joe said gleefully. And he a UOTC cadet?

I could not resist getting in a dig. "Is that a good thing or a bad thing?" I asked, all innocence.

"It's a —" he said, and stopped short, giving me a nasty look.

Rangoon fell on March 8, and the Andaman Islands two weeks later. With the Japanese now at India's eastern gates and their navy prowling the Bay of Bengal, the British at last sent in Sir Stafford Cripps to negotiate with our leaders. Our hopes rose but the talks dragged on. The tide of war began to turn in the Pacific; perhaps emboldened by America's successes, the British offered few concessions. At the end of it all, the Mahatma said, what that elegantly tailored man offered us was no more than "a postdated check on a failing bank." Frustrated and angry, we were ready to join in whatever course of action Gandhi chose.

But Father Burgoyne drew the line at all-out political activism. "I support the cause of India's freedom," he proclaimed at a college-wide assembly. "It is India's inherent right and destiny. But you owe it to your country to finish your education first. To govern itself, to move forward in a modern world, India needs an educated cadre." I could feel his eyes on me as he continued, "So I call on you to focus on your studies and help others to remain focused. Get your degree and prepare to join the intellectual elite—whether as educators, civil servants, civic leaders, even politicians. *Then* join the fight for independence."

When some of us applauded, the Communists booed; the more they booed the louder we clapped. However, the vast majority remained silent; while disappointed, they knew Burgoyne's call made sense. College closed in mid-April, and the question of political activism, for the moment at least, became moot.

Ayesha joined Saint Ignatius that June of 1942, when I had just gone into my second year, and Moira promptly introduced us. She seemed lively enough, and had tomboyish ways, but aside from a few pleasantries I paid her not much attention. A freshman is a freshman, there only to be ignored, though that had certainly not been true in my own case; right from day one, I had made sure I counted.

Ayesha's coming, however, did complicate my life in one small respect—in chapel the very first morning, I walked up as usual to kneel next to Moira at the communion rail only to find Ayesha slip in ahead of me. Though somewhat chagrined, I chose to say nothing. When again on the following day, however, I lagged behind Ayesha and tried to edge discreetly past her, she without turning her head stuck an elbow in my ribs hard enough to make me wince.

Naturally, I confronted her after Mass. "What's going on, Ayesha? You mind my kneeling next to your sister?"

"Good Lord!" she cried. "Was that you? I usually kneel next to Moira when we hear Mass together, and here I felt some pushy guy was muscling in from the side. If I'd known it was you, I wouldn't have tried to break your ribcage. Sorry!"

"I'm sorry, too," I said, and meant it. But she didn't look all that contrite. "You're smiling?"

"Of course," she said, smiling more broadly still, "if you feel kneeling next to me instead of next to Moira is some form of punishment, why don't you offer it up as penance? Maybe that'll earn you a couple of days off in Purgatory!"

"Two days won't help all that much," I said, only too willing to continue the banter. "With my load of sins, my time in Purgatory could be not days but years. So why don't you join me in making a sacrifice, kneel somewhere else, and offer it up for me as well?"

"I'll do it," she said. "But only because you might miss Purgatory altogether, and wind up down below, being roasted on a spit by devils with pitchforks."

"Small chance of that, with Burgoyne counselling me," I retorted. "But you should know that, since he's counselling you, too."

"No, he's not," she said. "When I saw how happy Moira was with Campana, I chose him as well."

Next day, I knelt at Moira's right, with Ayesha moving to her left. Though we were now friends, for the next few weeks Ayesha continued to move in her own freshman circle, and our paths crossed but little.

In the second week of August we students were once again galvanized. "Quit India!" a saddened but exasperated Mahatma publicly demanded of the British on a Saturday morning. "Freedom immediately, this very night—before dawn, if it can be had." Never had we heard such a stirring call, and neither had our masters. That was on the eighth. That very night, well before dawn, the British gave Gandhiji their answer, arresting him and hundreds of his followers across the length and breadth of India. With the leaders who preached nonviolence now thrown behind bars, a spontaneous uprising gripped the nation. Railway lines were torn out of the ground, bombs set off, police stations set ablaze.

In Dharghat the disturbances began within hours, on Sunday itself, when a crowd of two hundred thousand attending a protest meeting were dispersed with lathi charges and teargas. Next morning, thousands of workers shut down the city's textile mills and factories, while angry students closed schools and colleges. By the time I had walked to Saint Ignatius (streetcars and buses were not running), a crowd several hundred strong milled outside the campus gates; the police, busy patrolling the city's already riot-torn areas in force, were here nowhere to be seen. Green, white, and saffron-colored Congress flags and placards were being waved everywhere. I looked for Moira and Ayesha, in vain; I did, however, find Joe.

"What, you here?" I said, quite surprised. "I thought you were one of His Imperial Majesty's minions."

"I was never a minion," he shot back. "This is my country as much as it's yours; I've quit the UOTC."

The signs being waved aloft bore the Mahatma's own words: "Do or Die!" read one; he had called it his mantra. Another sign carried the same slogan in Hindi: "*Karange ya marange.*" Another proclaimed: "We shall either free India or die in the attempt." And yet another: "We shall not live to see the perpetuation of our slavery." That was the one that was handed me.

The excitement of the moment had gotten to us, but now I remembered our principal's advice.

"Old Burgoyne won't like this," I said to the student who handed me the placard.

"Old Burgoyne be damned," the fellow said. "Consider him extinct. Everything's changed! Wait till we graduate, while the country's on fire? The hell we will."

Before he had quite finished speaking, the police arrived, leaping nimbly out of their trucks, a grim-faced British inspector at their head.

"Join us," somebody shouted to the policemen in Hindi. "We are brothers in this struggle! Do not obey that *feringhee*." Despite that plea, the policemen lined up smartly when the *feringhee* barked an order, and they were stone-faced.

I looked anxiously around me. Most of us out there facing the police were young students who had come early, anticipating some action, and we were about to get it. Although by now our group included many young women, the two faces I kept looking for were still missing.

"Have you seen Moira?" I asked Joe. "Or Ayesha? I'm worried about the two of them."

"Don't you know?" He seemed surprised. "People have been lying down on the train tracks, and service from the suburbs has been disrupted. Since they're not here already, chances are they're stuck on a train somewhere in-between, and won't make it here at all. So relax—they're out of harm's way."

At a shouted order the police began to advance, metal-tipped bamboo lathis held at the ready. My stomach began to churn even before the first blows were struck.

"We're only a stupid bunch of unarmed students, not trained *satyagrahis*," Joe said as the police, prodding, shoving, and striking, rolled back the front rank. They were now just yards away. "Run!"

In seconds we were driven onto the college grounds. Was that Burgoyne at the window up there? From behind the safety of the gates we found the courage to turn and taunt the police; they charged again, and this time the inspector led his men in a sweep that took them right inside the main building. I ran, but Joe was among the twenty or so students trapped in the Common Room.

"Quit India!" came the cry once more, this time shouted and shouted again in anger, and hundreds of students took it up, as they converged from all sides to the rescue of their fellows. The police, who had been flailing away with their lathis, now found themselves encircled and outnumbered.

And then, all of a sudden, Burgoyne appeared. In his white cassock he seemed to float unscathed through the maelstrom of bodies, until at last he confronted the now sweating inspector.

"Why are you here?" Burgoyne asked him coldly, but his eyes blazed.

"Putting down sedition, padre," the Brit replied. "I'm placing some of your young hotheads under arrest."

"This is private property," Burgoyne said, "and your authority stops at the gate. I'm in charge here. Get your men out right away."

The Englishman bristled, but hesitated. In the sudden and intense silence, all eyes focused on the two of them.

"I'll give you one minute," Burgoyne said, "one minute—and if you're not out of the grounds by then, I'm calling the Governor."

Still the man did not move. I looked at Burgoyne, and at that moment this one small man seemed to be staring down an Empire; he was growing in strength and stature before our very eyes.

"You're down to seconds," Burgoyne said.

As the police beat their retreat, a spontaneous cheer burst from our throats.

"*Inquilab*," the ritual chant then began.

"*Zindabad!*" we shouted in answer. "Long live freedom!"

"Burgoyne—"

"*Zindabad!*"

I was still carrying my placard and lustily chanting "*zindabad*" as Burgoyne walked past, stolidly oblivious to the tribute. My voice died in my throat as he looked at me and through me. Had I then let him down so badly?

But with the crowd surging and roiling around me the feeling of guilt was short-lived. I felt a tug at my elbow. It was Ayesha, flushed and sweaty and quite out of breath.

"You!" I cried. "Are you hurt?"

She shook her head.

"Where's Moira?"

"Home with the flu. I'm fine."

"But the trains are not running!"

"I left home early. Mine was stopped only a couple of miles from here, so I just got out and walked; it took long because of the crowds.

I was looking for you when the police waded in."

The police by now had regrouped on the street and the crowd around us began to press forward, sweeping us along in the crush as we moved right up to the campus gate. "Quit India!"we cried, and with Ayesha by me I had found my voice again, we both calling out exuberantly, calling not just to the Englishman but also to the Indian policemen who had so unquestioningly done his bidding. "Quit India! Quit India! *London chale jao*!"

"Over here," the inspector called back, mockingly. "Over here, and I'll *chale jao* all of you, all the way to London. Just step over the line. Come on! Who'll be the first?"

We answered with hoots and jeers. But all over India the British held firm, and by November Winston Churchill sent us a chilling message. "I have not become the King's First Minister," he declared in London, "to preside over the dissolution of the British Empire."

At St. Ignatius, Burgoyne's firm intervention had had its impact—he was now our hero, and though the unrest in the city continued for weeks, the campus itself quieted, and we settled down to our studies. Still, I approached my next meeting with him with some unease, even trepidation, but to my relief my role in the demonstration never came up for discussion. He inquired instead into my forays in English literature, and suggested I explore other literatures as well. Then we talked back and forth, as we normally did, on philosophy and theology and the importance of having a goal in life.

"It must be more than a material goal," he said. "It must be an idea, a vision, a *mission*. A mission demands ardour, a surrender of the self, towards a higher purpose. Sometimes, a divine purpose."

From that point on our sessions grew more intense. It was always a game of wits. He sought to find out obliquely whether I had a vocation to be a Jesuit. I knew I didn't; he felt I did, but that the desire lay hidden. Still, there was never a direct question asked, nor was a direct answer ever volunteered.

On one point we eventually agreed, when I began my third year: I did have a strong sense of mission. But my mission, as I saw it, was

94

purely secular—to write, that others might read.

"You have said that even sport can be a prayer," I pointed out, "if it's cleanly played and offered to the Almighty. Surely writing—and literature—can be a prayer as well."

"Of course. We have brilliant writers among the Fathers of the Church."

"And among the laity as well. There's Belloc, whom you admire."

"And Saint Augustine," he said.

"G.K. Chesterton."

"Saint Thomas Aquinas."

"Alice Meynell."

"Saint Theresa of Àvila; Thomas à Kempis; Cardinal Newman."

"A.J. Cronin. Joseph Conrad. Stephen Leacock." I waited for him to throw up his hands; he didn't. "I see you smiling at me now, Father Burgoyne, but if we keep this up, sooner or later you're going to run out of saints and cardinals."

He laughed. "The point is, there's room for writers in the Church. And certainly within the Society of Jesus. All it takes is a commitment, but not everybody is willing to make it. Are you?"

I fell silent.

"There are marvellous opportunities to study overseas," he continued. "In the United States at Marquette—"

"Not Notre Dame?" I asked, incredulous.

"Certainly not Notre Dame; all they think of there is football," Father Burgoyne replied, his nose wrinkling, somewhat disdainfully. "Football, and marching bands. For that, one does not need a university. Now, in Marquette, you'll find serious scholarship. And if the U.S. is too far away, there are other choices. In Spain, you have Madrid, Valladolid, Salamanca."

"Salamanca, yes," I agreed. "A tradition dating from the Renaissance. Certainly that could be a most enriching experience."

"The Society provides its members with innumerable enriching experiences," he said. "Join, and you will never cease to learn."

"You have me standing on a mountain top," I said, "and you're showing me the universities of the world."

In the instant before he answered me I realized my error. "But I'm no Satan," he said evenly and without rancor. He did not add, "And you are no Jesus."

But I got the point. "I apologize. I wasn't thinking."

"The novitiate's a long process, and you'll have ample time to change your mind," he said. "The last thing we want is young men who join the Society for the wrong reasons."

His blue eyes were fixed on me; I sensed by the look on his face that this was a crucial meeting, that what I said next could elate or disappoint him deeply.

"I've had, so far, five years of close contact with the Jesuit order," I pointed out. "The last two years of high school, and three here at Saint Ignatius. My admiration for the Jesuit way of life is unbounded—both for the intensity of the spiritual lives you lead, and your extraordinary life as scholars. If I felt the call, I would join in an instant. But I'm sorry, Father, truly sorry. It's a commitment I cannot make. I feel no call whatever for the priesthood." I did not tell him that what I felt instead was a warm glow for Moira in my heart.

His face turned grave, but he gave no indication of any disappointment he may have felt. "You have formed an attachment," he said at last, somewhat sadly. "But I'm looking beyond it. True, it's understandable; whether it's realistic is another matter. I, too, at your age—"

He rose abruptly and went to the window, something I'd not seen him do before. He stood there framed by the light, not moving except for a clenching and unclenching of the hands, and beyond him lay the sky, and clouds drifting idly eastward in the afternoon breeze. For a moment he seemed deeply, terribly human, and I had to push the mad thought out of my mind that I should get up and go to him, this vulnerable mentor of mine, to touch him and comfort him. Instead, uneasily, I waited for him to regain his composure.

"When the call came," Father Burgoyne said, returning to his desk but not looking at me, his face pale but drained of all emotion, "I had to go." His voice dropped to a murmur. He fiddled with the papers on his desk, straightened them out, put them down. "I simply had to go."

Why did I get the feeling that he was justifying himself to himself, and to the love he had so long ago abandoned, and not just to me? That it was something he found himself doing, time and time again, despite the passing of years?

"You went, even though you were deeply in love?"

"It tore me apart." He shuffled the papers again. "I knew heaven and hell, at one and the same time. But I had the call. I was bound to heed it."

And now I am to give up Moira? I decided not to give voice to the thought that sprang to mind, but to my surprise I still heard myself speak. "Sounds to me not so much like a call but a conscription—conscription into an army. Obey or get tossed in jail, and never mind the broken heart one leaves behind."

"You forget, when I made the choice, I broke not just her heart, but mine as well," he said. "One prays, and prays very hard again, that God will heal the hurt."

"But is the hurt necessary? What if one refuses?"

"A call to the Army of God," said a voice at the door. "Dare one refuse?" How long had Father Campana been standing there, listening?

He came into the room.

"One should have the freedom to dare," I said, "since God also gave us the gift of free will."

Father Campana tugged at his beard. "Free will, of course," he said. "That's a given. Nobody ever went to Hell who didn't freely choose the path that took him there."

"It's our life to live, isn't it?" I persisted. "We're in charge?"

"Life has its twists and turns," Father Campana said. "If you turn down a direct call from God, to whom might you turn next?"

Leaning forward, he placed a hand on my shoulder, his beard wagging as he spoke, just inches from my face. "Remember Francis Thompson—'*All things betray thee, who betrayest Me.*'"

"The Hound of Heaven."

"The very same."

As I left the room, I ran into Ayesha, looking less than cheerful. "How's it going, kid?" I asked, knowing that just minutes earlier she had had a session with Campana.

She rolled her eyes.

"Relax," I told her then. "No matter what, this too shall pass."

She smiled, bleakly, and went her way.

In the three years Moira and I had known each other I had never once told her that I loved her. Looking back now, that does seem strange; what held me back? The fear of rejection? I think not; rather, a formal declaration seemed unnecessary. We spent so much time together, I knew that she knew. After the first few weeks, each time I sought her out in the library, the seat facing hers was always vacant, as though it had been saved, deliberately, for someone special, someone she was expecting. Coincidence, you think? I thought not.

When I finally summoned up the courage, I found I did not have courage enough. The prompt came from my mother, who innocently stopped me one morning, when I'd gathered up my books and was almost out the door.

"You'll be out of college in less than a couple of years from now," she said. "Have you thought of what you'll be doing then?"

And I thought, sure, I've thought about it, I'll get me a job and marry Moira. But my mother didn't know about Moira, except that she was one of many friends; neither did my siblings know or even suspect I was in love with her, or with anybody else.

I said, "I'll find me a job, either teaching or writing, I'm not sure which. Most likely with a newspaper."

"We know someone at the *Darghat Times*," she said, naming a distant relative. "I could talk to him."

"Don't," I said, preparing to shut the door behind me. "I haven't decided yet. Now I've got to go."

"When you're ready," she said. "Whatever you decide to do, you know we'll back you."

She was right, of course; they would back me, whatever my decision. Even if I told them I'd be marrying Moira, and settling down on my own, before my older siblings! In any other family, that would not have happened; I would have had to wait my turn.

So as I ran down the steps from our apartment I decided I would ask Moira that very morning to marry me. I was at once elated at the prospect, and deathly afraid. What if? But I brushed the fears away: I'd just take her aside, the first chance I got, and ask her, straight out. She would say yes, yes, and we'd kiss, and for the rest of that day I'd be walking on air. And that very evening I would have an answer for my mother.

To get to college I had to follow the streetcar tracks, walking south a mile along Byram Hospital Road, veering off to the right towards Dhonwadi, then following bustling Masjid Road to Market Street. Despite my euphoria my mother's question had truly unsettled me; I dawdled, trying to sort out my thoughts.

Soon, the doubts came flooding back, and a debate raged in my mind: Sure, I planned to marry Moira; we enjoyed each other's company, even sparkled when we were together; what could be more natural than that we should marry? But what if she had other plans? And if I actually proposed, out of the blue, and she had other plans, might I not be risking our friendship? It was then the solution came to me: rather than propose, I would merely tell her I loved her. And if she told me she loved me too, then—

Perhaps at that moment my feet acquired wings; I got to St. Ignatius without quite knowing how I got there. But then I faced endless frustration—each time I saw Moira, there were just too many people around. I did not get to speak to her alone till she was headed home, and I had walked her to the train terminus.

We had minutes to go before her train pulled in, and the platform, for the moment, was deserted.

"Moira," I said, and stopped.

She looked at me quizzically.

"Moira—"

She put a finger to my lips and said, "Don't say it."

Taken aback, I could only splutter, "Don't say what?"

"That you love me."

Peeved at being so transparent, I asked: "How did you know I was going to say that?"

"When you, of all people, are at a loss for words, and your ears turn a bright lobster pink, that's a dead giveaway."

"Well, you said it for me," I said sulkily. "And it's true—it was true from the day we met—I do love you." And I leaned forward to kiss her.

"You've woven me into your dreams," she said, holding me off, her hand against my chest. "You and me, together, for the rest of our lives. It will not work."

I looked away. She clasped my face between her hands, forced me to meet her gaze. "I'm older than you. I'm going to be nineteen—and you've just turned seventeen."

"That bothers you? I'm not exactly callow."

"Didn't say you were."

"If that's what you're concerned about, your being older by a matter of months, that's an excuse, not a reason."

"We can be close friends," she said. "Very close. Close as can be. Don't ask for more."

I swallowed hard. If I agreed, that would buy me time.

"I can read your mind," Moira said. "Much as I like you, don't get your hopes up."

"Not even in the future?"

"Not even then." She studied my face. "Look, there's another reason, that I only told my family about a couple of nights ago. I'm not yet ready to tell the rest of the world yet, but I see I must tell you now, so you'll understand."

I thought of all the other possible reasons, all of them wearing trousers, who might be standing in my way. Clarence was one of them.

"Is it—"

Again she put a finger to my lips. "Wrong guess."

She waited, I waited. It couldn't be Joe. Lord, anyone but Joe.

"I'm going to be a nun," she said.

"A nun!" The nuns I knew all wore forbiddingly dour faces; they never laughed or smiled; nuns knew no joy in their lives. And Moira?

"You can't be serious. You, in a nunnery? You're not putting me on, just to put me off?"

"Would I bury myself in a nunnery just to escape your evil clutches?" she teased. "I have heard the call. Look, we're a deeply religious family; you know about my brothers!"

I nodded, glumly.

"You look as downcast as Ayesha did, when I told her," Moira said. "But then, as my sister, I guess she's entitled. You, too; I should have discouraged you more thoroughly months ago, but I just wasn't sure then that I had a vocation. I'm quite sure now."

"Then—for a while, you did love me?"

"More than a little."

I felt hot anger rising within me. "And something tipped the scales. It's Campana, isn't it? He talked you into this?"

"He talked to me, yes, but I consulted him. It's not an idle decision, don't you see? It takes time to sort things out; you've done some soul-searching too, in your sessions with Burgoyne. You haven't felt the call; I have. Can you accept that?"

I swallowed hard, saying nothing.

"I feel badly for you," Moira said. "Look, Ayesha's meeting me at the cafeteria for lunch. She's not just upset, she's quite angry with me. Why don't you join us? You two could console one another, if nothing else."

We could, and we did. Ayesha and I had drawn gradually closer since the incident in the chapel, and over the next few weeks she and I did a great deal of consoling, because we were both truly desolate. I found she could be consoled best when the tears were flowing and I had an arm around her, and when I held her hand. It was warm and soft, and she did not pull it away, as Moira used to do, when I held it between both of mine.

Moira and I continued to be close friends, with no awkwardness between us whenever we met. Indeed, she encouraged my growing involvement with Ayesha.

"Now you're really in love," she said to me, beaming. "I can tell the signs. With me, you were just infatuated."

And she knew all this, even though she had not seen me hold Ayesha really close, nor kiss away Ayesha's salty tears.

I was now almost eighteen, and Ayesha, a full year younger, was gangly no longer but an athlete, lithe and high-spirited, the university's one-hundred meter women's sprint champion. She had her eyes set on the two-hundred meter event; though I was only a shade faster than she was, I helped her train. We ran, fleet as Arab steeds, free into the wind. Weekends, on my beat-up racing bike—a birthday gift from a friend who had no further use for it—I rode deep into the suburbs to see her. For fifteen miles the wind blew hot in my face as I leaned over the handlebars. Then, partners in a mixed team of neighborhood teens, on an arid plot of land we played a spirited game of field hockey together, dodging and weaving and chasing pell mell after a bouncing leather ball, laughing hysterically as it dribbled in erratic spurts and caromed off the trunks of scattered coconut trees.

That first year that we went together I was still stone-poor. And Ayesha a rich man's daughter! Competitive scholarships were still seeing me through college; but while my tuition was paid, I got no spending money, and no allowance from the family because there was none to spare. I could not even afford the price of a regular movie ticket; fortunately, Wednesday afternoon movies on campus cost just four annas a seat. A quarter of a rupee! Tram fare for students was half an anna each way, so by walking to college or riding my bike there and back home again I saved enough every two weeks to treat her. So we saw movies in the assembly hall twice a month, sitting on uncomfortable metal chairs, the boys on one side of the aisle and girls on the other, while fat and ruddy-faced Brother Figueira kept waddling up and down with a flashlight to make sure no one held hands across the three-foot wide divide. What went on in his mind as he did this?

A metaphysical question plagued my own mind, and it concerned once again the dilemma of free will, much debated in our philosophy classes; and one afternoon before the lights were dimmed

I passed it on to the ever-watchful keeper of our morals: How can one accumulate guilt and qualify for redemption, I asked, if the bright beam of a flashlight in someone else's hands takes away one's freedom of choice?

Across the aisle Ayesha giggled, and others joined in. The blood now rushed to Brother Figueira's head, making him look more than ever like a ripe pomegranate.

Just one circumstance gave me cause for concern: Father Campana was still Ayesha's spiritual adviser. I contrasted his tenacious and unyielding zeal and narrow focus with the principal's more humane and humanistic approach; through his counseling Burgoyne had indeed enriched my life.

At one of our very first sessions he had talked about a daily examination of conscience. Surprised, I said, "Father, I do examine my conscience every night."

"But I'm not talking of a daily catalogue of your sins," he had said, smiling. "The focus of this examination will be not on sins but on positive actions. Each night, before you go to bed, I want you to ask yourself just three questions, three simple questions that may change your life profoundly."

I waited.

"The first question concerns the talents God has blessed you with. Not only must you use those talents, you must improve on them every single day. It's a sacred trust."

"I remember the parable."

"So ask yourself: 'How have I improved on my talents today?' If you haven't, you still have time to set that right before going off to sleep."

"That would save the day."

"But only in part. Saving more of it would depend on how you answer the second question. 'How have I, this day, touched the life of someone I know?'"

"Most days, answering that would be a cinch."

"Then answer the next one. 'Have I also touched the life of someone I don't know?'"

"A total stranger?"

"Perhaps, but not necessarily. Someone you don't know can wear a very familiar face."

In the extended silence my thoughts focussed on how I spent my days—partly in study and partly in prayer, true, but mostly at play and in pursuit of pleasure. But I follow the Golden Rule, I told myself; isn't that enough? And the answer, which came from within, from the burgeoning Jesuit within me, was—the Golden Rule is in a way a negative exhortation; where does it say I should touch, really touch, the life of someone I do not know? And that, precisely, was what Burgoyne was demanding.

"Well?"

"In the light of that last question, my life does seem a bit like the Great Thar Desert."

"But from now on it can be an oasis." He rose. "Already you have much to think about. Three little questions. All you need do is make them a part of your daily life."

"I can think of nothing I'd like better," I said. My life a continuing oasis, refreshing and healing the lives I touched, friends and strangers alike. Imagine that!

I tried it, that very day, and it worked.

I told Clarence my trust in Campana had eroded. "He seems as fanatical a figure as Savonarola," I added. "I'm almost beginning to fear him."

"Savonarola was burnt at the stake by those who feared him," Clarence responded drily.

Finding no sympathy in that enigmatic reply, I decided to speak directly to Ayesha. "Are you comfortable going to the Hound for spiritual advice?" I asked her.

"Oh yes, very."

"He doesn't pressure you?"

"Oh no; in private sessions, not as much as you would expect from his public persona."

"Which means he pressures you still. Restraint from the Hound of Heaven would be too much to expect, don't you think?"

She laughed and tossed her head. I let that go; I believed her. No matter how hard Campana tried, our love would prevail.

A week later Ayesha asked me about my sessions with Father Burgoyne.

"I enjoy them," I said. "But are you worried? You have no reason to be. I have now told him, flatly, absolutely, positively, 'no'."

"But I do worry. He doesn't give up easily, does he?"

"Neither does Campana."

"True, but I don't know that Campana even really tries any more. I think with him now it's really like a pro forma exercise. My family has given the church three sons, we are giving Moira as well—four from one family should be more than enough."

"Amen to that. Three was too much already."

"Of course, if only on principle, the Hound might not agree. He says one should not fight Divine Love, no matter what the circumstances—and he cites Moira as living proof. He says one does not realize the full power of the Almighty until one comes up against Divine Love. Capital D, Capital L—you can hear them both in his voice."

"To me, Ayesha, despite what you said earlier, this means Campana may not be engaged in a pro forma exercise, after all—he could still be looking for yet another recruit from your family."

"Then he'd be better off looking somewhere else."

"Still," I said, "why don't you change advisers? Switch over to Burgoyne?"

"I'll think about it," was all she would say.

Days later I asked her again: "Just what does Campana do?"

"He listens, he talks, and he encourages me to pray for divine guidance. And that's about it."

"And you're doing that?"

"Continually." She took me by the arm, planted a small kiss on my cheek. "Divine Guidance keeps telling me what my heart keeps telling me—I have made the right choice. I love you."

I drew her to me, and clasped her hands in mine, quoting Robert Bridges.

I have thee by the hands,
And will not let thee go.
"Nor I, you," she said.

Ayesha's parents always welcome me, whatever the hour. My lack of means doesn't seem to bother them unduly. The first time I visit, Ayesha has invited me; I get off my bicycle at the gate and see a garden that seems to stretch for ever, and at the end of it her house, not so much house as mansion, with the front door ajar. I'm here on time, but Ayesha's nowhere to be seen; when the door is pulled open seconds later it is not Ayesha but an elderly lady who steps out on to the broad verandah. I'm drenched in sweat and now I'm anxious—this must be her mother; what will she think of me? I should have ridden on awhile, cooled off, pedaled back, and now it's too late; she's seen me.

She smiles warmly and waves a greeting and calls "Ayesha!" into the house. "Ayesha!" Her voice now has a rising inflection, rising all the way up to an exclamation point, and before the sound has quite died away Ayesha is out the door and running down the steps to meet me, her face aglow. Under her mother's eyes I respond somewhat cautiously; in my family we're not used to quite so much exuberance.

"My, but you've had a long ride," the mother says sympathetical-ly, when at last I get to greet her. "Go in and wash up and Ayesha'll get you some fresh cold lemonade."

"Moira's not home yet," Ayesha tells me, as she leads the way, but to me Moira's presence is everywhere.

The wash and the cool drink help. The mother takes my glass. "Both Moira and Ayesha have talked a lot about you," she says.

"All the bad things," Ayesha says. "I prepared my parents for the shock. Come on, let's go."'

Hockey sticks in hand, we head for the playing field.

On my third visit, a Saturday, as Ayesha and I are almost at the gate, her mother calls me back. "Will you stay for dinner?" she asks.

I'm quite unprepared, and torn, also nervous at the prospect. What if—what if I reveal myself to be an unmannered lout? What do I know of fancy ways?

"It's a long ride back,"" I say, "and I haven't told my parents I'll be late. They'll worry."

"Perhaps another time?"

I nod. "With pleasure."

"Tomorrow, then?" she says, and there's no escape.

While pedaling home later that evening I think about this. She has assumed so matter-of-factly that I will be back next day, as I have been for three days in a row; is my heart now beating on my sleeve? I have been most discreet in her presence, and so has Ayesha; how then? Lost in my thoughts, I have to swerve abruptly to avoid hitting a bullock cart creaking along in the same direction; another instant and I would have been thrown.

I think of the invitation to dinner, and the pleasure and discomfort it can lead to; mainly, the discomfort. Standing there, in their sumptuous home with the elegant furnishings, I have seen the table set for formal repasts. At home we don't eat in this fashion. All that multiplicity of cutlery—what fork do I use first, which knife do I pick up? I wonder about this, wonder what they will think if I blunder, as I most certainly will. But when I get home and consult my brother he tells me not to worry; just hold back, he says, keep talking, that's something you have no trouble doing, thank God; it's wonderful to have your gift of the gab. Play for time; see what knife or fork or spoon someone else picks up, and follow that example.

So at the dinner I'm less apprehensive. I'm not the only guest; Ayesha's favorite great-aunt, all of ninety years old, is visiting and has joined us at table. Her hands tremble slightly, but she can still feed herself; her voice trembles more than her hands. We bow our heads as the father says grace. It gives me a chance to catch my breath, control my nervousness. Still, there's an awkward moment when the servant brings the first dish around and stands by my chair and the mother invites me to help myself first; my brother had not warned me this would happen. In the instant that I hesitate, Ayesha moves to fill my plate. I thank heaven she can read my mind.

The father has sad eyes. Even when he laughs the laughter quickly fades and the sadness comes welling back, as though a reservoir of sadness lurks behind the eyelids. Ayesha has added to what Moira has already told me—how proud he was when her oldest brother joined the Jesuits, how resigned when the second son insisted on joining as well, but how he grieved for all three when the third also decided to join the order.

"And now, with Moira, he's taking it very, very hard," she said. "Thank God there are five of us left, still."

Watching him now, I feel that perhaps he has not cried enough at these amputations of his family; perhaps, if he did, in one vast torrent of tears the reservoir would be emptied.

"We're having caramel custard for dessert," Philomena, Ayesha's younger sibling, tells me, above the bustle at the table. "Save some room."

Her parents smile; we are still on the first course. I look at them and wonder at the strength of their faith. Four in a row. Could I, in the father's place, have accepted such a sacrifice? Would Ayesha, as my wife? The sudden pressure of Ayesha's shoe on my foot brings me back to the present: her great-aunt has just called my name, again. I apologize.

"Did you know," the great-aunt says, graciously and proudly, in her high-pitched, quavering voice, "that our dear Moira has decided to join the convent? Within a year or two, she'll be gone!"

Ayesha's father coughs and turns away from the table and reaches for his napkin; her mother puts down her knife and fork and reaches out to touch him, wordlessly. Moira's eyes are focused on her plate; she has stopped eating.

The great-aunt is oblivious. "She—"

"He knows, Aunty, he knows," Ayesha cuts in quickly.

Nobody shows anger. The upset dissipates. The meal over, the great-aunt makes her excuses; Moira puts an arm around her waist and gently walks her out of the room. We watch them go, the father most closely of all. When they are out of the room he tells us funny stories about Moira as a child interacting with her great-aunt, and we laugh heartily, but still the sadness does not leave his eyes.

At the time that I speak of, I can read Ayesha's thoughts and she can read mine. She finds this amusing. Sometimes after a little silence we both come out with the same idea, couched in exactly the same words, simultaneously. When this happens, we stop in midsentence, again together, and collapse with laughter. "Soon we won't have to say a thing to each other," she exclaims. "I'll be living inside your head, and you in mine."

"Perhaps we were twins in a previous existence," I tease, "or perhaps even happily married, and now we've found each other again we must hold on. Forever."

Since I have no telephone we resort to sending each other telepathic messages. Sometimes messages get through that were not even sent. As happens the time I arrive at her house unexpectedly to find her expecting me.

She laughs, delightedly. "I just sensed you'd come," she says, humming "I'll be calling you."

"I will answer too!" I sing back, a Nelson Eddy to her Jeanette Macdonald. There's no one else around. I nuzzle her cheek.

Philomena pops up out of nowhere, and comes dancing up the steps from the garden. "I saw that," she cries, giggling. "I saw that! Do you do that a lot?"

"Mena!" Ayesha aims a slap at her sister's buttock, but the child nimbly evades it.

"Do you kiss, too?" Mena asks solemnly, poised by the steps. "I bet you do. Does Mummy know?"

"We do and she does." Between the two of us we corner Mena in the garden, and I trot between the bushes carrying her on my shoulders.

"I like you," Mena sings. "Can you kiss her now? Once more? Can I watch?"

The weeks pass, and I'm introduced to all and sundry as a friend. Not just as Ayesha's and Moira's friend, but as a friend of the family. I wonder if they'll still welcome me, poor as I am, if and when they suspect that Ayesha and I are serious about getting married. Because we are.

"When we graduate," I tell her. "As soon as I graduate, and get a good job, we'll marry."

She makes a face. "But I must graduate, too."

"But that could take forever," I tease.

"Naturally. I'll stretch it out as much as I can."

"If you really want to stretch things out," I suggest, "we could wait till the Brits really quit India. That could take even longer."

She is serious again. "When I graduate," she says. "Let's marry just as soon as I graduate. Then, when India gets its freedom, we'll celebrate that freedom together, husband and wife, side by side, hand in hand."

Then I tell her of my fears. "Your parents may not agree."

"But they love you," she says.

"Only as your friend."

"As a son. Indeed they do." Finally, she convinces me.

Ayesha and I don't talk much about the future. Some things we take for granted. Coming from large families as we do—she with her eight siblings, I as one of five—we both know the joy that large families can bring. That we will have a dozen fleet-footed black-haired kids, once we both graduate and have married, that much we know, tacitly. The thought that sex would be the means of achieving that end does not even enter our minds. In homilies and at annual religious retreats we've been told that sex will be holy and pleasurable. We accept that. But, for now, we think in terms of love and companionship and warmth, not sex. We do not even touch one another where it matters; not even when in my final year I get a job tutoring two wealthy kids, and at last have some money to burn, and Ayesha and I are huddled together week after week at a brand new movie house. In dark and scandalous cubicles for two, we find a leather couch instead of seats, and no one prowling around with a flashlight to mar our privacy. On the screen unfolds a story we have not the least interest in seeing; yet even here, in this iridescent darkness, it is enough to look into her eyes, hold her hand, and feel the tingle run up and down my spine before I so much as kiss her lips, her eyes, her hair. We kiss, we kiss, and we hold each other close.

After one such tryst on a Friday afternoon, the credits start rolling across the screen, people are leaving the theater, but she does not pull away. My lips on her honeyed mouth, should I complain? Then "Take me back," she cries suddenly. I feel her tremble.

"Take you back? Where?"

"To Saint Ignatius. I have a late appointment with old Campana."

I don't like the way that sounds. I'm about to graduate; she still has a year to go—a year laced with spiritual advice from the Hound of Heaven, without my presence at her side to counter it. I become immensely nervous.

We hail a cab. "Cancel the session," I tell her in the taxi. We have been riding long minutes in silence.

"Why? It's just routine."

"I feel uneasy."

"But why?"

"Because I sense that, suddenly, you're greatly troubled. And because I don't know why, now I'm troubled, too."

"Put it out of your mind."

"I'm trying, but it doesn't help at all."

She searches my face. "Are you afraid? And of what?"

"Of losing you."

The cab has stopped by the college gate, and her hand is on the door handle.

"I just don't like the man," I tell her.

"The man, or the priest?"

Her eyes are on my face; I sense that it is not an idle question, that she is really trying to sort something out in her mind. Who is it that is advising her, Campana the man, or Campana the priest?

"Call him what you will," I answer shortly. "To me, there's no distinction."

She opens the car door, then leans back in, her hand caressing my cheek. "Stop worrying. I'll see you in the morning."

As she reaches the Gothic entrance she turns to wave. "I'm staying with a cousin in the city," she says, and mentions a name. "You know where she lives. Mena will be there too. Come by at eight, I'd like you to teach me to ride your racing bike." Ayesha, Ayesha, how I love you, Ayesha.

Next morning, having awakened ahead of the alarm I had set, I arrive well before the hour, and do slow turns on the deserted road to kill time. I brake till the wheels barely move; finally, I sit balanced astride the bike, immobile. It's a quiet road; there's no danger.

The minutes pass; it is eight, and soon it is after eight, and Ayesha, usually so joyously prompt, still does not appear. From the road the house seems unusually quiet, but as I mount the steps I can hear the sound of a child crying. I ring the bell and wait. The crying redoubles in intensity, comes closer. And then of a sudden Mena is at the door, her eyes swollen, her face streaked with tears.

"Ayesha doesn't want to see you any more," she wails. "Not ever again. Never again. Don't ever come back again." And she turns weeping into the house, slamming the door behind her.

At St. Ignatius, beyond the deserted Common Room, the carved stone cross inset into the open niche above the chapel casts an elongated shadow on the tennis courts in the quadrangle. No one's playing there this late June morning, nor are the cadets at their drill, even though the monsoon's backed off and the sun is shining. The quadrangle is deserted. But Moira should be here; I've asked her to be here; she cannot let me down. Ayesha will not talk to me, not tell me why I'm being shut out of her life, and I want Moira to tell me why.

Father Campana enters the quadrangle at the far end at the same time that I spot Moira by the Assembly Hall and she sees me. He sees me, too, and begins to tug at his beard. Moira and I walk towards each other, she slowly, I in a rush, and—even though Father Campana is watching—she takes my hand, the way I used to take her hand precious seconds at a time before she decided she really wanted to become a nun.

"We can't talk here," Moira says, as she walks me through the quadrangle back the way I came. I have come to her in utter despair;

with her beside me my despair gives way to hope.

"Why is she so angry with me?" I ask. "You must know, Moira; she won't talk to me, but surely she has told you why? Whatever I did or said, tell me what went wrong, so I can make things right again."

Moira stops and I turn to face her. But she takes her time speaking, and when she does her voice trembles.

"It's not you," Moira says gently. "She's not angry with you, because you did nothing wrong. Nothing! She's angry at herself, and blames herself. She just can't face you."

I grab her by the shoulders and she winces. "For heaven's sake! Why, Moira? Tell me why."

"You have no clue?" she says, and now her eyes do not leave mine. "Can't you even guess? She can't face you because she too has found she has a vocation."

This I cannot accept. "She asked me to meet her next morning, then found a vocation overnight?"

"Not so—she struggled for weeks before making up her mind."

Anger and bitterness well up within me; I feel myself suffocating.

"I feel for you," Moira says. "Yet, look—you're not alone. Though I should be happy for Ayesha, I'm crying, too."

"Once again, it's Campana, isn't it—it's that damned Campana. He has struck once again."

"Don't blame him," Moira says. "No matter what he said or did, it's really between Ayesha and God, not him. Her vocation, like mine, is very real."

"What's real is that she and I have loved each other. And I still do."

"And as far as she goes, that hasn't changed."

"Then I must see her."

"Don't insist," she says. "It would destroy her. Believe me, it would destroy her."

"Moira, just once—I've got to see her just once more. Where is she now?"

"I can't tell you. But she's not home."

"Explain this to me, Moira," I say, quite exasperated. "Explain this, if you can. I loved you; and though you decided to become a nun, we're still close, we still talk freely, still meet as friends. But when Ayesha, whom I now love, also feels the call, I cannot see her? Can't see her at all?"

"Because she loves you," Moira says. "Don't you see? She loves you far more than I did. And she loves you still, but she loves Christ more. Do you get it? Seeing you suffer would tear her apart. Is that what you'd want?"

Oh, the unfairness of it all! "It's like a death, Moira, a death! It's as though she's died on me."

"My parents feel that, too. We're all upset, Ayesha most of all, and believe me, we're upset for you as well. My parents love you, too," Moira says.

And that should make me feel better?

"Try to understand," Moira says. "You gave me space. Give her the space you gave me, so she can sort this out by herself."

"By herself, or with Campana's help?"

"He is her adviser."

"Pleading a special cause. Why can't I plead mine?"

"Because you are emotionally involved."

"And Campana?"

"That is different."

And I ask her again, "Why?"

For answer she bursts into tears.

"Let's go home," Moira says, finally, taking my hand again.

"Will she be there?"

Moira shakes her head.

We take the train to the suburbs. Moira talks, but her words are blurred by the question throbbing in my mind.

Why, Ayesha, why?

"That's what we asked her," the mother says. "Haven't we given enough to the church? Three of our sons already priests, Moira on her way to the convent, and now you're going, too? That's what I said. I wept. Her father wept, strong man though he is. 'Not you, too, Ayesha. Marry him, Ayesha,' that's what I told her," the mother says. "God has demanded enough sacrifices from our family; He can expect no more."

"She says she loves you," the father says. "She loves you still, but says it's beside the point. That I can't understand."

A nun. My Ayesha leaving me to become a nun.

"Perhaps in time she'll be willing to talk to you again," the father says. "What a shock, a terrible shock." He looks at me, seeking comfort. From me?

I make no answer, my head bowed. Campana—to think I admired him once, and this is how he paid me back.

"We love you," the mother says, reaching for my hand.

"I love you, too." Now there's no holding back my tears. Her words bring hollow comfort, for Ayesha, whom I love the most, has abandoned me. Despair in my heart, I hear a voice ringing in my head, see a hand tugging at a beard:

> And is thy earth so marred,
> Shattered in shard on shard?
> Lo, all things fly thee, for thou fliest Me!

"Ayesha told me," the mother says, pulling me close and peering up into my face, "that you once told her you'd go to the ends of the earth to find her if ever she went away. We raised her in the lap of luxury, and now she talks of improving the lives of tribal women, deep in the forests, digging up roots and eating berries and wild honey. How will we find her there?"

She weeps.

Ayesha living in the jungle, grubbing for food? The world gone mad.

"Stop her," the mother says, her nails digging into my wrist. "You alone can do it! Stop her! Stop her!"

The months pass, much too slowly, my grief a cloak against the world, finding scant comfort even in what little good news there is. The British set the Mahatma free, but only after a fast unto death puts his life in jeopardy, and after wondering long and hard whether it would be worth their while to let him die. The war ends, finally, not with a whimper but with nuclear blasts. At my mother's prompting I enroll in the Master's programme, but drop out within a month, unable to face the halls of St. Ignatius and all the memories they hold.

I drift from job to job, then find one I like, and throw myself into my work. The country feels more strongly the winds of freedom; in February of 1946, a mutiny shakes the Royal Indian Navy, the country riots in support, and still the British cling to empire with bulldog tenacity. In Dharghat alone a thousand people die. But the Indian Army is also restive, and a lesson has been learned. Independence comes at last the following year, in a rush, and we celebrate.

On the night of August 14 every building is ablaze with light. I leave the apartment at eight, and join the stream of pedestrians heading for the center of town; all along the arterial highway, cars packed with revellers sit with their engines idling, with nowhere to go. The closer we get, the slower our progress. It takes two hours to walk the four miles, but at last I am out in front of Prince Albert Terminus, this vast monument to a fading British presence, and around me the throng is packed shoulder to shoulder, a dozen horse-drawn gharries marooned in our midst. The normally patient horses are now restive, so the coachmen stand close by their heads, holding on to their reins, stroking their necks and backs and foreheads, whispering into their ears. Over to the right, a lively group of young Parsis roistering in an open convertible begins to sing "*Hindustan hamara hai*"; others nearby pick up the popular tune, till thousands upon thousands of throats are affirming that, at last, Hindustan is indeed going to be ours.

Everywhere, miniature flags are being waved aloft; Congress flags and those of the Muslim League, and the new national flags of India and Pakistan. In between shouts of "Gandhi ki jai!" and "Jawaharlal Nehru ki jai!" we hear the chant, "Gandhi-Jinnah eki hai!" Such is the euphoria of the moment that yes, in our eyes even

Jinnah, who carved our nation in two, must now be embraced. On the facade of the station itself, the giant clock points at a minute to midnight; the crowd shushes itself. At the stroke of the hour, the air resounds with the joyous hiss and crackle of myriad fireworks, with thunderous shouts of joy. I too am seized with a wild elation; freedom from a foreign yoke is being celebrated; not just India's freedom, but Pakistan's as well, and the now redoubled chants reflect this feeling of fellowship: "Long live Nehru!" "Long Live Gandhi!" "Gandhi and Jinnah are one." Hindu and Muslim, Christian and Jew and Parsi, we raise our voices and dance in the streets. And then I remember, *she* had said that when this moment came, we would be together, celebrating. Husband and wife, side by side, hand in hand. The moment turns sour, threatens to overwhelm me, but from somewhere within I find the strength to turn it aside. India is free, is free, is free, and for now, that's all that matters.

The next day dawns and reality sets in—we are no longer one India but two nations, India and Pakistan. Gone is the feeling of brotherliness; we are instantly at each other's throats. Mass killings begin in the north, on both sides of the border, then sweep swiftly across both countries. Dharghat, too, is engulfed in bloodshed. Gandhi fasts now to stop the madness, and we are at last brought back to sanity; then, five months later, a fanatic shoots the Mahatma dead, and there are more things yet to forget.

Years later still, I move to New York. Though all the bitterness has now drained out of my heart, Ayesha is still a hidden, loving, hurt-filled memory. But I have also found great happiness, a wife I deeply love, children and grandchildren who now fill my universe.

And then one day the phone rings, and it's Clarence. Like Moira's brothers he too has joined the Order, he tells me. He is in town on a visit to Fordham and other Jesuit educational institutions, and on the last day of his stay has managed to ferret me out. Bless him. I pick him up at a Jesuit residence in Manhattan, and there is a moment of awkwardness when he walks into the parlour where I have been waiting for him; it is close to twenty years since I saw him last, and this is the first time I am seeing him in a cassock. The religious habit suits him, lending him an air of quiet authority. How do I greet this once dear friend of mine, now a greying priest?

"To you I'm still just Clarence," he says, as we hug.

I bring him home for dinner. My wife welcomes him warmly, and we sit down to a quick and simple meal, because he is due at the airport in an hour. We remember our college days, and over wine we laugh a lot.

"The Order has been good to me," he says.

That was, after all, what Burgoyne had promised. "Fair enough," I point out, "but these things have a way of balancing themselves. No doubt in turn you've been good to the Order."

He laughs. "At least my superiors thought so. You remember the things Burgoyne used to talk about—the opportunities for scholarship, for study overseas, for an intellectual as well as a religious life—for me they all panned out."

I am glad for him, and I say so. But I look at my own family, and have no regrets. I too have been rewarded, and I don't have to tell him so; he is acutely aware of our happiness.

On the way to Kennedy Airport he brings me news of the others. Burgoyne has retired and gone back to Barcelona; I ask for his address, and he scribbles it for me. Campana stayed on and died while still at the college. I do not react; I have long ceased despising the man. Joe became a clerk with a British shipping company, and is a bitter man, having never been promoted; senior posts for which he qualifies are filled instead by young Brits sent out from England as soon as they have finished high school. Moira is in Madras, the much-respected Mother Superior presiding over a much-respected women's college. He carefully avoids talking about Ayesha.

I pull up at the Air India terminal with minutes to spare, determined to find out.

"Ayesha. How is she?"

He has the car door open, and he hesitates; he had not expected that I would ask so bluntly, after all these years. "She suffers terribly from arthritis," he says.

I feel a sudden, intense, stabbing pain in my left arm and shoulder. I have to know. "Is it here?"

"How did you know?" he says, surprised. "Have you been in touch, then? That's just where she has it."

How can I explain to my old Jesuit friend, in the few seconds before a skycap hustles off with his bags, that the telepathy Ayesha and I once enjoyed might just have come alive, that even long-parted lovers' minds can reach out and touch in most mysterious ways?

"Do you know where she is?" I ask.

"Still in the jungle," he calls back, and in that moment, before I can ask him where, what jungle in which benighted state, a cop orders me to move the car.

The years roll on once more and Ayesha is now finally out of my mind. And then, three nights in a row, I dream of her. I am lying sleeping next to my wife in bed and in my dream Ayesha and I are planning to be married, but she calls it off at the last moment, and I wake up sobbing.

The next night, after I drift off to sleep, I find myself at Saint Ignatius's once again. I hurry through the deserted Common Room, stand in the arch looking to where the carved stone cross, inset into the open niche above the chapel, casts an elongated shadow on the tennis courts in the quadrangle. No one's playing there this June morning, even though sport itself, properly offered to the Almighty, is itself a form of prayer; I had Father Burgoyne's word for it, and I have Father Campana's word for it. Now I see him at the far end of the quadrangle. He beckons me over, but it's not him I have come to see, not him at all; it's Moira. I have to talk to Moira about Ayesha. Ayesha, who does not want to see me anymore.

Moira by the Assembly Hall catches my eye and waves. We walk toward each other, she slowly, I in a rush, and she takes my hand—even though Father Campana is watching us closely.

Campana walks towards us.

"We can't talk here," Moira says, as she hurries me through the quadrangle back towards the main road. "We're all upset, and believe me, we're upset for you as well."

We walk past the squat Arabian palms, out the gate. The city evaporates before our eyes; we walk through fields that seem to stretch forever. "I don't know quite what to tell you," Moira says, turning to face me. "Didn't you see it coming? Ayesha never told you? Not even a hint?"

I shake my head.

"She's been agonizing over it," Moira says. "Day and night, yes and no, torn this way and that, it's been driving the family half-crazy."

Why did I fail to see it? I turn the question around. "And you yourself, Moira, sat back, told me nothing, didn't try to stop her?"

"I thought you knew," Moira says. "And me try to stop her, me? I answered the call first, remember?"

Did I, twice blinded by love, twice shut out the signs?

"There's a knife in my heart," I say, "and twice you helped put it there."

She makes no answer. By now we have reached the crest of a hill. "When you get the call there's no fighting it," she finally says. "She loves you still. She still loves you. It's heaven and hell for her." Where have I heard that before? "Do you understand that? Do you?" Moira's voice seems to be coming from elsewhere; I hear it but it does not touch me; "Do you, do you?" echoes insistently from surrounding peaks. Looking down, I see we are standing no longer on a hill but a mountain. A village we had left minutes earlier lies far below.

We walk towards a group of picnickers; I spot her father, her mother, sitting on the grass. They greet me anxiously. Of Ayesha there is no sign. Had she been there, what could I have said to her?

"Stop her," the mother says, rising up, weeping, her hands outstretched, beseeching. "You alone can do it. Stop her, for us, for yourself."

Stop her. I have to stop her from throwing all our lives away.

I move away from them and look for Ayesha among the people still on the grass. Not finding her there, I turn to look at the top floor balcony of the seven-story building now suddenly looming up behind me. I see her parents there, and Moira leaning over the railing, waving me away, pointing down the mountainside, as though saying, "That way. Hurry! You'll meet her down the road."

I take a deep breath and run down the slope at a steady loping pace, covering much ground, leaning back to control my speed, not risking breaking my neck before finding Ayesha. I'm in my track outfit of white shirt and shorts and running shoes, and the spikes built into heel and toe bite sharply into the dirt.

Despite the darkening sky, bright slanting sunshine still bathes the road. I feel the crunch of gravel underfoot and hear it scatter behind me with each strong kick from the ankle. A half-mile down, two ragamuffins are playing with a stash of ten-rupee notes. Already the trees are closing in. I ask them if they have seen Ayesha, see them spread their hands and shrug, not understanding the question. In this part of the country they do not speak my language. I look back; perhaps Ayesha is there by now, perhaps even sprinting down the road, running at last faster than I can. I see the mountain, but the house is gone; the road is empty; even the boys are gone.

The sky is black; lightning flares. In that instant I see Campana moving resolutely up the road. His voice cuts through the darkness above the rising howl of the wind:

Naught shelters thee, who wilt not shelter Me.

Hurry, Ayesha!

I shut my eyes against a blinding squall.

When I reopen them my pillow once again is wet with tears. Beside me my wife of a lifetime stirs in her sleep. Gently I turn and put my arm around her. She sighs contentedly and snuggles up close. Life has been good to me, perhaps because, through it all, I've followed old Burgoyne's advice, and sought to answer each night the questions he posed to me so forcefully so very long ago: someone I know, and someone I don't—have I touched their lives today? The questions have already been asked and answered for the night, yet I ask them once again, and once again the answer is, yes, I have; however imperfectly, I have. Comforted, I drift off to sleep, only to have the dream frighteningly recur.

Ayesha, why did you break into my sleep this night, and all those nights before; why have you crept into my dreams? It's been fifty years, Ayesha; it's been that long. What happened on that Friday afternoon, those fifty long years ago, that a door was slammed in my face next morning, a message inexpertly delivered, leaving me bereft, blaming myself, half-crazed with anguish? Did Campana recite "The Hound of Heaven" to you one more time, and with those piercing eyes of his, was it then that the message finally got through? Should I have tried to see you yet once again, laid siege to your home, to speak to you once more, just once, even though you sent word through Moira that I absolutely should not? Not even to say goodbye? Folly, all folly. A lesser rival I could have struggled against; how does one wrestle a bride from Christ, when He holds your heart and soul—and mine—cupped in His hands?

It took years to ease you from my dreams, Ayesha, and now you are back. I have raised a loving family, placed two continents and vast oceans between us, and still you are back. And I ask again, why? Coming thus unbidden into my nights, from there into my waking thoughts—you can't turn back the clock, Ayesha, pretend that nothing's changed. Can't just stir up old emotions, tormenting me in the twilight of my life with the remembered innocent touch of a soft warm hand. So enough, enough of mind games. No more reaching out; the old telepathy won't work any more. Project your thoughts, if you must—this receiver is shutting down for good.

And yet—

How shall I touch your life today, Ayesha, whom I know and have loved? From deep within those jungles you chose to make your home, with that forest-bound tribe whose women you hoped to gentle—is it in an hour of need that you are trying to find me now, at the ends of the earth, as I once said I'd find you?

Are you all right, Ayesha; tell me, are you all right?

2

The Immigrant Experience

Author's Note: The fact that some immigrants speak in an ungrammatical manner just means that they are not as familiar with English as they are with their own language; it has nothing to do with their level of education. Speakers in such cases will tend to use the syntax and word order they are most familiar with—that of their mother tongue. This can lead to such inversions as "Then only he came," or "Alone I was left." Examples of immigrant speak occur in "Lonely Aging Chinese-American New York Neighbor Lady," in "Wooing Mr. Ram", and in "Uncle Prabhu's Special Y2K Party". Enjoy the diversity.

New York

Peter and the Battle
of the Ants

Peter, having just finished eating a home-cooked meal that night, had said to his wife, "Rukmini, there's a nest of ants multiplying behind the refrigerator; get rid of them, won't you?" And because he cared about her safety, he had thoughtfully added, "But be careful how you zap them, Ruki, they look like Brazilian army ants to me," and she had sharply and uncharacteristically replied, "I'm still eating my dinner. There are no ants in my kitchen. If you find any, get rid of them yourself." The response was so unexpected that he doubted he had heard it right. So he had rephrased his request, this time very quietly and very patiently, taking care not to sound like the domineering white chauvinistic paranoid schizophrenic American male his mother-in-law proclaimed him to be.

This time around he got an even shorter answer. "I'm eating. Kill them yourself."

Even then he had understood quite clearly that the statement did not come not from his normally docile Indian-born wife's inmost being; deep in his heart he knew she loved him dearly and admired everything he stood for. Still, it was possible that she—being highly literate and an avid reader—had now succumbed to the wiles and preachings of feminists, especially Gloria What's-her-name. In his mind the possibility quickly became a certainty; what could have been a gentle question he blurted out as a blunt accusation. When she had hotly denied being a women's libber, he had lost his cool, and, for the night at least, his mate.

Their shrill quarrel did not go unnoticed—downstairs, old Mrs. Mulligan reached for her broomstick and pounded on her ceiling. Usually she only did this late at night, timing the thumps to match the creaking of their bedsprings and interrupt their very vocal lovemaking. He had often wondered why she did this; was she an avowed racist, or did she just disapprove of miscegenation?

Gazing out the window of their Manhattan penthouse, he stubbornly avoided looking at Rukmini as she packed. Outside, he could see the city still going about its nightly business; the East River glistened and rippled under a benign moon; a seaplane droned noisily as it taxied towards the 34th St. marina; the bridges arching towards Queens sparkled with strings of dazzling white pearls streaming in, and ribbons of red rubies flowing out. The world seemed obscenely normal, normal everywhere, that is, but in his eat-in kitchen. And of course, in his bedroom.

He had reviewed the situation again later, while lying in bed. He had reached out in his sleep and his hand, not encountering the warm comfort of his wife's pneumatic shape, had come down instead on bare cold mattress. Reality set in—she had indeed gone home to her mother. Jolted awake, he had blinked twice to bring his thoughts into focus. He saw then that perhaps he had been wrong to assume that feminists were to blame; perhaps Rukmini was reacting, not so much to the order he gave, but to its specificity. Why couldn't he just have said "army ants," and left the "Brazilian" out of it? Why couldn't he just have said "ants"?

He chided himself. That she resented the preciseness of his speech was no news to him; she had hinted at it more than once. "Must you always be so damn specific?" was how she had phrased it the last time around, her voice low and husky and intense. He did not relish the irony in their situation; he, a red-blooded American male, had married her because she was a gentle Indian woman, anachronistically ladylike in her demeanor; he had not expected her so quickly to acquire such abrasive Western ways.

He had explained that he couldn't help his penchant for the precise phrase. He had reminded her that by training he was a scientist, a researcher, a mathematician. Fuzzy math aside, accuracy and specificity were treasured qualities in each of these disciplines. Brilliant at all three, it was not his fault that as yet he was hardly known outside the walls of the tiny lab where he worked, bending his energies to de-scenting compost. "If you're really all that good, why aren't you famous?" Rukmini's mother had asked him once, in that needling tone mothers-in-law sometimes cultivate. Her voice was high-pitched and had a sing-song lilt, both qualities that greatly annoyed him. He would have pointed out that one does not receive Nobel Prizes for de-scenting organic fertilizer, had she not pointed that out first. She was the only person he knew who could get in both the first word, and the last.

Of course there had been advantages to the marriage. He had provided a secure home while Rukmini worked towards her doctorate at Columbia, her thesis focusing on an unlikely oxymoron—the emergence of unreal realism in contemporary world literature. He did not understand the concept, and said so in the mildest yet strongest of terms; it did not matter, she said—tenuous logic was the stuff of doctoral theses, providing gainful employment to countless doddering advisers. He let that pass. In return for being agreeable and coping with Mrs. Mulligan's thunderous broom he got more than satisfactory sex and service, to say nothing of love and sustenance.

Alone now at his ill-made breakfast, munching on a charred English muffin between sips of lukewarm coffee, he reflected bitterly on the contrast between past idyllic mornings and the unreal reality of his present condition. Should he call her?

He decided not to. To pick up the phone, as he was doing now, in spite of his resolution not to; to dial the number, as he had begun to do, that would be abject surrender. Even knowing this, his fingers and his brain continued to work at cross-purposes. The phone rang, twice; what if the mother answered? Hurriedly, he hung up.

His frustration mounting, he had just picked up the *Times* Sunday magazine to distract himself when a movement on the wall caught his peripheral vision: a large ant, of the type he had seen skulking behind the refrigerator, was supervising a mass of smaller workers, who were dragging the carcass of a dead cockroach up the kitchen wall. Before his very eyes. "Get rid of them yourself," his wife had said, and by golly, though a peaceable man himself, he would show her that he could do it. In one smooth movement he was off his chair, had pulled off his right shoe, and bam! there lay a mess of dead ants and one twice-dead cockroach.

"One hundred and ten," he said to himself, and, because he prided himself on the accuracy and swiftness of his estimates and predictions, he did a body count. One hundred and eleven, counting the ant in charge. Well pleased, he bowed repeatedly to imaginary applause.

No sooner had he sat down again to his now quite tepid coffee than two hundred and twenty-two ants showed up—one hundred and eleven to retrieve the ones he had killed, another one hundred and ten to drag the cockroach up the wall, and a new ant in charge, fractionally larger than before. "Well, now," Peter said, "you've asked for it." And off came his shoe again, and with a single mighty blow he killed the lot of them. "Three hundred and thirty-three with just two whacks," he thought with some satisfaction. "Not bad at all. Can't be too many left— I'll keep bashing them as they surface."

When four hundred and forty-four ants marched up in military formation, he despatched them with ease; and the very next skirmish, with a regiment of eight hundred and eighty-eight, also lasted just seconds. "Ex-ter-mi-na-tion!" he shouted exultantly, matching each syllable with resounding blows from his shoe. By now he had fathomed the ant commander's strategy—a new warrior was assigned to carry away each battlefield casualty, and an extra one hundred and ten were sent in to retrieve the prized cockroach. And always, there was the officer in charge, growing ever more imposing in size as the numbers mounted. "This is going even better than expected," Peter said to himself. "Come on, brave military ants! Come on to death and glory! The sooner you come, the faster you die." He waited, shoe held aloft, a Joe DiMaggio aiming to smite whatever came, right into the bleachers.

Fresh reinforcements now began pouring in so quickly that he no longer had time to sit. He wished he could have had an extra pair of hands. Rukmini could have helped, had she not stalked off so hastily and in such high dudgeon. He would have even welcomed

Mrs. Mulligan, provided she brought her hated broom along. How quickly the numbers escalated: One thousand seven hundred and seventy-six; three thousand five hundred and fifty-two; seven thousand one hundred and four; fourteen thousand two hundred and eight.

His adrenalin surged as he discovered that the ant formations now being committed to battle had been trained to scatter and re-group. Even units that he had decimated resurfaced as roving guerilla bands. Peter now found himself damaging his own environment as he savaged the enemy. True, ants still died by the hundred at each blow, but the faster and harder he hit, the more dents he kept putting in the plaster walls of his kitchen. He rethought his strategy. Dropping the shoe, he now armed himself with the *Times*, the rolled-up Business Section in his left hand, the bulkier Real Estate in his right. He slapped at the wall with great sweeping motions, but though he was prepared for the ants' numbers he had not counted on their dramatic shift in tactics: entire elite regiments had learned to let go of the wall and float to the ground in free formation microseconds before he hit. Once again he needed new weapons; remembering the success of Operation Desert Storm, he looked around for smart bombs, and found them close at hand.

In a frenzy, Peter abandoned the *Times* and hurled pots and pans at various concentrations, scoring direct hits on units that were maneuvering even way beyond arm's reach. To psyche himself up and demoralize the foe, he accompanied each lightning strike with explosive sound effects. "Kaboom!" he shouted, as he flung a large frying pan. "Kaboing!" He had just launched an expensive slow cooker—Rukmini's prized Crock-Pot, a birthday present from her mother.

The din was immense. Dead ants and plaster dust exploded off the wall. Backing off, he leaped high and twisted in midair to land simultaneous rapid-fire kung-fu kicks on two ant columns that had deployed to the right and left of him; and he congratulated himself on this brilliant maneuver until he saw the floor leaping up to greet his face. After he had picked himself up he stomped on the remaining ants, yes, he stomped on those that like him had fallen to the ground, as they deserved to be stomped on, showing them no mercy, but he used the *Times* once more to smash and smash again the ones who were running off with his shoe.

A strange and acrid scent assailed his bruised nostrils. A scientist once again, he told himself, "That's formic acid," changing that to "No, that's formic pulp," and made mental note to check on its potential value as a possible de-scenter of compost. Given the right formula, the Nobel might still be his.

In the silence he became aware of Mrs. Mulligan, now angry and seemingly besotted, pounding on her ceiling and cursing, screaming at him to stop beating his wife. The witch! As though he would do such a thing! Why didn't she put her broomstick to better use, riding it straight up, up, and up, to incineration in the sun?

"I'll call the cops!" she screamed again.

"Go to hell!" he yelled back. The pounding eventually stopped. Quiet descended on the kitchen.

His coffee by now gone cold, his muffin inedible, his nose intruding hugely into his field of vision, Peter nevertheless felt greatly elated. True, his heart pounded so fast he had trouble breathing, but nothing else stirred in that now ravaged room. Not unconditional surrender, but extermination had been his goal, and he had achieved it. He surveyed the field of battle: on the credit side, twenty-eight thousand three hundred and five of the enemy accounted dead, injured, or missing; no prisoners. On the debit side, a once immaculate kitchen in shambles, soiled and damaged walls, some dented pans, a throbbing nose. He'd have to replace the slow cooker, naturally, before his mother-in-law discovered the damage; whatever the cost, it would be a small price to pay, just to keep that woman off his back.

He was glad now that it was he who had waged war on the ants, and not Rukmini. He loved his wife, and he could see now that fighting all these ants she could easily have been hurt. Her sari would certainly have gotten in her way; the ants would have swarmed up the folds faster than she could have gotten rid of them. It reinforced a point he had often made before, particularly when that first lone woman cadet had quit the Citadel military school—in Virginia, was it—just days after having been admitted. He had cheered the woman's departure, while Rukmini wept. And he had told her firmly then: "Soldiering is a man's business. Absolutely. No women in the trenches! Not even in military academies." How right he had been!

He cast his mind back through history, recalling the great military victories of the past—not just those won by the likes of Eisenhower, and Rommel the Desert Fox, nor even by Powell-and-Schwartzkopf, and certainly not Joan-of-Arc's flash in the pan, but by the true military geniuses, the empire builders. And he wondered: had he not been at heart a pacifist, who would he rather have been?

Alexander the Great came instantly to mind, at twenty-one already master of half the known world; then Genghis Khan; then Babar, not Babar the elephant, but Babar the first Moghul to invade India, galloping his mountain pony across the snow-cloaked Hindu Kush passes. After Babar, he thought of Napoleon. Napoleon! Indeed, as Napoleon he would have functioned even better than Napoleon himself. Then there would have been no abandonment of Egypt, no withdrawal from Spain and Portugal, no retreat from Moscow, no defeat at Leipzig, and therefore no rout at Waterloo.

And think what it would have done for Rukmini—she would have been Empress, the first Indian woman to become Empress of France; indeed, Empress of all Europe, presiding over the Tuilleries and Malmaison. Perhaps, even, Empress of India, if he as Napoleon then chose to follow in Alexander's footsteps and led his victorious army across the Indus. If she—ungrateful woman!—dared run off to her mother's, he would not care, but turn at once to the voluptuous and dusky Josephine. The thought of the elegant Beauharnais waiting in the palace wings enthralled him; his mind lost itself in visions of her cuddly form, reflected and re-reflected a thousand times in the great Hall of Mirrors at Versailles.

To celebrate his triumph he picked up the telephone, and re-dialed his mother-in-law's number. It felt good to be making the first move—it would be something he could harp on should the situation ever recur.

At the ninth ring Rukmini picked up the receiver. He decided to be casual, nonchalant even. "I did it, Ruki," he said. "I did what you asked—killed off the ants myself. The whole lot of them. Not a one in sight anymore. Shall I tell you how many there were?"

"No."

"Twenty-eight thousand three hundred and five." He kept his voice level, waiting for her ecstatic reaction.

"So?"

How sad and lonely she sounded! She needed cheering up.

"So, Ruki—you can come home now." He smiled into the mouthpiece, encouragingly, projecting positive mental images of connubial bliss. "Everything will be hunky-dory, you'll see." He paused, to lend emphasis to what he was about to tell her. "I have forgiven you, dear."

Hearing her sharp intake of breath, he felt he had finally touched her, and forced himself to wait through the ensuing silence; overwhelmed by his noble gesture, she obviously needed time to pull herself together.

"You're sure you got them all?" she finally asked, her voice quavering. "Every last one of them?"

Her words confirmed his thinking. Although hungry for reassurance, it was clear she had been greatly impressed.

"Every last one," he said, savoring each word.

"Then take a goddamn selfie and send it to the *Guinness Book of World Records*," she snapped, and slammed down the receiver so hard his ear hurt.

His victory had put him in a magnanimous mood, however, and on reflection her suggestion did not seem to be such a bad idea. He saw no sarcasm in it; as for the slamming of the receiver, that was surely an accident. What bothered him far more was the fact that Rukmini had thought of the *Guinness Book* before he did, when in matters involving thinking he preferred her to be not so much a leader as a loyal retainer, tagging along three mental steps behind the master.

With eight snapshots left in the old Polaroid he took out of the closet, Peter took three of various sections of the kitchen for insurance purposes, following up with a close-up of his shoe with the dead ants lying around it; then, with a whisk broom in one hand and a scoop in the other, he began to gather up the ants in one giant heap for the final pictures for Guinness's. As the pile grew he decided at first to shape it into a rounded burial mound, but with the sun now slanting increasingly through the window he changed his mind. In a minute he was done. And he was well pleased with the result— the ant pyramid he had created cast a long and impressive shadow.

A funeral march seemed in order. With a mournful face he began humming the slow movement of Beethoven's "Eroica" Symphony. At the deliberate pace he set, the cortège would last a good fifteen minutes. So involved was he in his own scenario that even as he hunkered down, camera in hand, Peter imagined hearing the measured tread of myriad marching feet. It was only when he was inching back to increase the width of coverage that his peripheral vision alerted him to a tidal wave sweeping across the floor and cresting swiftly towards him.

When he turned his head it seemed to him that an army of one million one hundred and eleven thousand one hundred and eleven ants had deployed into the kitchen. He did not even question that figure because it had sprung spontaneously to mind. He could see at once that the situation was absurd. He wondered why so vast a horde had been sent in, when mathematically speaking twenty-eight thousand four hundred and sixteen were all that the situation called for. Or as few as one hundred and eleven, if the ants would only forget about all their dead comrades and settle for just taking that stupid cockroach away. After all, the cockroach had caused the whole problem in the first place, by being found dead where it had no business being found at all.

Peter felt it ironic that the Brazilian ant high command was employing against him, an American citizen, the American tactic of ensuring victory through the use of overwhelming force concentrated on a specific target. Before he could pursue that line of reasoning and devise a counterstrategy, he found himself being toppled violently forward.

The sudden assault on his person outraged him. "Take your damn cockroach," he cried out in desperation, as he fell onto his hands and knees, scrambling to retrieve the camera that had bounced and rolled just out of his reach. "Take your damned cockroach, but leave me to my work." He remembered that some ants were carnivores. He thought of the Nobel, and the mention in Guinness's, both now slipping quickly out of his grasp.

Perhaps even now, if he took a picture of the ant army trying to take him captive, his place in history might be assured. Rukmini might find the print and send it to the *Times*, with a suitable news story. A headline sprang to mind: "Scientist Tragically Dies Battling Ant Invasion", with the subhead: "His Formic Pulp Research Held Nobel Potential". And the body of the story could hint at international intrigue, with the ants being controlled by sinister foreign agents.

He grabbed for the camera again, futilely. A large ant contingent had seized hold of it and were turning it around so the lens faced him. Others stung him on the fingers. He felt pain and numbing. "Damned insects!" They were all over him.

He struggled in vain as the main body of the enemy flipped him swiftly on to his back and pinned his hands to his sides. He felt and then saw a creature clambering up his face, its feet digging into his cheek. The leader of the ants, as big as his thumb and with both antennae aquiver, was soon straddling his nose, the better to control the action. Peter felt like sneezing, but dared not. This insect might not brook being sneezed at.

It occurred to him at that moment that the ants he had been battling were all female, as were those that were taking him prisoner. Given all his pronouncements on women in the military, Rukmini would certainly have felt vindicated. He had assumed that the ant army was composed of males; his mother-in-law would have set him straight. She would even have reminded him that in ant societies the role of males is to be confined to the bedroom, after which they die.

The ant on his nose now reared up on her hind feet and raised an antenna. Somewhere to the left the Polaroid's flash went off. He thought he heard massed cheering. The ant leader signaled again; the flash went off again.

Her followers redoubled their activity. He felt himself being raised and trundled out of the kitchen, feet first. He hoped they would take the elevator, rather than risk the stairs, where if they lost their footing he would surely break his neck. Besides, the elevator would work to his advantage—he was so tall they would have trouble fitting him into that cramped space. He locked his knees, to be as difficult as circumstances would allow. So let the ants struggle! Every second he gained would increase his chances of being rescued.

He hoped that Mrs. Mulligan had finally phoned for the cops, something she had often threatened to do, and never done so far. He hoped they would respond in time, rushing in with guns drawn; but then—even if they did, what good would it do? Would "Police! Freeze!" produce any results at all?

He regretted having to leave in this unseemly manner—unable to wish Rukmini goodbye, leaving the kitchen a mess. He became especially concerned that, now that in him they had captured an almost inexhaustible food supply, the ants might at last have forgotten all about the cockroach; Rukmini was so neat in her housekeeping, so concerned about health and vermin, she would hate finding the dead roach in her kitchen. He sensed now that he must have caused her much pain in the past; he did not want to give her further cause for unhappiness. And she would certainly blame herself, he knew, once she realized that the roach, ultimate cause of their final quarrel, ultimate cause of her beloved husband's downfall, was like her obviously an Asiatic.

"Take it," he pleaded, time and again, hoping the stupid insects would understand. "Please take the roach." The ants paid no heed. Only when they were maneuvering back and forth to get him through the penthouse door did he realize, because of his excellent peripheral vision, that the bug too had been secured.

He thought again of the *Times*, of how painstakingly it would reconstruct his final moments, and the accompanying obituary. With luck, it might make the front page, especially if it contained a suitable final quote. But a quote needed an earwitness; where was Rukmini when he needed her most?

And then he realized that he could, indeed, reach out to someone—someone from whom he could expect an instant response. All he needed to do was think what his final words should be, and say them out loud. He thought of Napoleon when he too found himself trapped in similar circumstances, being shipped off willy-nilly first to Elba, then to St. Helena. Yet, despite having been given two chances to speak to generations yet unborn, what immortal quotes had the warrior emperor left behind? Alas, none at all.

It was then that Peter remembered a true Twentieth-Century hero who had functioned much closer to home—MacArthur at Corregidor (or was it Bataan?). Ah, redemption!

"I shall return!" he shouted with all his might.

The ants stopped short, but did not let go of him. Nothing stirred. His rallying cry was greeted with prolonged silence. The ant leader climbed back onto his nose, antennae pointed at the door.

There was no time to lose. "I shall return!" he shouted once again, pitching his voice much higher.

As the ants began to move him once again, from the floor below there came at last an encouraging thump and an answering battle cry. Help at last!

"Oh, go to hell!" shrieked old Mrs. Mulligan. "Nobody returns from there!"

A Kiss for Nandini

Last night in church, I looked longingly at Grace, a bride lost to me irrevocably. Lost, yes, lost, lost for ever! The more I looked at her, the more I became convinced that I, J. M. Mulrooney, should have been the one standing proudly next to her at the altar rail, not that weird-looking man with the pointy ears, poufed-up hair and too-large feet he does not know what to do with. I would have pulled it off, too, but the first time I saw her, six months ago, and fell in love, she was a bridesmaid at a wedding reception I had crashed; I was asked to leave before I got to meet her. Last night's wedding was just the third I have crashed this month; how was I to know that this time Grace would be the bride?

"Isn't that a strange coincidence, Ma?" I ask my mother, after I have shared the details over lunch. "Isn't that odd? Seeing her first as a bridesmaid, then seeing her as a bride?"

Ma now no longer answers my questions directly, countering them instead with one of her own. "You're into crashing weddings now?" Ma says. "That's what's odd, Jay Em—that you, a grown man, get your kicks now from crashing weddings and wedding receptions. You like weddings so much, why don't you get hitched yourself?"

"What's the hurry, Ma?" I ask her.

"You don't know what the hurry is?" Ma says, acting like she's very surprised, which tells me there's a zinger coming "You've been living here too long. Time you moved out."

Any other man I know would have given his mother a sharp answer, but I know Ma only talks like that when she's in one of her moods, and when she's in one of her moods I don't pay her much mind.

Still, I must admit, she's right: I have been getting my kicks lately by crashing church weddings, even though the sight of all those lovely brides paired off with strange-looking men in monkey suits is a downer for me. So after weddings I go straight to receptions, because receptions, unlike weddings, give me hope. I see all the eager young women lining up to kiss the bride, and I say to myself, "JayEm, there's a whole lot of pretty mermaids waiting to be scooped up in your own little corner of the world's vast oceans. Today, buster, could be your lucky day!"

The feeling of hope has persisted, and grown, even though Ma keeps reminding me the lucky days keep passing me by. "You think you're getting younger?" she snaps at me. "Why aren't you getting married?" she keeps repeating. "At least then, you and your bride would be out of my house."

"Ma," I remind her then, "it'll happen soon enough. For me, it's like winning the lottery. You lose today, win tomorrow — just a matter of time."

Of course I haven't told Ma this, but in the ten years I moved back in with her, the only thing that's stopped me from moving out again is knowing that Ma will be lonely. And the older she gets the lonelier she'll be without having me around to nag at. "Ma," I have wanted to say to her more than once, "think of the future. Yours. Once you think of the future; it will help you appreciate the present. Like my being present here." Somehow, every time I've wanted to blurt that out, the moment has never seemed right.

Ma may not know it, but I too am feeling the pressure of bachelorhood, so I've become much more proactive in my search for a bride. At a couple of the most recent receptions, I have waited for the bride to take her place, then staked out a strategic spot I call Square One; that's the spot from which, the moment the bouquet gets tossed in the air, I can waltz across the floor, quick on my feet, to be first to talk to the babbling young woman who has snatched the flowers in midflight. I figure that at that moment she is vulnerable, dreaming as she is, with her eyes closed, of white knights and marriage. When her eyes blink open again, I'll be the first person she sees, standing there tall, handsome, and available. I'll be imprinted on her mind, know what I mean? Like the farmer who gets imprinted on baby chicks if they see him before they see their own mother hen. If I have struck out both times so far, it's because other guys have muscled in unfairly. No sweat; another chance lies just around the corner.

Which is why today, after a rather late brunch at three in the afternoon, which Ma served in a strangely moody silence, I'm getting ready to go out on my Sunday afternoon jaunt. I'm putting on my shoes while Ma is doing the laundry, and since she doesn't seem to be doing anything much at the moment, I ask her, "Ma, do you think I should get a new pair of shoes now, or later?" "Get them later," Ma says, "'cos there's two other things you should get done first. Get married and get out." Ma says it without turning her head, in that deadpan tone she has, and if I didn't know what a great kidder she is, it could easily have gotten us into another one of those ugly knockdown drag out fights dysfunctional families sometimes have.

I let her be, and set out calmly in my antique collectible two-tone blue-and-white '56 Chevy Bel Air convertible, heading nowhere special but tooling east on Long Island's Northern Boulevard with the top down and my seat belt fastened and my blond hair blowing in the wind. Dressed as I am in my favorite red shirt and gray-blue suit and tie, I figure any cop who pulls me over for running a light while I'm ogling a pair of stilettos on the sidewalk will see that he's dealing with someone who matters; not one of the top upper crust, maybe, but certainly not someone who can casually be pulled over and ticketed, either. So when after an hour or so of cruising I see a stretch limo awash in buntings pull up in front of a church across the street, with not a cop in sight, a quick U-turn across a double white line is all it takes to let me pull up just a couple of cars behind. Serendipity, 'swonderful.

I leave my car at the curb and join the crowd of guests and passers-by waiting expectantly to one side. A guy in a suit hurries to open the limo doors, and when the bridesmaids step out I see they are a whole bunch of nutbrown babes in bright blue saris flecked with gold. They're wearing pink flowers in their hair, and for me it's an "Ah ha!" moment — I've stumbled on my first-ever Indian wedding, and am I in for an exotic treat! The crowd on the sidewalk gasps. I gasp. Then it's the turn of the bride to step out demurely, and a bridesmaid moves quickly and sinuously to help her, and though the bride is pretty I see that this particular bridesmaid is prettier still. Stop racing, heart. Move over, Grace! This time it's true love. Really.

"Thank, you, Nandini," the bride says, smiling tenderly.

Nandini! What a musical name, I think, and so absolutely apt, as fluid as the way she moves, as rippling as the way she walks.

Nandini smiles back. Tenderness being in the air, I too send her a smile and add a gentle wave of the fingers for good measure. Unfortunately her eyes are focused on the bride and my slight but meaningful gesture goes to waste. No matter. I know right away this day will be different beyond my dreams, so it's Nandini that I keep my eye on as the party swirls up the church steps and I follow discreetly behind.

In the church it's almost wall-to-wall Indians. Some of the women are in saris and some in dresses, about sixty-forty I would say, but most of the men are in suit and tie except for some who are wearing what looks like a tight male corset that buttons right up to their earlobes. I know from reading the Daily News that ninety out of a hundred Indians are Hindu and the other ten are Muslim, so I whisper to the suit who just came in and has sat down next to me: "What are these people doing in a Catholic church? Isn't there a temple or mosque nearby they can go to?"

When he looks at me cross-eyed, I notice he is as brown as the rest of them; he's the guy who opened the doors of the limo. "Indians can be Catholic or Protestant too, just like other Americans," he says. Blow me down.

Then I catch a glimpse of the groom. "She's marrying a white guy?" I whisper again.

"A while ago, her parents would not have allowed it," he whispers back. "But now we realize some of you white guys aren't so bad."

Reverse prejudice? That sets my mental wheels spinning, and now there's one more question I have to ask. "What about his mother? Won't the bride have ma-in-law problems?"

"Not at all," he says. "Problems? Indian girls are trained from childhood to love and respect their mothers-in-law. That's the whole foundation of the joint family system. Once the groom's mother sees this, no problem."

A latecomer plants himself in front of me, his turban blocking my view; Nandini I cannot see at all, but from time to time I get a glimpse of the pink-faced young priest who is officiating. This gets me antsy. When it's my turn to get married, whether in six months or a year, I'll want an older priest to be the celebrant, not someone who's younger than me. I know how tough it must be for young priests to officiate when young couples are getting married, especially tough since they themselves are not allowed to marry. They might have lustful thoughts, don't you think, and then have to flagellate themselves in the sacristy? Older priests, on the other hand, have had time to adjust, know what I mean?

Has my mind been drifting? The organist is playing the Recessional; I've missed the homily, and all the rest of the ceremony. What contrasts do I see as the bride and groom come slow-marching down the aisle, Nandini floating behind them; other bridesmaids tittering nervously, Nandini serene; the little flower girls losing their place, the now ringless ring bearer tripping over his own feet, calm Nandini there to set things right again. My Nandini, my Nandini now, knowing what to do, always in charge. Trained to cope, even with someone like Mom.

Minutes later in the foyer, I hug the bridegroom heartily, twice, and slap him on the back, so it won't seem odd that I kiss the bride on each cheek, also twice. The kisses come out sounding really heartfelt, and I'm thinking that's a good thing, because Nandini's turn will come next, she's standing right behind. But when the bride moves, Nandini's not there.

Playing for time, I follow the bridal couple down the church steps. So many people now come up to wish them that I get in line again, knowing that Nandini will have to come back to join the bridal party because the limo has now glided to the curb. By now I'm face to face with the bride again and there's still no sign of Nandini, so I try for a third kiss but just as I'm leaning forward, someone pushes in between us. I have a sudden rush of anger until I realize—surely that lightest of perfumes comes wafting down from Heaven! Who could be wearing it but my lustrous Nandini?

Before I can call her name, or even move, there's a commotion behind us. "My car!" a man is shouting. "They're towing my car!" In his rush to get to the towtruck the man pushes roughly past, sending me and others lurching forward and knocking Nandini off balance. To keep her from falling I quickly grab her arm, at the same time that Nandini, making her own desperate effort to save herself, spins around sharply to the right, her elbow crashing into my ribs while her right foot keeps flailing for a foothold, stomping on my right foot, not once, but time and again. Ah, the exquisite pain of it all!

I let go of Nandini's arm to grab my toes. "So sorry," she murmurs. "Did I hurt you?"

She cares! My darling cares! My ribcage is on fire, my toes have been turned to pulp and I can barely stand, but my Nandini's apology rings in my ears as mellow as church bells pealing at dusk. Are we going to be soulmates, or what?

"I should be the one to apologize," I tell her. "Did I startle you? You seemed about to fall."

She doesn't answer. Instead, she reaches for the limo's rear door and as I gallantly open it for her, I see I had better introduce myself in the few seconds I have left.

"I'm Jay Mulrooney, at your service," I tell her, bowing smartly. I want my precious sweet to know that I can be sensitive to the courtly ways of the old world, even if it means bumping my head on a too-high car frame.

She gets in and settles herself. As I gently push the door shut, I wiggle my fingers as I'd done an hour earlier and smile at the lightly tinted window. Quickly she turns her face away, but is that a hint of an answering smile I see lighting up my winsome angel's face? Shy, shy, she cannot bear to let me see her blush!

The driver puts the limo in gear. "Nandini!" I cry, and tap quickly on the window. It stays shut. The limo glides away. Oh, rats!

A hand grabs my elbow; it's the man I'd been quizzing in church. He'd been bustling about just moments ago, getting people organized in car pools. Now he opens the door to a waiting limo and says, "I see you know our Nandini. You missed your ride? Get in please. Not to worry—she's my favorite niece. I'm Ashok. Make yourself comfortable; you'll be able to catch up with her at the reception. I'll be driving you there myself."

Who is this man, Ma, is this Cupid? Thanks to him, I'll catch up with Nandini at the reception. We'll chat and we'll dance and if all goes right I'll even pop the question. You and I couldn't have planned it better if we had tried, Ma. It must be fate.

"By the way," Ashok says, as he pulls away from the curb, and picks up speed, "it's a good thing you did not drive up to the church and park right where that other guy was parked. Now look behind you: another team has just hitched a two-tone Chevy Bel Air to their tow truck. Beautifully kept, too. What a shame."

Lonely Aging Chinese–American New York Neighbor Lady

Very lonely my aging Oriental Chinese neighbor lady must be, so few visitors she is having. One month now I've been watching her, ever since my son Ganpat brought me to stay with him in America after his father died. "Ma," at that time my son is saying, "with me you'll have a home in New York. Who's left for you in India?"

You're from small town here, my neighbors in India are telling. Almost like a village it is. You have never even traveled more than few miles. Now you are going to Amrica?

Nobody's safe in Amrica, again those neighbors are saying. This is 1960s. Wild it is. Don't go! People shooting right and left, bullets flying through street, shots coming in through windows, just like in Hollywood movies. Indians also may have died. You haven't heard?

What about rioting in India? I am asking them. Many of our Indians we ourselves are killing.

That is by mutual consent, they are telling me. Here our people are rioting only when both sides are agreeing it's time to kill each other. When you are getting murdered in Amrica, no warning you are getting, neither any consent you are giving.

"Nothing bad is happening where I'm staying, Ma," Ganpat is telling me. "I'm living in a very safe neighborhood, safest in New York, perchance even safest in U.S. of A. It's really a white neighborhood, Ma! What can happen?"

Never mind about white neighborhood, my neighbors are saying. People are people, you know that! Good people and bad people are living everywhere. Under every skin color you will be finding them, good and bad.

"I'll only come if you are needing me," I am answering Ganpat.

"Most definitely I am needing you," he is telling me. "Very much I am needing you. Now surely you will come?"

If your son is genuinely needing you, most definitely you must go, my neighbors are agreeing.

So I came, an aged widow lady. Even though New York is frightening me, so big it is, I came. Months it took to get visa, very tough it is in these days, Russian is banging shoe on New York table, big *bandobast* American Immigration is making, even more objections American Consul is raising. But visa I am getting. And then very long flight it is, Bombay-London, London-New York. Plane is leaving in middle of night; even with window seat when I am looking out nothing I can see. For long time we are moving in airport, slowly slowly plane is turning this side and that side.

"Pilot must be having trouble seeing," I am saying to man in next seat, pointing to small yellow lamps someone has put on ground; very little light they are giving. He is not answering. Then plane is stopping. Long time it is simply not moving. I am thinking, Ganpat will be waiting in New York. How long long time he could be waiting for me, standing alone in airport, if this is way we are getting to America?

"What is going wrong now?" I am asking man in next seat.

"Pilot must be walking back to gate to get bigger lamps," man is saying. Then loudly he is laughing; why, God only is knowing.

Then engines are roaring, seats are shaking, and so fast aeroplane is going, where my stomach is I don't know. But man in next seat soon is snoring, all people are sleeping, air hostesses are switching off lights. I am thinking of asking snoring man, if hostesses also going to sleep, who will be telling pilot if plane is falling down? So no sleep I am getting; very scary it is, to be first time on plane, and you are only person who is caring about safety.

Now with my son I'm living in Jamaica, New York City. Private house it is, such homes I am seeing everywhere, big big but not big like Empire State in Manhattan. In all other houses I am seeing white Americans, and only that one single aged oriental Chinese neighbor lady living in house across street. At eight o'clock morning time of second day I am looking through upstairs window, and in her garden she already is. By side of house she has small narrow vegetable plot, and bending down from every plant she's putting something in basket. I'm thinking when finally straight she stands, her face I'll see. But still she's bending, even when turning and going back inside house. So slowly she is moving, bending at waist, stopping at each step, and no son she has in her house to help her.

"Where are Indian neighbors living, *beta*?" I am asking Ganpat after neighbor lady has gone in. "On next street?"

"No Indian neighbors here, Ma," he is answering. "Nearest Indians are living in Flushing and many more in Jackson Heights."

"And that is where? Not nearby?"

He points at front door. "Fourteen-fifteen minutes by car."

We have old Chevy car that Ganpat drives. Very wonderfully he is driving. This way, that way, wherever we have to go, that car is taking us. But fifteen minutes! Very far away those places must be. My son works all day. How I will visit those people?

"No Indians living closer?"

"There may be, Ma. Sometimes I see people walking by. But we don't talk, when we pass each other. This is New York, Ma. You don't talk to strangers here."

"But you talk to Chinese lady?"

"I'm late for work," he's telling me. He walks to front door and I am walking behind and watching him getting in car. Long after he is gone I am standing by front door, looking at what all is happening outside. Some neighbor people are passing by. Like statues they are walking, not once they are turning their heads. I'm standing there, looking, waiting to see warm faces, friendly eyes, like I'm used to seeing before. But here nobody is looking. Still, Ganpat is speaking truth. I'm widow woman. Which relative is left for me back home? There also only neighbors are left.

Every morning 8.00 o'clock aging bent-over Chinese neighbor lady is opening her door; slowly slowly she is climbing down three steps

149

and slowly slowly bending she walks into garden. Bent over she is, so it is taking her more time. Everytime I can see what all she is doing, from my upstairs window.

Next to door she has big rose bush. First she goes to bush and is smelling red *gulabs*; long time she is standing there, touching and smelling. I too am taking deep breath, remembering sweet rich smell, wonderful smell of my rose bush in India. Jasmine and champak also we had in our garden. Then she is walking to left side where vegetables are growing. Tomatoes, and I think other things that like me she must also be liking—onions, cucumbers, brinjal, hot peppers, ginger, coriander, beans; same things we are growing in India; after all, Chinese she is, our neighbors also they are in Asia, same people like us.

I am wanting to walk about, go on next street, stand on sidewalk and look at other people's houses, not just Chinese neighbor lady's house. At gardens especially I want to look; I want to see what all different things different people are growing. But Ganpat is telling no need to look; here at least Chinese lady is growing vegetables, he is saying; other neighbor people are growing only bushes and grass. Lot of time they are uselessly spending, he is telling me, first watering grass to make it grow, then giving it American-style crew cut.

Ganpat is always telling me not safe to leave our house without him. "Ma, this is New York," he is saying. Yet I am seeing other women walking about alone, even elderly ladies.

"They are used to walking in city traffic, Ma," he is telling me, when I'm pointing this out. "Look at the cars. You could get killed! When I have time we'll take long walks together. I'll show you when to cross, and when to wait."

Rarely Ganpat is coming home before dark. Then only we are walking to end of street and back. When he will show me, hard to tell.

"What about walking on next street, beta," I am saying? "That also must be safe?"

But there he won't take me. "Not to get you too tired, Ma," gently he is telling me. "You are old lady now." Very caring and thoughtful for his mother, my Ganpat is.

Ganpat works in very big office, he is telling me. He is holding big post there, very big post, that's why so late he is coming home. "Be proud of our son," his father always was telling me. "He is one high-ly industrious fellow." At other times he would say, "He'll go far, our Ganpat. Very far he will go." He was saying this even when our son was still in high school.

What all my husband is foretelling is coming true. But that time when Ganpat is telling he's going very far, going off to New York, at that time Ganpat's father and I both are not liking it. But we are telling each other, "It's his life, what to do? So long as he's happy."

"Let him go," Ganpat's father is telling me, when still he is see-ing me crying. "Dry your tears, *mataji*. Our young eagle has grown wings; let him test his wings. Better in America than in Europe. Other fellows are making money in New York. Look at Rockefeller; though ancestors were poor, now he is rich and also Governor. Why not our boy, hunh?"

But I am worrying that in New York he will marry some painted foreign woman.

Now I am here, I am seeing how hard life is for him. No time he has for friends or women, young or old, painted or not. And his secretary is a man also, he is telling me.

Very hard my Ganpat works, morning to night. First two days I am here he is drinking cup of tea early morning and rush rushing to office. Now I'm getting up at five, to knead flour for chapatis. Five chapatis I roll out and heat on flat *tawa* I have specially brought from India; ghee I am using, not oil, because ghee is fattening and Ganpat is looking so thin, people will say his mother is not feeding him. From one side to other I am turning chapatis as *tawa* heats up, sprinkling little little water till dough quickly puffs like ball and is getting little gold brownish spots. Then soon soon I am taking and putting next one on.

"Ma, that's most wonderful smell!" Ganpat is saying, first time I am making them. Now every morning after completing ablutions he is having tea with four chapatis.

"Eat more, *beta*," I am urging him. "Look, there's still one remaining. I can make two-three more if you want."

"I'll be late for work, Ma," he is insisting, but I think he really is leaving fifth chapati for me.

After he is going I am having plain tea. Tea only I take in mornings, with sugar and little little milk. Milk in New York is costing more; not everyone is having their own cow or water buffalo. Careful I am; nothing is wasted. For lunch I am always eating yesterday's remaining curry with fifth chapati. Every evening one new meal I am cooking; then too five chapatis I must make. At nine o'clock we eat. Always Ganpat wants to eat at nine; but sometimes when he is in room working, then I have to heat, reheat, heat, reheat, until his work he is finishing and he is sitting down at table.

One month is passing and still I am not leaving house by myself, but Ganpat says I can unlock front door and stand on front steps few minutes at one time during day. Such loving boy he is, so caring for his mother's safety. Standing on front steps is big help because during daytime hours no Indian TV programs one can see. Not even at night. No Indian radio stations on dial. But Ganpat has Indian LP records, and these I have been playing. Sometimes *filmi* music, songs by Lata Mangeshkar, thin thin voice she has like young child or bulbul bird that I am liking very much.

Mornings I am listening to sacred bhajans, to bhajans also late at night. So beautiful they are sounding, I am playing them little bit loud so neighbors also can relax and enjoy. One night when loud banging we are hearing I am telling Ganpat, "Don't open door, beta!" But he is looking out window and says it is okay, police are doing knocking. They have received complaints, police are saying; neighbors are feeling troubled. At once I am telling Ganpat to explain to police that hearing sacred bhajans early morning and late at night can be very healing to person's soul, also soothing to troubled neighbors. Police are then telling Ganpat that that can be true in India, but after 11 p.m. ticket for noise pollution and disturbing of peace can be very hurtful to disturber's pocket in New York. Then he is writing something on paper and giving to Ganpat and going away.

"Has he given us permission, beta?" I am asking.

"He has given us warning, ma," Ganpat is replying.

Not more I am playing music in daytime or night; instead I am talking to myself, remembering old old times, especially remembering neighbors in my old town in India. Never they are calling police; how big party they gave when I am leaving, how they cried, how many hugs they gave! Several times I am trying telling these memories to Ganpat, but too busy he is with his work. Sometimes he is saying, "Keep talking, ma," and sometimes he is saying, "I'm listening!", but his mind is becoming busy with big big things, while fingers becoming busy with number machine. Always he has to think how to get promotion and how to make more more money. Why I should bother him with old woman's thinking? So foolish it would be, to be talking about past, when his future he is thinking about.

If I had cat I would talk to it. At home always we had two three cats. Cats sit and listen. We would eat together, I would feed them bit of my chapati and bit of curry rice, and I would talk and cats would be purring. Or one would jump in my lap while other one rubbed against my feet. Very good company cats can be, always rubbing lovingly, always listening with sleepy half-closed eyes, always purring. Even spicy hot food cats will eat, just to keep company, but no cat Ganpat is keeping in New York.

"Why keep cat," he is asking, "when we are not having any mice?"

"Ganpat," I am finally saying, "never mind about getting cat. I would just like to say hello to Chinese neighbor lady. Will you take me there now, beta? Five minutes only I am needing for little chitchat."

"Next week, ma," at once he is answering. "Next week I take you there. Tonight I am little bit busy."

But next week also very busy he is. Best to wait, I am thinking. So daily I am opening front door, and from front steps I am watching people walking by—one short fat dogwalking lady with short fat look-alike dog, tall woman taking small child to school, very high heels she is wearing walking fast fast so child has to run; more women hurrying hurrying to catch running bus. All are passing at fixed times; no need to look at clock; simply by seeing them I am knowing what time it is.

And every day across street same people are walking by Chinese Oriental neighbor lady in her garden, not saying hello to her, good morning, how you are feeling, what you are doing, how nice vegetable garden you are having, not only grass like ours. Finally I am thinking, that is not right, lonely she must be. So looking for cars this side that side I am quickly crossing street and talking to her. Ganpat will not be knowing I am crossing road, if Chinese lady not going to tell.

"Good morning," I am saying. "Namaste!" But Chinese lady is having back to me and not hearing. Then turning, frightened she becomes. But I am smiling, and with palms pressed together am saying to her again, "Namaste".

"I am living in that house," I am pointing and showing her. "Your new neighbor I am. Mrs. Desai. Sushila Desai."

Chinese neighbor lady is nodding her head, and smiling. Nicely she is smiling, even though like me some teeth she has missing. "Neehowma," she is saying.

"Nee how ma!" I am repeating. That only is her name? Funny name it is, that Chinese ladies are having.

"Neehowma," she is saying, more quickly.

"Neehowma," I am saying, also quickly. "Such very lovely name it is."

Then laughing she is showing me her hands, how dirty they are, pointing to ground where she has been planting.

"Bhaji?" I am asking. Puzzled she looks. "Spinach?"

"No Inglish," she is then telling me.

"No Chinese," I am telling her. We both are laughing.

For minutes we are standing, talking and laughing, not understanding words, only feelings. Happy she is that I have come to see her. Happy I am, too. Happy because memories are wonderful things to have and tell, I am thinking. But to have value to teller, listener also must be valuing them. Otherwise, what's point of sharing? Look at Ganpat, I am thinking; now no time he has for my memories, but once he is getting promotion, others will be doing his work, more time there will be for him to listen. Then I can tell him what all I am remembering. With Ganpat's father I could share anytime. I'd be talking and he'd be answering "hunh, hunh," until he finally falling asleep. Very peacefully Ganpat's father is sleeping, after I'm sharing good memories with him.

With Neehowma also I can share. About Ganpat's father, and our marriage, how it was arranged, which people came, from how far; how I was dressed, what all I felt, even what sari I was wearing, and gold embroidery on it. My mother did embroidery, Neehowma knows that now, I am telling her that. Also how many gold bangles on which hand, and other jewelry. Everything I am telling her, she is nodding her head. Then I am telling her about Ganpat, his work, and how one day I am wanting to get him married. She also is telling me her story; three children she is having, and eight grandchildren, they all living far away or dead. Only that much I am understanding, and that she is wanting to stay in this house until she herself is dying.

Now every morning to her house I am going, and for one hour we talk talk talk. Sitting on front steps, we are talking in our different languages, sometimes she first, sometimes me first, nodding our heads, waving our arms, we are laughing and talking. Sometimes she is telling me happy things, and she is laughing and I am laughing, and sometimes she is telling sad sad things, very sad things, and then she is crying. Very softly she is crying, without making sound. Then I am putting my arm around her and with my sari pallav I am wiping her tears. Then touching her cheek I am making her smile, and then again I am making her laugh. My Neehowma, how she can laugh! Older she is than me, almost no teeth she has, still she laughs.

Sometimes I am one with tears flowing, and she is listening, and with my own sari border Neehowma is drying my eyes. Very good friends we have become, understanding each other without knowing words. And often I am thinking, how very lonely Neehowma would be, if Ganpat had not needed me and brought me to New York. Look, I am saying to myself; even when big big trouble is coming, how nicely fate sometimes is arranging some things. After Ganpat's father died, alone I was left, alone and needing someone. How lucky woman I am, very lucky, finding two people in new country who now are needing me. Perhaps some day, I am thinking, other neighbors will be needing me, too.

The Specials of the Day

When Jerome had first seen her at a writers' conference at Marspeller University some weeks earlier, in mid-July, she had been a cool presence in a sea of sweltering registrants; cool, and serene, though she alone seemed unprepared to face the steamy summer's heat, wrapped as she was in those endless pastel-hued yards of gossamer silk. Bemused, he stood aside and watched as, oblivious of his presence, she moved from table to table, glancing at and picking up materials on sessions that caught her eye.

As was his habit, he made quick assumptions: she would need mentoring, he decided, perhaps a great deal of mentoring, yes, especially if she were new to this country, spoke with an Indian accent. And she seemed to be filled with unsettling humility; he sensed it from the way she pulled back and smiled an apology whenever someone else reached for a handout she too had wanted to pick up.

"It's quite different, isn't it?" a voice murmured at his side. "Fascinating, even."

Startled, he turned, to find a heavyset man leering in his face. "What's different?"

"Their walk," the man said, nodding towards her. "Indian women, the way they move. Must be the saris, way they wear them. I mean, makes them move like models on a runway, knee before knee, only not strutting and frozen faced, far from it. Far more graceful. Demure. Seductive, almost; see what I mean?"

"Really," Jerome countered, dismayed at having been caught. "You may well be right—but I hadn't noticed."

"Your eyeballs were popping out of your head," the man said. "Funny way you have, a very noticeable way, of not noticing."

He ignored the remark. And then, when he looked at her again, he saw she was looking at him.

Mrinalini had noticed him right away at registration. It would have been hard not to; in that crush of T-shirts and loud Hawaiian bush shirts, he was the only one in a suit. White, all white, except for a discreet blue tie that bore a spattering of gold fleur-de-lys. She sized him up quickly as a man absolutely sure of himself, a francophile, a traditionalist as well, and so a kindred spirit, since she saw herself that way, too—as a traditionalist in a changing world.

She turned her head slightly, to look at him askance through lowered lids, and found he was staring at her bug-eyed. She continued smoothly with what she had been doing, moving with deliberate grace the way she had seen her mother move, and her mother's mother before her. When she felt it safe to look again, a balding man in brown shirt and faded jeans was whispering in his ear. She wondered what the stout man was saying that suddenly had Fleur-de-lys looking so flustered. When he turned to look at her again, she looked away.

Being a forthright person, Jerome had pushed past the other man, then walked right up to her and said it out loud: "You exude humility."

She had answered, quickly, "My parents will cherish that compliment; it's they who taught me the value of humility." No accent there that he could place, neither Indian nor British nor American. But he seized his chance for a quick retort.

"And mine taught me the virtue in pride."

"Is pride then a virtue?" she had teased. He had not expected that sally.

"But of course! Aren't you proud of being humble?"

She had laughed, and though they parted right away—he to go to a workshop on "Fiction as Reality, Reality as Fiction", she to "Ghostwriting as Self-Revelation", she told him—already his opinion of her had begun to change. He had liked her laugh, and the repartee. And she had been quick to pick up on his bon mots.

At lunch break he looked for her in the cafeteria and saw her in the line ahead of him, picking up her tray, then looking with faintly wrinkled nose at the steaming meat dishes before turning to the salad bar. He gathered that she was almost certainly a vegetarian; only her degree of commitment remained to be established. Did she draw the line at eggs? Would she touch fish? Not having a clue yet, he kept watching.

By the time he had filled his tray and paid the cashier, most of the nearby tables had been taken, but he spotted her at a far corner, at a table for two, and she was alone. He maneuvered his way towards her; she was too busy leafing through some handouts to notice. Her salad bowl sat to one side, untouched; and also untouched was the entree, a *truite meunière*.

"May I?"

She looked up, startled, then smiled warmly.

"But of course." And as he set down his tray, she added: "The proud soon-to-be literary lion asking leave to sup with the humblest of lambs. It's almost biblical."

"To be biblical, we'd have to lie down together, not just sup," he said, and watched her blush. Impulsively, he stuck out his hand. "I'm Jerome Smollens."

"And I'm Marguerite Madhuvela."

It had not been her intention to lie. But seeing him there face to face, wearing a tie that flaunted a centuries-old symbol of French royalty, she gave as her own the first French royal name that came to mind. Royal and literary; not Marie-Antoinette, who after all lost her head, but Marguerite. Mrinalini he would never have been able to pronounce.

"I'd wondered about your name," he said. "I thought you might be a Nalini, or Indira. But Marguerite, an Indian name? Never crossed my mind. How did that happen?"

"My family's from Pondicherry," she lied again. She was born in Bombay. Invention piled on invention piled on invention; something Jerome would surely understand, given the workshop he was involved in? "It's a former French colony just south of Madras. You want French names, we've got plenty of them there. Now, your tie—

all those fleur-de-lys. You are certainly French, yourself?"

He laughed, pleased at having discovered in her a brilliant conversationalist. How easily she had turned their idle chatter around, to focus on him instead!

"I'm just a francophile," he said. "Don't get me started on how that happened."

She did not need to, she realized; he got himself started. The man loved to talk about himself. But then, didn't they all?

In between sessions he began to seek her out; and when she asked for copies of stories he was working on, he gave them to her, trustingly but a bit reluctantly, because they had not yet acquired that high gloss at which he normally allowed his work to be read. His fellow participants agreed with that assessment—he confessed that they savaged his prose, gleefully.

She was appalled. He countered by pointing out that Somerset Maugham and Graham Greene in their day had also had their detractors.

Flaubert and Dostoevsky as well, she reminded him. Let the dogs bark, she added; he did not need a caravan to plough ahead. Too late she realized she had mixed a metaphor, and was glad he was too preoccupied to notice.

He agreed he could march on by himself.

She attended the final session as his guest, her own workshop having ended in disarray a day early. He found he had called in a champion. Where others found fault, she came to his defense, rising hotly to proclaim, "Jerome is a master!" Then and there he decided that marching through life by himself would be less rewarding than having her march alongside, in lockstep.

"Lunch, the first week we're back in New York?" he whispered.

Should she reel him in already? "I'll be busy all that week," she told him.

"Dinner, then?"

"Still, not that week. Sorry."

"The following Monday, perhaps?"

'I'll be out of town." That much was true. "Perhaps the week after? It'll have to be; the following weekend I'm flying back to India."

He was dumbfounded. "To India? For good?"

"I don't think so. But my mother may have other plans."

He jotted down her New York number and address.

The summons from her mother had been no invention. *Mataji* had indeed called from Delhi, two days earlier, and the hoarse voice, made hoarser by the crackling on the line, still rang in her ears. "*Beti*, child, you should come home to visit," her mother had said. "Your father's gone old, who knows how long he'll last. You should be here, couple of months, couple of weeks at least. The family are very anxious to see you. Uncles, aunts, other people also."

She knew what that meant. She'd be paraded before a succession of brideseekers, or the brideseekers would be paraded before her; *mataji* wanted an Indian son-in-law, and so did her aunts. Fortunately, her mother did not add, as she so often did, "You're almost thirty, *beti*. Time you got married."

Jerome put his first week back in New York to good use, choosing the restaurant with care. The Golden Dahlia in the East Village he dismissed out of hand; Tex-Mex was not the food he had in mind. *La Vie en Rose*, on Restaurant Row, he found more attractive, certainly for its cuisine, and also because each table was bedecked with a tiny vase holding intertwined miniature roses, locked in a kiss. But he finally chose *La Crème Brûlée* on the Upper West Side because, besides its ambience, the maître d' sported a certain *hauteur*, that *je ne sais quoi* that puts the hoi polloi ill at ease. Having made his choice, Jerome had then monitored, over an entire week, the sequence in which the canned classical music selections were played, including the love songs; had checked out the lunch menus; and even savored the various dishes, jotting down—surreptitiously— the specials of each day.

On Thursday, true, there had been that small incident with the receptionist. Each day as he ate his solitary meal he had been watching that handsome young woman with a cascading mane of golden hair. Literate, too; since she had so little to do at that hour, she used the time to improve her mind, keeping her nose buried in a book. He had gone up to her on his way out, and wondered to her idly, recalling a line by W.B. Yeats, whether her young man loved her for herself alone, and not her yellow hair? He had expected her to catch the allusion, and smile; how was he to know she read only the romances of Danielle Steele?

She had glared at him. "He loves all of me," she had said frostily, thrusting her breasts at the vase of orange daylilies glowing before her. The bitch! He had smiled back, but on Friday he had taken his revenge. On a sheet of the pale lavender notepaper he never left home without, he had written, in his elegantly styled hand, "Your receptionist should smile more often. *Merci!*" and dropped the note, unsigned but crisply folded, in the restaurant's suggestion box.

Monday was the day he chose, and he called Marguerite to tell her so. Of all the menus of the week, he felt Monday's held the greatest possibilities for a true cultural exchange; it included such choice vegetarian items as *Crabe farci le fish spot*, and *Écrevisses auvergnate*. She would like that. Not only would he order the dishes in impeccable French, a skill he was proud of, but taking advantage of her name—Marguerite—he would speak of his favorite opera, Gounod's *Faust*, and when the taped orchestral arrangement (saccharine, but lushly performed) actually came on (as it invariably did at 1.20 p.m., he had timed it), he could speak of Faust's great love for Marguerite, and—if the place were almost deserted—could even sing to her, in his finely honed tenor (plangent head voice, pianississimo, but passionately) the first few measures of *Salut! demeure*. Starting with the *récitatif*, of course.

Even the mackerel dish he would be ordering—the *Maquereaux au vin blanc provençale*—had its role to play. He would segue into the glories of Provence, ancient and modern, where they could spend their honeymoon—if, that is, she accepted his proposal, which he had tentatively set for 1.30 p.m. The idea had grown on him during the preceding week: since she alone, of all the women of his acquaintance, had seen through his stoic façade to the genius surging within, it was proper that he offer her the privilege of becoming his wife.

Now, as they entered *La Crème Brûlée*, he smiled as she gasped in delight at the ambience. "Wait till you taste the *crabe farci*," he murmured in her ear.

The blonde-tressed receptionist, busy buffing her nails, barely looked up as they approached.

"Good afternoon," he said. "Table for two, please."

She did not return his smile, but reached out languidly for a day-book. Was his helpful suggestion, that she smile more often, gathering dust at the bottom of the suggestion box?

"Mr. Krakov? We were not expecting you until one."

"And I'm sure Mr. Krakov will not disappoint you," he said. "But I am not Mr. Krakov. The name is Smollens. Mister Jerome Smollens." The 'mister' came out lightly stressed.

"I don't see your name here, Mr. Smollens," she said, running her finger down the page. "Did you make a reservation? We require one." It was as though she had never seen him before.

"Is this something new?" he said, nonplussed. "I've had lunch here all of last week, and never needed one."

"It's been our policy all along," she said. "Says so in all our ads. We may not have insisted before, but we're doing it as of today."

"But the place is empty," he spluttered. "Just look around you—empty tables all over the place."

"Jerome," Marguerite said, "it's just not worth the hassle. Let's go eat someplace else."

"I'll go get the maître d'," the receptionist said, sliding off her perch. "Perhaps he can make some sort of accommodation." Over her shoulder she flashed him a smile, a pearly baring of teeth.

Jerome watched her saunter towards the kitchen, her walk delicately sinuous, returning moments later with the maître d' in tow; the man could hardly take his eyes off her.

"Is there a problem, m'sieur?" the maître d' said.

"No problem at all," Jerome said, "but perhaps a question of attitude. Why do I need a reservation today, when I didn't need one all of last week?"

"I have explained to Mr. Smollens that it's our rule," Yellow Hair purred, baring her teeth again.

"It's because of the way our kitchen's set up," the maître d' said. "Our chef prefers not to be surprised."

"Jerome," Marguerite said, her hand now tugging at his sleeve.

"But certainly we'll accommodate you, this one time, because I remember you from last week," the maître d' said. "It's not that we don't value your patronage. Follow me." He led them to a table by a window.

"I'm sorry," Jerome said, when they were seated. "I had meant this to be a very special lunch, but it's gotten off to a rocky start."

She patted his hand. "It'll turn out all right, you'll see."

"I'm your waitress, Francine," the cheerful redhead said, floating into their consciousness out of nowhere. "I'm a trainee, actually. I'll take your order whenever you're ready, but meanwhile, would you like something to drink?"

Marguerite ordered a gin and tonic, he a whisky sour, straight up, and when they were halfway through their drinks Francine was back.

"Are you ready to order, madam?"

"We are," Jerome said.

"Before you do, let me tell you about the specials of the day," Francine said.

"Please don't bother, I'll just start with the *crabe farci*," Marguerite said, but Jerome looked encouragingly at Francine. On previous visits it had amused him the way Francine in particular would not be denied, but reeled off the specials as breathlessly as though she were auditioning for a role on Broadway.

"Our first special is a Crab and Tomato Bisque," she said, leaning earnestly towards Marguerite, "a delicious blend of crab meat and delicate seasonings, gently coddled in a butter-and-cream sauce, its flavor enhanced by a long simmering in freshly squeezed tomato-citrus juices."

"It's excellent," Jerome said to Marguerite, "but it's not a patch on the *crabe farci.*" He turned to Francine for corroboration.

"Our next special is a Stuffed Flank Steak *pommes de terre*," Francine went on, reddening slightly but otherwise not responding to the interruption. "A select flank steak, scored lightly crosswise, stuffed with a balanced mix of cubed bread, celery, onions, and sage, spiced with herbal butter, and served in a steamy nest of finely shredded potatoes."

"Mind you, it's a royal treat," Jerome said. "Yet, the *crabe farci*...." He looked again at Francine.

"Lastly we have Fillet of Sole Marguery," Francine said, her voice now pitched fractionally higher, "your choice of baked fillet of sole or flounder, bathed in imported sauterne, lavished with diced lobster and your choice of no-neck clams or tiny raw shrimp, topped with grated Parmesan cheese garnished with watercress and a single ripe strawberry, served on a fragrant bed of aromatic vegetables." She paused, looking expectantly at them both.

"They all sound wonderful," Marguerite said, "but I'll stick with the *crabe farci*." She handed Francine her menu.

"And I'll have the *maquereaux au vin blanc provençale*."

"Dressing with your salad?"

Marguerite picked a *Niçoise*.

"And I'll have the Russian," Jerome said, "à *l'Audélan*, and tell the chef I would like the black caviar folded in carefully, yes, but not too thoroughly."

"Would you like a soup for starters."

"What's the soup of the day?" Marguerite asked.

"*Vichyssoise* à *la Ritz*. It's the chef's specialty."

"Does it have milk in it?"

"It's vichyssoise," Jerome said. "Vichyssoise! It ought to be good."

"Then I'll have the vichyssoise," Marguerite said. And to Jerome she said, "I've never had it before—it'll be a treat."

He was touched by her innocence in culinary matters. "If you like it enough, you can have vichyssoise each time we dine together," he said, reaching out and patting her hand, then hesitated briefly over the *potage* à *la Caravelle* before ordering the *cressonière* for himself.

For wine he chose the suitably expensive *Chateau Neuf du Pape* '93. They toasted their friendship and the future; Marguerite glowed.

Obviously he's smitten enough that he sees us dining together a great deal, she thought. But is that really what I want? I find him charming, yes, sophisticated, and complex, and yet in some ways so disarmingly simple; to please me he offers not a weekend in Acapulco but vichyssoise each time we dine together. It must be some dish!

But when the soups were placed before them she hesitated a moment, took a sip, and blanched. "This is loaded with milk," she whispered.

"That's what makes it a vichyssoise," Jerome said. "Milk, and cream. Something wrong with the taste?"

"I'll be sick," she said. "I'm allergic to milk."

"Then we'll send it back." He signaled to Francine, with a flip of his fingers.

"This soup has milk in it," Marguerite said. "Please take it back."

"It's a vichyssoise," Francine said.

"I asked you if it had milk in it," Marguerite said, "and all I keep hearing is, 'it's a vichyssoise.' If I'd known it had milk, I wouldn't have ordered it. I'm allergic to milk."

"I'm terribly sorry, but I thought you wanted soup with milk in it," Francine said. "My mistake." She looked pointedly at Jerome, who began buttering his roll and remained silent, not sharing the blame. To Marguerite she said, "May I bring you the *Consommé Argenteuil* instead? We recommend it highly."

"Yes, thank you," Marguerite said, relieved and grateful. "It sounds wonderful."

Francine did not look at Jerome when she returned, but there was something about the way she set the soup before Marguerite that let him know the chef was less than pleased.

The trainee continued to hover nearby as Marguerite reached for a spoon. "Is the consommé to your liking now?" she asked, her voice showing genuine concern.

"Yes, it is," Marguerite said. "Thank you."

The maître d' had been seating two new arrivals, and stopped by their table. "Is everything all right?" he said, looking from one to the other.

"Yes, thank you," they said, in chorus.

But he was back in a moment. "Is the consommé to your liking?" he asked Marguerite.

"It's delicious." She dabbed at her lips with her napkin. It was her last spoonful.

Jerome looked at his watch: 1 p.m. The *Faust* selections would come on in exactly twenty minutes. Nearby, Francine was telling the newly seated couple the specials of the day. The man looked bored; he must be Krakov.

"She has the Ancient Mariner touch," Marguerite said.

"Just what I was thinking." He pushed back his plate.

"Fate must have meant for us to meet," he said. "You from far-off Pondicherry, I from New York—yet we have so much in common."

Francine, ever watchful, came to clear the plates.

"Was the soup all right?" she asked.

"Yes, it was, thank you." But to Jerome, after Francine had left, Marguerite said: "If they ask one more time, I'll scream."

"I'd like us to spend more time together," Jerome said, reaching for her hand, grateful that she did not withdraw it.

Francine was back with the salad. "Pepper your salad, sir?" she said.

Jerome saw the giant peppermill in her left hand, her taut outstretched pinkie steadying the barrel, her right hand waiting to turn the handle. He waved her away without looking up, not meeting her eyes, but Marguerite said "Yes, please!" and regretted it the next moment, as Francine spattered her plate with a heavy coating of black pepper, and disappeared.

"Redhead's daring you to send it back," Jerome said. "I would, if I were you."

"I'd rather die first," she said. "I'm not going to ruin the rest of our lunch."

"I have planned it to be a rather special occasion," he confessed, letting his gaze flicker around the room.

"It certainly is that," she said.

The maítre d' had seated two more couples. Each time he had done so, Marguerite and Jerome had paused in their small talk, to hear the specials being recited. Francine's enthusiasm never flagged; the inflection never changed; listening to her was like listening to a recording.

"Now I too know that spiel from memory," Marguerite said. "I'm not sure I can take many more repetitions."

"Just block it out," Jerome said. "Stay cool." In five minutes, he'd get to sing the Faust aria after all.

"I'd like everything to be to your absolute satisfaction," the maítre d' said.

She was delighted with the way the *crabe farci* was served. "It's a work of art!" she cried, hands clasped together.

"Wait till you taste it," Jerome said. "Then you'll agree, it's heavenly. And the presentation! That's nouvelle cuisine for you. Why, I've had dishes here that looked like Modigliani paintings—richly textured, too, almost too good to eat."

The Faust selections had already begun, and though there were now more people around than he had expected, he composed himself, and cleared his throat.

Was he going to sing, then? "Here, have a taste!" Marguerite said, and mischievously offered him a forkful.

He dared not refuse. "Heavenly!" he said again, and chewed as quickly as he could. "Heavenly, like the music."

"My favorite opera," Marguerite said. "Have another bite?"

Hurriedly, his hand said no.

"My favorite, too." He looked deep into her eyes. "What wouldn't I give to sing Faust to your Marguerite!" He still had a few crab morsels in his mouth, but the music would not wait.

"Sing, Faust!" she cried, ecstatic, and as the violins played the muted introduction to the récitatif and air he leaned forward and once again gently cleared his throat. He would have to sing very softly, with so many people around.

"Is everything to your satisfaction, madame?" the maítre d' said. They had not seen him coming.

"Yes, dammit, yes!" Marguerite exploded. "Everything is to our satisfaction! We have told you so so many times that I've reached the point of stupefaction."

"Then, everything is not all right?"

"All right, you imbecile!" Jerome was furious. "How can anything be all right when you and your staff keep butting in like this?"

"I shall leave madame and m'sieur alone," the man said, frostily. "I was merely being solicitous of madame's welfare. My apologies. Madame, m'sieur!" And he was gone, leaving the hint of a bow behind him.

They were silent a moment. Then, "I blew it, didn't I?" Marguerite said. "The mood is gone? You were going to sing, and then—and then he laid a guilt trip on us, and the mood is gone?"

"*Au contraire*," Jerome said. "When you jumped on that sap the way you did, I knew in a flash—you love me."

She felt herself blushing. Lord, she thought, not this. The joke's gone much too far. In love, with him? She had been drawn to him, true, had been flirting, even, but *love*? And yet, her heart was beating fast and strangely.

"And you," she cried, "how do you feel?"

"I love you too. Madly."

At least they were even. "I'd like a more formal declaration," she said. "Something a bit old fashioned, if you please." She could still play the game.

He plucked a rose from the centerpiece and touched it to his lips, then went down on one knee.

"Marguerite, light of my life, will you marry me?"

Relishing the moment, she looked at him tenderly before answering; to him, the silence seemed to stretch beyond enduring. He became conscious then of people looking fixedly at him—Krakov and his date; the maítre d', and the young couple he was escorting; the receptionist; Francine; other diners with their hands frozen in midair—all staring at him there, at him, down on one knee at her

169

feet, and in a public place. But that too was the stuff of opera, was it not? The tenderest, most intimate scenes worked best before an eager and appreciative audience. The chance to sing had been lost to him, but he could still salvage the moment, and to the sound of throbbing violins as the aria itself faded to a close, he sang the *récitatif*'s closing phrase:

"Ah, Marguerite! Behold me at your feet!'

In the profound stillness that followed, while not just the pleading timbre of his voice but the remembered shimmer of violins still softly floated in the air, while other diners held their breath and Marguerite was still wondering whether, how, and at what precise moment she should reach for the rose so beguilingly being offered to her, Jerome could stand the tension no longer.

"Will you, or won't you? Choose, Marguerite!" he cried.

His words broke the spell, and Francine came alive, addressing the couple who had just been seated.

"Before you make your choice," Francine said, "let me tell you about the specials of the day."

How I Missed My Chance to Become a Porn Star

The whole thing starts one cool November evening when Terpinsky opens the limousine's door, slides into the driver's seat, and says, "Man, these bleepin' tinted limo windows are so bleepin' dark, we could ride naked into bleepin' Manhattan."

Well, actually, it starts earlier in the day, when I've just yanked the drum set out of my beat-up 4x4 and am trundling it towards the Terp's basement door. That's when the chick strolls up and says, "Hey, guy, you with a band?"

I'm a freshman at the local community college, but man, this babe's such a looker, of course I say, "Yea, I got a band!" Even though it's just me and my neighbour the Terp, getting together this morning for the very first time, and he's the one has the guitar.

"Is it, like, famous?"

I just stop and look at her, open-mouthed. Famous? We haven't even started yet. Tell her that, my mind warns me, and you'll lose her. Go ahead, Zlotsky; tell her the truth; lose her, you dumb ape.

" 'course you're famous," she says. "Sorry I even asked."

Oh, that was close, very close. "We're 'The Two Terps'," I say. Hey, when there's quick thinking to be done, I'm the one who can do it, just like that.

"Oh!" she says, "the *Terps!*" as though she's heard the name. Her eyes have opened wide; she's thinking, "He's so tall!" Which I am, but thin as a lamppost, which makes me seem taller still. She says, "I'm Delia."

"I'm Zlotsky."

We 'pleased-ta-meetya'd.'

"Is it Something Zlotsky?" she asks. "Or Zlotsky Something? How do you spell Zlotsky, anyway?"

171

"Just Zlotsky," I say, spelling it for her. I'm tired of spelling out my family name, Tzcherbattschoff. And I want to stop her asking all those questions. "You a singer?"

"I wish." She makes a face, then smiles. "But I've always wanted to, you know, like, sing."

"Stick around." I nod towards the Terp's basement door. "We'll be warmin' up in a few minutes. Wanna listen?"

"Gotta go," she says. "But I'll be back."

Down in the basement the Terp's waiting for me. I'm hoping he'll give me a hand with the drums, but he's got himself a shiny new guitar and he's practicing jerking his head over to the right and back down again while doing deep knee bends and twanging on the strings.

"Guess what," I tell him. "We may have gotten ourselves a singer."

But the Terp's not listening. "Got a coupla chords down pat," he says. "Think that'll do?" He turns up the amp and the sound is earshattering.

"Sounds great," I yell, as I begin to set up. "Now all we need is a hit song."

"Whaddya say?"

"Need a hit song."

"Ain't got a song?"

"I'll think of one."

"Ain't got all week," the Terp yells back. "Today is Monday. Get me one by tomorrow."

Tomorrow! Straightaway that gives me an idea. The Beatles latched on to 'Yesterday'; we'll glom on to 'Tomorrow'.

"Got one now," I shout. I certainly have; my creative juices are flowing. "Give me a chord, Terp! Let's go!"

He jerks his head, flexes his knees. TWANG!

"You didn't come in," he says, surprised. "I give you a chord, man, you'd better come in quick."

"I was chewin' on the words," I tell him. "Hit it again."

He does, and this time I start off right:

Tomorrow will be Tuesday,
We're-gonna-make-the-news day,
Ain't-gonna-get-the-blues day,
Tuesday! News day! Yea!

"Man, that's truly Awesome!" the Terp says. "You're a regular stinkin' Poet. Let's bang out some More Verses."

I can tell when the Terp's really excited because then he takes to using Initial Capitals on Key Words, just like Martha Stewart when she's telling you how to dress up a Pot of Geraniums in silver foil Before your Dinner Guests arrive. (I watch Martha a lot on TV because, like her, I too someday will own a home in Connecticut and a slice of the ocean in East Hampton. When that happens I'll want to be ready, Pots of Geraniums, silver foil, Dinner Guests, and all.)

So we belt out a whole slew of verses. While I'm singing I'm also working the drum set, boom bang boom babang baboom boom sssssscrash! It's a small basement and the Terp's got a powerful amp with speakers to match, so one feels the floor throbbing and the walls pulsing and the ceiling about to come down, but above the banging and the twanging and my own lusty singing we hear some high-pitched shrieks, and they're not from the mike or the speakers.

We stop, and the screaming's right next to the house.

"Someone's gettin' killed out there," the Terp says, and we rush up the stairs.

But it's only Delia, back with a friend. The two of them are jumping up and down and shrieking, with their eyes closed, not knowing the music's stopped. The way they're going, they could keep this up for ever.

I look at the Terp, and he looks at me. He gives me a high five. We've found ourselves our very first groupies – and they're good. Damn good.

"Hey, guys, this is Luizie," Delia says, when they open their eyes and we finally connect. If Delia's a looker, Luizie's a knockout. The Terp's impressed, but tries not to show it, and I'm down to thinking: If this is how good it gets at the beginning, what'll it be like when we're as famous as, say, the Rolling Stones? And then I think: it won't be good at all, at least for me, if all of the groupies can't take their eyes off the Terp, which is what's happening with these two now. It's time to take charge.

"You're in," I tell them, and that gets Delia to jumping again.

"We're gettin' in on the ground floor," she squeals at Luizie.

"It's better'n that," I tell them. "We're lettin' you in at the basement level."

We usher them down the stairs, so they can practice squealing while we rehearse some more. Our playing may not be much, but the way those girls can shriek, even from up close you'd think we're the Beatles. Maybe even better.

Later that evening we get together again: the Terp wants to go bar-hopping. Turns out the girls are underage; Luizie tells us so. No matter, she adds; they both have fake IDs. Also, they're nicely dolled up, they certainly are, so nicely that no barkeep in his right mind would turn them away. As it is, the Terp and I are having trouble keeping our eyeballs inside our head. Both girls are the soft, clingy type: they listen, they laugh, they sigh. If we get a gig, who knows? They might even adore. The price of fame—I'm all for paying it.

Our evening starts off well. We are welcomed into the first two bars we visit, no questions asked, but in the Crescent 'ar and Grill—the B's been missing for months—the barkeep stops me cold.

"You have to look up when you talk to me," I tell him, "and you still want to see my ID?"

"I don't serve nothin' to smart-arse minors like you," the barkeep says.

And I say, "Joe Baby, you've served me many times before," which is partly true, since he has served me once.

And he says "Don't you Joe Baby me, you snot-nosed infantile beanpole."

I don't like being called names, not when there are chicks around, and one insult leading to another, Joe grabs me by my shirt collar and the seat of my pants and gives me the old heave-ho; problem is,

174

when he throws me out the door he's looking at me instead of where he wants to throw me at.

I can see, even as I'm doing my imitation of John Glenn girdling the globe, that a very compact man's hightailing it through the door. I wish Joe Baby had seen him too, so we could have jointly aborted my launch. Now it's becoming plain that my orbit and the Robot Man's are going to intersect, and I can tell from the look on that oncoming face that colliding with him, even involuntarily like this, is going to be one big mistake. He's short and chunky like a large pickup truck that's been put through a car compactor, but the way he's moving, his powerful legs have just thrust him into overdrive and he's picking up speed. Bad news, for both of us.

Before I can shout 'Red alert!' I slam into his chest and we drop to the ground together. Lights start spinning inside my skull and I'm having trouble breathing. When my eyeballs refocus I see he's sitting up straight and he's holding me up with his left hand squeezing my throat and his right hand cocked into a fist. Where is friend Terpinsky when I need him most? Why aren't the girls screaming?

"Let 'im be, Shorty," a deep voice says. The voice seems to be coming from below the two of us, and that's when I realize I must have knocked down not one person but two, something to tell the grandchildren, if I live long enough to have any. Deep Voice must have been trotting in right behind Shorty; I'm certainly glad he's somewhere down there beneath us; cushioned our fall, for one thing. Besides, anyone who says 'Let 'im be' when a guy like Shorty's about to bop me in the schnozz could be my buddy for life. But actually I'm not thinking survival. I'm thinking, 'Shorty'? That's a funny nickname for such a short guy. Why isn't he called 'Big Guy'? I think to ask—then I see again that large clenched fist. *Now* I'm thinking survival.

"Ain't his fault he swooshed into you," Deep Voice says, soothingly. "He got throwed." As though Shorty didn't know.

"Don't care," Shorty says. "He must've done sumpin' bad to have got throwed that hard. Lemme bop 'im one. Just one." But he stays his hand. Obviously, he needs permission, and Deep Voice is the one to give it. Or not.

"Can't start a ruckus now," Deep Voice says, smooth as Chivas Regal. "Can't have 'em cops comin' down on us, when we still gotta make that last special delivery. Unfinished business, heh heh! We made the pickup, we gotta deliver, before them goods gets spoilt. Perishable produce, get it? Bop 'im next time you see 'im."

This seems like darned good advice to me, because I'm hoping the next time is never. This is the first time I'm seeing Shorty, and once is enough. He seems to think so, too, because he gets off the floor in one smooth motion, and I come up with him, a movable object being moved by an irresistible force. Then Shorty picks me up much as Joe the barkeep had done and throws me farther out into the street than the barkeep would have. A slightly higher angle and I'd have slid right into the fancy limo that's sitting there, going nowhere at all.

As I pick myself up I check for bruises. The palms of my hands and my forearms have broken the fall; aside from a few scrapes and scratches, I'm okay. Then I hear Shorty tell the barkeep, "Make it a double, Joey Boy. An' easy on the rocks!" Hearing this makes me really mad. It's what I'd been meaning to order for myself before the barkeep got so ornery.

"Did'ja know, the guy tried a real fancy move," Terpinsky tells me, admiringly. "He tried to land a kick on your arse soon as he let go, but kinda lost his balance. Spoilt his aim. Guess you gotta be one of those superstar foreign soccer goalies, an' then you learn to dropkick an' connect, all at once, no problem at all." A mine of information, that Terpinsky; a real fountainhead of knowledge.

I find a pay phone outside the corner deli but it's been rigged to trap suckers; I lose two of the Terp's quarters in it before I figure that out. Then I look for another booth

"Who you tryin' to Call, Zlotsky?" Terpinsky says, when I bug him for more change; I'm too embarrassed to ask the girls.

"It's a toss-up," I say. "Between the cops and the FBI's Ten Most Wanted list, that guy must be wanted for something. And I'd like to see the look on his mug when his 'special delivery' of perishable goods gets derailed."

"Ferget the bleepin' cops," Terpinsky says. "This looks like it's Shorty's bleepin' black limo parked out here, bang in the middle of the street." He's walking around it, and eyeballing it, with lust in his heart. He's been a car freak for years, our Terp has, but so far he's specialized in sporty models; good old Beetles, Turtle Porsches, Grand Ams, he has driven them all, taking me along for the ride. And he's always left them close to where he found them, in good working order, except maybe for a scratch or two, or a dented rear bumper, so the owners never could tell for sure they'd been borrowed. Unless, of course, they checked their odometer, which so few people do.

"Bleepin' Mafia Squad Car," Terpinsky says admiringly. "Hood's still warm. Could be your Payback Time, Zlotsky Baby. Why not have some Fun with it? Set Off the bleepin' Alarm, an' have Shorty gag on his Drink an' come Runnin' out in a Rage? We could Hide an' Watch!"

Hide and watch! What can the Terp be thinking? "What if Shorty found us?" I ask. "I'm the one he'd come after, bopping me at will and throwing me halfway to Kingdom Come."

"Then you an' the girls go an' Hide," Terpinsky insists. "I'll set off the alarm myself. Hope Shorty's enjoyin' his Double, what's left of it."

But the Terp's timing is off, or maybe those drinks we had at the first two bars have begun to kick in. Anyway, before we can split, he up and yanks sharply at the driver's-side door. It springs open—surprise!—throwing him off balance. But the alarm never goes off. And I thank God for that, because I can't see Delia and Luizie running very far, not far at all, in their slinky too-tight skirts and clunky high heels. Now the three of us laugh as Terpinsky staggers back and falls on his behind.

"Shit!" Terpinsky says. We laugh louder still.

"Shit!" Terpinsky says again. He doesn't much like being laughed at. So that's when he quickly gets inside the limo and says—but I've already told you what he says: "Man, these bleepin' windows are so bleepin' dark, we could ride naked into the bleepin' city."

He steps back out and peers into the windows again.

"So what's stopping us?" I say to him. "The key must be in the ignition—that's why the alarm didn't go off."

"Zlotsky, you're almost a bleepin' Genius," Terpinsky says. That's the most praise he's ever given me, and I do mean ever. "Let's bleepin' do it!" He points to the rear door. "Hop in, girls. We can Strip Inside."

I look at Luizie, who says nothing. She and Delia seem to be at that halfway point in barhopping when their guard swings midway between up and down, yes and no, and guys on the make like me wonder whether just another drink'll tip it our way. Delia's moving slowly to the front passenger side, and it's making Terpinsky drool. So she'll be sitting next to the Terp. That figures—they've been acting like they're already an item, while me and Luizie, we'll get there, I hope. She's modest and I'm virginal, sort of, I swear.

Right now I can barely see Luizie's face, the street's that dark. The only light comes from the neon sign blinking fitfully on the Crescent 'ar and Grill, and its reflection on the shiny black limo. On pause off. On/off. It turns Luizie's face a kind of reddish purple, like her lipstick that I'd like to have rub off on my shirt collar at least, if not elsewhere.

"Wait," Terpinsky says. Delia has the door open, but stops.

We wait.

"Maybe we should Strip Right Here on the bleepin' Street, before we gets in," Terpinsky says.

Wish I'd thought of that! On the other hand—strip on the street? It's deserted for now, sure, but what if a car comes along? I look again at Luizie, who still says nothing. Reddish purple Luizie, here pause gone, here/gone, with the flashing Crescent 'ar and Grill sign. She and Delia seem frozen.

"You wanna join the Band, guys?" Terpinsky says. His voice curls upwards towards the stars, and the girls and I understand it's not a question, it's a no-option option. Big decision, being made for us.

That does it. The four of us strip, I as fast as I can, which is not all that fast since the cargo pants I'm wearing to impress

Luizie are so new and so stiff you can almost hear them crackle. The Terp's a comedian; he takes his time, just as he does when he's going into one of his fab 'drunken perp' routines. Delia joins him, but Luizie won't even begin to take her clothes off until I turn my head away.

When Terpinsky's done and we've stopped laughing we throw our clothes pell-mell into the back of the car, and then we throw our shoes in too, and we pile in, the Terp and Delia in front, Luizie and me in the back. I tell you I'd have been a lot more comfortable sitting next to the Terp and cracking jokes, rather than being here in the back, this being the first time I've been naked in public, so to speak, in public even though I'm in a dark limo with tinted windows and there's a naked young woman seated beside me, and that too the Luizie of my newest dreams.

I'm not sure what to do, reach out and grab her or wait for her to make the first move. I mean there's this sexual harassment thing out there, and if you watch the evening news you know lots of innocent guys like me get nailed and thrown in the slammer when all they wanted was have a little fun.

But Luizie does nothing and now I'm feeling rejected, so to break the tension I do some heavy breathing. I mean, really heavy. Hunh hanh hunh hanh hunh hanh. Hunh! Luizie giggles and Delia laughs. Even the Terp laughs.

"Broadway, Here We Come!" Terpinsky says. "Bleepin' Road Show! Live bleepin' Theater! Naked Broads! Horny Studs! PRIVATE BOOTHS! Free, Free, FREE! Too Bad y'all won't get to See It!' Then he turns the key and the engine purrs to life and his left leg starts hunting for the clutch and can't find it.

"It's gotta be an automatic transmission, Terpinsky," I tell him.

"I know that!" he snarls back and puts the limo in gear, but I know his foot is still feeling for the clutch because it keeps hitting the brake instead. Each time this happens my body jerks forward and my head jerks back and I'm beginning to wonder can I sue him for neck injuries.

"Easy there, Terp," I say, "Luizie here's gettin' whiplashed somethin' awful."

"Go to hell," Terpinsky says. "Luizie can speak for herself."

Does he care so little for Luizie? Can't he see that if we lose Luizie, we'll be losing half our groupie following?

The Terp finally figures things out gear-wise, sort of. The limo jerks back and forth and on one of the backswings we hear the tinkle of breaking glass; he has backed into a lamppost and we have lost a taillight. "Gotta go!" the Terp says now, and pulls out into the street; in minutes we're lurching over the Queensboro Bridge into Manhattan. How quickly time passes when one doesn't have to fake heavy breathing! Actually, nothing much is happening with the four of us, action-wise. Traffic's moving almost bumper to bumper, and the Terp's so busy working the imaginary clutch-cum-brake he has no time to clutch at Delia; we in the back have had to fasten our seat belts to stop from being thrown to the floor.

Going down Second Avenue the best Terpinsky can do is pray for the lights to turn red. But even when he turns west on Fifty-Seventh Street he's plumb out of luck—the green lights stay green and the red ones turn green just as he gets his hopes up.

Delia pleads with him to drive slowly. "There's no clutch there, Terpy honey," she wails. "There's just the brake pedal. My neck's beginnin' to hurt, Terpy honey baby."

Nobody's called him "Terpy honey" before, let alone "Terpy honey baby," and I can see he's touched. He reaches out to massage the back of Delia's neck but tries to change gears at the same time and we narrowly miss hitting a Mercedes. Now several drivers honk at us, and one by one as they pass they give Terpinsky the one-finger salute. It bugs him that he can't roll the glass down to return the insults, what with the four of us in the state we're in. He hurls curses at them through the closed window, and it gets him madder still that the others can neither see nor hear him.

At last we turn on Broadway, and down the Great White Way we go, heading for Times Square. "We'll turn on Forty-Second an' head back home," Terpinsky says.

But he misses the quick zigzag left and right where Broadway and Seventh cut across Forty-Sixth, so at Forty-Second we are now on Seventh Avenue and heading south instead of south-east, but you knew that already, didn't you.

"Holy Shit!" Terpinsky says, and I'm glad that this time at least he has sanctified the excrement. Then he makes a left on Forty-second anyway, which as you know is quite illegal, and a cop steps out of the shadows and motions him to pull over. I'm surprised to see the Terp oblige, the cop being on foot and all. But then, the way the Terp keeps working that imaginary clutch, a one-legged man could have run us down, without breaking a sweat.

The cop comes up on the driver's side and even through the tinted glass I can see he's an older guy, forty at least, probably been years on the force. One thing about these older New York cops—there's nothing they haven't seen, except perhaps four naked people dreaming of making out while riding down Broadway in a hiccupping blackened limo. Perhaps the same thought crosses Terpinsky's mind, that this cop's been denied that one life enriching experience; he rolls down his window, and we see the cop's got a flashlight in his left hand and his right is resting on his holster.

Delia crosses her arms as the light shines in on us but Luizie reaches for the floor of the car, grabbing for something to cover herself with, and what does she come up with but my pair of cargo pants, which of course is just what I myself most desperately need. We wrestle for it and I get one foot in but it's in the wrong trouser leg, because Luizie's holding the pants backwards and tugging. I'd have pulled harder if I'd known how strong she is.

The cop's sharp eyes pick up the movement in the back seat; he trains his light on me and Luizie, and yells, "Hold it!"

And the next thing he yells is, "OMyGawd." Not, "May I see your licence and registration, sir?" nor "Keep your hands on the wheel and in sight at all times," which is what they say on cop shows when they pull someone over, but "OMyGawd." With initial capitals, just like the Terp.

His two-way begins to crackle and a thick voice rasps, "What's going on there, McDermott? You been hit?" and the cop says, "No, Sarge, but you gotta see what I see."

We've been pulled over right off the heart of Broadway. This being closing time, the theatres are spewing thousands of people out onto the street, and, thanks to the prowl car's flashing lights, they all seem headed our way.

Above the chatter of the crowd we hear the shriek and howl of approaching sirens, coming down Broadway and from both ends of Forty-Second Street. Could there be a fire somewhere? That would certainly take the heat off of us.

"Everybody out!" the officer snaps, waving both his gun and his flashlight. "Everybody out, nice an' easy."

Before we can move, the sirens converge, and flashing lights surround us. "Get 'em all out," a burly sergeant says. For a man walking into what might be a tense hostage situation he looks surprisingly jolly; but I suppose he can tell, from the state we're in, that we're not carrying any concealed weapons. Besides, look how much backup he's brought along! "This we all gotta see," he chortles.

The night has turned nippy, and the road feels cold and grainy underfoot. Next time I strip, the shoes will stay on.

"See What You Did, Stupid!" Terpinsky says. "Big-Mouth Bleepin' Zlotsky, Big-Time Stupid Bleepin' College Nerd. Nerd Nerd Nerd. Smart enough to be Dumb Dumb Dumb."

Could he be talking to me? Talking about me? I realize at once this isn't the Terpinsky-I-Know. It's just the Terp-I-Know, Buckling under Pressure.

"Broken taillight," Officer McDermott tells the sergeant. "Illegal left turn. And now public nudity."

More sirens, more flashing lights. The crowd scatters for a fire engine.

"Anyone here need CPR?" a fire captain calls, as he leaps off his rig. "My lips are trained and ready to do their duty." The cops laugh. So do the firemen.

"Anybody need pryin' apart?" a fireman follows his chief. "We brought the Jaws of Life along, just in case." He holds the heavy gad-

183

get up high above his head and bows to the crowd, acknowledging applause and more laughter.

"Could we have our clothes now, please?" Luizie asks the cop who pulled us over.

"Get the girls back in the car, and give 'em their clothes," the sergeant says. "Give the guys their jocks, that's all."

By now more flashbulbs are popping around us than at a big-time Broadway opening. Luizie and Delia, now dressed, stand close, shielding each other; Luizie has tears running down her face, and I see Delia reach up and wipe them away.

"You're the one should be wiping her tears, Shorty," a male heckler calls. "You were in the back with her, weren't you."

"That's enough of that," the sergeant says, suddenly grim. His men push the crowd back, into a rough circle. By now the spectators are standing more than five deep, and more are joining each minute.

"What's going on here?" a tourist asks.

"Looks like it's a Happening," a bystander says.

"Street theater?"

"Something like that, but unplanned. Happens around here quite a lot."

"Theater in the round?"

"Also in the buff."

"Thought as much. Those four guys from Greenwich Village?"

"Probably."

"From Queens Village," I tell them, to set the record straight. "Actually, we're—"

At which point Terpinsky snarls, "Shaddupp!" One word, just like that, without even the usual added bleepin'. That hurts!

"Are they going to kiss?" a little girl asks, pointing at Delia and Luizie. "Are they? Why are they waiting? What are they waiting for?"

"Of course they're not going to kiss," the mother says. "Girls don't kiss girls. Now shush your mouth!"

"In that video you rented, two girls kissed a lot," the child says. "I was watching, when you thought I was asleep. They even—"

"I'm taking you home," the mother says. "It's way past your bedtime."

"That's a whole lot of cops." It's the tourist again. "Wow."

"Mayor may have sent 'em—he's big on this quality-of-life thing. Doesn't like people foolin' around, no way. These four could be arrested, you know. Yup, they sure could be."

I don't like this one bit, these two guys giving the cops ideas, as though the cops didn't have enough ideas of their own.

"Arrested for what?" I cry. "We're innocent!"

"ShaddUPP!" Terpinsky hisses, and this time I know he's gone beyond initial caps. Way beyond.

"Why arrest them?" Another voice.

"Disturbing the peace—or maybe they're starring in a porno movie."

"Starring? Couldn't be—certainly not the tall skinny one. He'd be a walk-on, at best!" says the tourist.

"Or the cuckolded husband. Ha ha!"

Do these people have no feelings at all? No tact? To be dissecting me in public, like this!

"I heard a lot of nudists had planned to gather here, and be photographed all together," another voice says. "A hundred or more. Mayor stopped it."

All together in the altogether, I think. Hah! I've got to share this joke.

"Hey, Terpinsky," I say, and seeing the look on his face I back off. "Okay, I'll shut up."

Now a news photographer's standing in front of me and he's using up a roll. Click-clickety-click. *Daily News* or *New York Post*? *National Enquirer*, maybe? No way to tell, but enquiring minds will surely want to know. Through the flashes I can see the headline already: NUDE NERD NABBED IN LUXURY LIMO. And a rival tabloid competing with BARE-BUTT BABES BUSTED OFF B'WAY. Both on Page 1, and my picture with each story. I remember to smile.

To my right I hear a furtive "Psst!" and see a man in the crowd waving at me. I think perhaps he's waving at the Terp but he hisses "Psst!" again and points at me.

"Me, producer," he says. "Movies." I can tell right away he wasn't born here, the way he speaks; these swarthy foreigners are all over the place. He frames a shot with his hands. "Like, y'know, adult. Big-time, big box office. Porno big stuff." A sweeping gesture takes in the four of us, his entire cast. "I'd like you to, y'know, star. Make big career. They lock you up, call me when you get out."

"All right!" cries an enthusiastic voice in the crowd. "Go for it, fellow. Dive right in."

"Right on!" says the tourist.

Fools! Why should I mess with something like that, breaking the law, when I have a clean future ahead of me, in a band?

The cops have been poking around in the car. "No drugs, no weapons here," one says, disgustedly.

"Open the trunk," the sergeant orders Terpinsky.

"It's not our car, sarge," Terpinsky says. "We didn't get to put nothin' in there."

"Open the damn trunk," the sergeant says again. He moves to the rear of the car, and raps on the trunk with a nightstick.

The Terp opens the trunk, and the smile on his face says, 'Hah! Gotcha!'

But when the trunk swings open, the crowd gasps.

The sergeant growls, "You call this nothin'?"

I don't have to crane my neck like the others; height brings its own rewards. What I see is a man, tied hand and foot and gagged, and butt-naked like the four of us had been. The 'special delivery'! The 'perishable goods'! He's very small, he's very old, he's very frightened, and he shuts his eyes against the glare of flashing cameras.

I see now that my moment of triumph has arrived, perhaps the greatest moment of my life. The cops are faced with not just any kidnapping, it's a major kidnapping, and I, Zlotsky—Big-Time Stupid-Nerd Zlotsky, is that what you called me, Terpinsky, hah; Dumb Dumb Dumb Zlotsky, remember?—I, Zlotsky, have first-hand (or first head, you might say, since that's the part of me that brought the two thugs down) knowledge of Who Did It. And what will the headlines say now, eh, Terp? COOL COLLEGE KID KOs CRAZED KIDNAPPERS, that's what!

"Sarge, I can explain everything," I tell him. "It's not us that kidnapped and tied up this nice old guy. I know who did it."

He ignores me. "Take off the gag and untie him," he tells his men. "Hand him a warm blanket."

To the man, the sergeant says, "Can you identify the guys that got you?"

The man looks at us and shakes his head. "Not really," he says. "They had their clothes on. But I know there were at least two of them, and they grabbed me from behind. Cowards!" He scowls at us fiercely and clenches both fists. Ugh! That would certainly have scared off Shorty and his pal!

My mind works coolly on his statement. On the one hand, he says he was grabbed by two men, and that looks bad for us, very bad. On the other hand, he's positive he can't identify us, since he was grabbed from behind. That's good. That's very good. Very very very good.

"Wait," the man says. "I remember now—one of them kept calling the other 'Shorty'. Shorty was the guy who wanted to bop me one, and then insisted on tying me up and tossing me in the trunk."

It figures! Tossing someone around is just what Shorty would do, and I have the scrapes and bruises to prove it.

"Shorty, eh?" the sergeant says. "Now aren't we lucky you heard that!" He turns and smiles at me in a most fatherly way.

"You're darn right we're lucky, Sarge," I say, smiling right back. I see that Delia and Luizzie too are looking relieved: things at last are going our way. "I know just where Shorty and his pal can be found— getting pickled right now at the Crescent Bar and Grill in Astoria, Queens. It's their limo we've been joyriding in, honest. Let's go get 'em now!"

"Tomorrow, Shorty," the sergeant says. "There's no rush. I'll go get 'em tomorrow. Myself! Not fair to bother them or you this time of night. But tomorrow you won't be coming with me. I like your story so much, you should be telling it to a judge. You guys are under arrest."

Blow me down. And no Miranda rights?

"Read 'em their rights," the sergeant says.

It's while the handcuffs are being adjusted to the right comfort level that the porn movie starring role offer begins to look attractive. I mean, aside from the fame, there's money to be made, and then there are the perks! I look around hoping the producer hasn't left, and when I spot him I give him an encouraging nod, and mouth the words, 'I'm ready.' He nods. He's holding a business card in his right hand, between thumb and middle finger; expertly he flips it my way, even as he turns and melts into the crowd.

The card spins and swerves and curls gracefully through the air, then hits me in the chest and falls at my feet.

I see what that card could lead me to. I see possibilities of a career opening up that would rival that of the major hoop stars—that Abdul Kareem guy excluded—or anything the rest of the business world could offer. Of course, college will have to wait. And I think, I won't let success spoil me, when it comes. The girls can be part of this, of course, Delia may want to, but since the Terp got me into this mess and then cussed me out, the best I can do for him is save him a place in my entourage. 'Cos, after all, I do owe him one: it's being thrown into this mess that's gotten me the movie offer, and I'm taking it.

I'll just have to figure out how one picks a business card off the asphalt with one's toes, when one's hands are cuffed securely behind one's back, and the free transportation the city has provided will not wait.

Wooing Mr. Ram

Many Americans who have met my friend Ramakrishna S— consider him to be a misfit in New York; specifically, an introvert in business, a reclusive and obsequious rabbit in a rambunctious world of bulls and bears. I, as a fellow-Indian, would call him merely gentlemanly, in an Old World sort of way, and I use every ploy I know to boost both his ego and his self-esteem.

For awhile Ram would have none of it. The first couple of times I introduced him to one or another successful business man, saying things like "I'd like you to meet my very good friend Ram, he's in import-export and on his way up," instead of being pleased he became embarrassed. "Actually, I run only a small business," he would say right away. "Believe me, really, it's a very small business."

"Ram," I finally said to him, "what makes you say things like that? Here I'm using up my breath trying to build you up, and what I build you promptly tear down?"

"I'm just telling the truth, Dev," he said.

And in a way he was. But I have learned from talking to my beautiful young wife Lakshmi, particularly when we are having a disagreement about something that happened in the recent past, or even an hour ago, that Truth, far from being one and indivisible, in fact has two distinct abodes—it dwells in the mind and mouth of the speaker as well as in the ear and the mind of the listener. The speaker can thus pronounce one Truth and the listener hear the same Truth or another Truth entirely. When they differ, can we truthfully say one is lying? Not if each of them remains true to what was said and what was perceived. In reality, of course, I usually have to surrender, most often if the person I am disagreeing with is my spouse.

Not wanting to explain all this to Ram, I merely said, "You must tell the truth in a way that will actually make listeners question the truthfulness of what you have said. While you may think this would

189

be counterproductive, it will actually work to your benefit. I'll give you an example: When you say, 'I run only a small business,' that is absolutely true and absolutely boring. But if you say, 'I do not run a very big business,' people will at once become suspicious. They will ask, 'Why is he saying that? He has an office in midtown Manhattan, he must be paying very high rent! Is he afraid of something? Being reported for underpaying taxes, perhaps? He probably runs a big enough business, and is just being modest about it.'"

Still, Ram looked dubious.

"You should give it a try," I said. "It's a concept called the Power of Positive Denial."

"Never heard of it, Dev," Ram said.

"It's one of my Three Power Business Secrets," I said, "a concept I developed myself. Part of my Seven Step Serial Success System I have been telling you about. I'm sharing it with you now, at no charge. Repeat after me: 'I do not run a very big business.' Repeat it often, aloud. See what happens."

My words bore fruit. Word has spread that Ram's small business has grown, that it is now at least a medium-sized business. Which of course it isn't, but you can't hold him responsible, Ram says, when people draw inflated conclusions from the patently true denial he makes. This makes me proud; without wanting to share in either the praise or the blame let me say only that Ram is being very well mentored.

Actually, the truth about Ram's business would become evident if, like me, you were sitting where I'm now sitting in Ram's twenty-fifth floor mid-Manhattan office; you would see at once that his is really a very small enterprise—just a one-and-a-half man business in fact, the half being Govind, who comes in for half a day. Though he is supposed to leave at 1, you'll often find him still there at 2.30 or 3 in the afternoon, cheerfully putting in extra time for no additional emolument. Not even comp time off.

In my line of work as an executive consultant, I often think I could use someone like Govind as my personal amanuensis. My son

Atul on the other hand, a teenage law intern, or my daughter Indira, still in eighth grade but obviously heading for Harvard, I could never employ; brilliant children that they are, they each would function as a supersecretary and would fluster me a lot, finishing tasks just as fast as I assigned them; I would then be in a dither, vibrating like freshly made guava jelly, just finding new things for them to do. But not with Govind; his skills, or the lack of them, give me the time I need for contemplation, meditation, and sometimes even for much-needed catnaps. The feeling of calm attained in these periods, which I call "Relaxed Interiorized Intensity", is my Power Business Secret No. 2, essentially a refinement of the popular American job prescription, "Take it easy."

I have often explained this concept to my Lakshmi, but to little effect; wives especially do not accept it when they think you are out working hard in Manhattan and instead find you catnapping at home. Once I even said to her, "My little bulbul," (I call her my nightingale because she sings the liveliest old-time Hindi film songs while preparing our meals), "if you catch me sitting in the rocking chair and snoring, then you can truly accuse me of being asleep. But has that ever happened? If on the other hand I'm merely reclining with my eyes closed, then you must know I am meditating. For me those are the truly productive moments, when my body engine is running on idle, and my mind is at its most agile and yet silently purring." At least for the moment, she seemed satisfied.

Right now, my chair jammed into a corner by the window, I must peek over a clutter of files on Ram's desk to watch Govind, dark skinned and smooth faced and skinny as they come, pecking away at a computer keyboard, using the index finger and thumb of each hand. Bollywood film videocassettes are stacked a foot high next to his monitor. He checks a title and types it in, checks a price list, pecks away some more, rechecks the title against the original, hits print and then the save key, then adds the cassette to a pile teetering on the floor.

"This invoice and package simply must go out today," he explains earnestly. "No invoice, no package, no money coming in.

No money coming means I don't get paid. Ha ha! That's not my joke, that's Mr. Ram's—he cracks same funny joke every day. But he means it, I think."

Carefully he pulls at the completed invoice as it slides off the printer, then catches me glancing at my watch.

"Mr. Ram will be here shortly," he says soothingly. "If you just wait another three-four minutes, he will surely be putting in an appearance. Perchance somewhat sooner even maybe."

"He's never been this late before," I point out. "Could he be sick or something?"

"Any minute now he is coming, saar," Govind says. "He also has another earlier appointment."

Hearing that *saar*, I feel I'm right back in India.

There are footsteps at the door, and I look up expectantly. But Govind shakes his head: "Those not Mr. Ram's footsteps. Mr. Ram's right shoe is squeaking." In all these months I have not noticed that; when one's mind is attuned to extracorporeal phenomena, it matters little which shoe is the one that squeaks, or who is wearing it.

"That sounds more like Mr. Pat," Govind adds, looking at his watch. "Already he is being more than one hour late."

"Not Mr. Pat, the insurance agent?" I've known him for years, going back to the time when we were classmates in a Jesuit college in Bombay, and he was a wizened snot-nosed wisecracking teenage prankster known not as Pat but by his full family name, which was Patwardhan. I didn't like him then, a pushy young fellow, elbowing people out of his way, whether we were chasing a cricket ball on a dead-end street or trying to get into a movie theater ahead of the crowd. Little has changed, except that he is now both wizened and bald. Does he realize how old he looks when he looks at himself while shaving each morning? Does he have a mirror he has trained to lie? Not to be judgmental, but some of us simply don't age as gracefully as others.

"Also now he is part-time consultant," Govind says.

This news sets off alarm bells in my mind. Ram is my client; is Pat here as an insurance agent, or as a consultant as well?

"Does he come here often?" I ask.

"Three-four times lately he has been here." Ha!

I watch the doorknob turn, the door slowly swing open. Pat enters cautiously, leaning forward at a sharp angle—first I see the hawk-like Patwardhan nose, then the scrawny head and neck, then suddenly all of him is in the room. When he turns and sees me, his eyes pop, but he recovers quickly.

"Hello, Dev," he says brightly, as he places a bulging briefcase on Ram's desk. "Hanging loose as usual, hunh? Executive consultancy going well? *Achcha, achcha.* Why should it not—there's one you-know-what born every minute. Ha ha! Everyone OK, otherwise? Your good self? Son Atul and daughters Bharti and Kamala, two birthdays coming up this month, your young wife Lakshmi, aged mother-in-law Parvati, they also OK? Good, good."

Pat adapted to New York ways almost as soon as he set foot on the Cunard Line's Hudson River pier; he arrived here as I did on one of the Queens in the mid-fifties, before planes and stevedores sent the giant liners into mothballs. Familiarity, he says, is his best business asset. But he stops short of slapping you on the back, and still greets any woman in a sari with a slight bow and a respectful "Namasteji", hands folded together and raised all the way to his forehead. Each time I see this hypocritical and too deferential obeisance to womanhood, I remind myself that this is the same fellow who, while we were sitting behind a group of coeds in college, snipped a couple of inches off one girl's extra long braid, dipped another's hair in an inkpot he had brought with him, and then got me blamed for both.

"They're in the best of health," I lie, expecting him to try to sell me yet another family policy, besides the three he has sold me already, one at each chance meeting we have had. Those are the vulnerable times, the chance meetings, when a Patwardhan on the loose can catch you unprepared. One moment you are discussing higher things, like life after death; you point out that the spirit lives on through metempsychosis, while the body is incinerated into a heap of worthless chemicals; next moment Pat is telling you that those same worthless ashes can be worth x hundred thousand dollars if you pay as little as y dollars a month now before another birthday rolls around. Before the earth gets much older, you are signing on the dotted line.

Today of course I could have taken umbrage at his remarks. One you-know-what born every minute, indeed! My clients are men of substance, even those whose substance lies in the future. Money is not my main pursuit in life—it never has been—and it comes as ordained in such lean or bountiful measures as the goddess Lakshmi provides. How fortunate I am, I sometimes think, that my wife also shares the goddess's name! When I bring her my earnings at the end of each day, my bulbul wisely puts some aside for the temple that's being built in our neighborhood, and some for our savings, and some for her household expenses, and the rest she returns to me, to do with as I wish. Usually there isn't much left over, and she sometimes says to me, "Atul's father, you are such a brilliant man, surely you could be a respected university professor instead of doing this consultancy thing? If you don't want to change what you are doing, I'll understand, but then you should at least be charging your clients a little more?"

I do not remind her how hard it was for us when we first arrived here, how no matter what job I applied for, the answer was either "You are underqualified and so we cannot take you on," or "You are overqualified and will soon leave us for a better job and so we will not take you." In the '50s we both knew it was a racial thing and I'm glad that's over; but when I finally got a job and then got laid off, she shared the humiliation I felt of standing in line for weeks before the first unemployment check came in. The money was coming to me legally but still I felt like a beggar. So when she suggests a professorship I give Lakshmi a reason that will not pain her—the age thing: "You must believe me, my sweet bulbul, the times have changed. Colleges are now looking for bright young people to teach postcolonial studies. Look at my face—I'm an aging pre-postcolonial man, not one of midnight's children, and so totally useless for their purpose. As for charging my clients more, I charge every dollar that the market will bear."

And indeed I do, which is why I do not set my consultation fee in advance. A potential client calls me? After telling him how busy I am, how full my schedule is, I allow myself to be persuaded to visit him at his office. When we meet, someone brings me tea, and while we chat about family I take the time to carefully look around me. What I see tells me what I can fruitfully ask for. If I see expensive furnishings, I can tell immediately that consultations will bring me a sizable fee and stretch over at least six leisurely lunches spread out over as many weeks, and perhaps a relaxed and protracted dinner a month as well. Meager surroundings tell me the business is going through hard times; consultations in such cases may call for nothing more elaborate than a well-spiced cup of fragrant masala tea. At the end of a session the masala tea clients don't have to give me even one penny; it is mutually understood that our conversation in itself has been a mutual reward. The six-lunches-and-dinner clients, on the other hand, stuff hundred-dollar bills into an envelope and, somewhat hesitantly—as if apologizing for the grossness of the gesture—hand it to me. Alas, with the economy stuck in a rut, my masala tea clients far outnumber the lunch-and-dinner buyers; but, as I often point out to my Lakshmi, are we in this life to complain? What good will that do, except generate unhappiness? Our time of prosperity will come to us when it comes.

I am hoping some of it at least will come today. Ram is only a two-lunch-no-dinner client, it is true, but at this moment he is one of my three regular paying consultees, and we meet every week. More, he walks around with hundreds of dollars stuffed in various pockets of his business suit. He has been doing this lately because, since he wishes to increase his cash flow, I have been working with him on the Value of Virtual Visualization, one of my Six Success Concepts. "You want more wealth? Visualize it," I tell him, "but don't just see it in your mind's eye; smell it, physically touch it as though it is already yours. Surround yourself with money. Stuff your pockets with tens and twenties, so each time you put your hand in a pocket, your fingertips will touch money. Real money. In time, wealthy is what you will become." Lest it be said that I don't practice what I preach, I too keep money in each pocket, in fives but mostly in singles; money is money after all.

My arrangement with Ram is that beside the two lunches, he regularly give me a hundred and fifty dollars a week for the mentoring sessions. Strictly speaking, this is not a formal arrangement, but it has been Ram's practice for the past few months, which I have tacitly accepted. At one point a friend had suggested I could have made more money as a yoga teacher, with dozens of rich American clients; but that would not have worked—with my tendency to corpulence, after sitting cross-legged for one hour in the lotus position, I would have had difficulty rising from it in a suitably dignified manner.

But never mind that. Just think: if blessed with more income, imagine how I would shower my Lakshmi with gifts! As it is, some two weeks ago she had said to me, after I had partaken of a particularly fine but frugal meal she had cooked, that while walking past Manganlal's sari-cum-jewelry shop in Jackson Heights she had seen a fine gold necklace with pendant and earrings in the show window. "Would you like me to get the set for you, my little bulbul?" I had tenderly enquired.

"A gold necklace for nine hundred dollars?" she had answered, much surprised. "What would I do with it?"

I was so pleased with her attitude that then and there I had decided to buy her the jewelry. After all, though she herself has become pleasingly plump, her throat has retained its swanlike elegance, and a gold necklace such as Lakshmi described would surely set it off. Manganlal, when I spoke to him, said, "Dev, because you have been long-time friend, for you the price will be eight hundred and thirty-five only." We finally settled for six hundred and seventy five and four consultations. Now, if Ram gives me one hundred and fifty as my fee today, I will have to persuade him to give me the balance as an advance. It will be a humbling experience, but I will do it for my Lakshmi, and I know he will not refuse. The only impediment is that Pat is here.

Months ago, even before I saw him as a potential threat, I had envied Pat his superior self-confidence and tried to find a strategy to deflate it. I even devised a working title: Implantation of Incipient Self-Doubt. I should have pursued the project to a successful conclusion instead of letting it drop.

Pat is distracted. "Ram not in yet?" He looks from me to Govind, then back again. "Do you know what's delaying him, Dev, Govind?"

I shrug.

"He told me to be here at 9 o'clock sharp," says Pat. "It is now 10.30. Still he has not come in?"

"Momentarily I am expecting him, saar," says Govind. "See, I have got you in the book! Both of you gentlemen, properly entered in correct sequence. First appointment, nine o'clock, Mr. Pat, comprehensive insurance planning. Ten-fifteen, second appointment, Mr. Dev, executive consultation. Mr. Ram insists I write everything in book, so I am puzzled by why he's not here. Usually by 9 he is here, sometimes by 9.30 maybe 10; rarely he comes in by midday. If not here by midday forget it."

Pat seems satisfied, and pats Govind on the back.

"Hardworking chap, this young man," he says, pushing aside a stack of papers and seating himself on a corner of the desk. "Yes, yes. Good man, good man, hardworking young fellow. I like that." He picks up an ashtray and gently blows across the top, watching a mini-tornado of feathery ashes spiral up and drift down towards the floor. "Has his problems, of course. Poor chap—has big problems." He is speaking in the confidential but quite audible tone family members use in hospital rooms when discussing a terminal illness in the patient's presence.

Aware that the patient is awake and listening intently, I say nothing.

"Probably has no working papers," Pat explains, jerking his head in Govind's direction. "Imagine what Immigration will do to him when they find out." He draws a finger across his throat and makes a sharp hissing sound even as Govind coughs convulsively.

"You got your papers yet?" Pat asks.

Govind's Adam's apple bobs up and down as he swallows hard and fights to regain his breath. "Not yet, saar, Mr. Ram's advocate is still working on it. Mr. Ram says advocate has told him, maybe we'll have answer this month, maybe next, not longer than within next six months most definitely."

"Pollyanna," Pat says, with another flip of his head.

"Not Pollyanna, saar, advocate's name is Mr. Ardeshir. He has big big contacts, Mr. Ram says. Some state senators, even."

"Smoke and mirrors," Pat tells me. In seconds he has the three of us back in the hospital room. "That's Ram's method for getting out of a crisis—bring on the smoke and fiddle with the mirrors." He turns to Govind again. "Ardeshir, hunh? Can't say that I know him. You've got his address and phone number?"

"Mr. Ram most surely has it, saar."

"Know where he lives, then? In Queens, perhaps—Jackson Heights, or Flushing? Or in Edison, or Iselin in New Jersey?"

"Mr. Ram only he knows that too."

"The guy's probably a shyster," Pat says, turning back to me. "If he were any good we'd have heard of him, don't you think? You'd have found him first, too, you hungry consultant, you. Still, I might try to sell him a policy or two, more if he is a family man. I better write his name down." He does so with a flourish, using a gold-capped fountain pen. "Your delectable young wife expecting again, Dev? You old hound dog! Number four, is it?" He punches me on the arm. "These North Indians never need an aphrodisiac," he tells Govind in an aside, causing him to blush, then turns to me again. "You need more coverage?"

"Sorry, Pat, there's no new baby on the way, so it's no to all those questions," I tell him. My demeanor is placid, my mind serene. I will not let Pat have the pleasure of rattling me.

Govind has gone back to his typing; I have no such escape. So I think instead that if only Ram and Pat had kept their nine o'clock appointment, not only would Pat have come and gone, but by now I would have spent at least a half-hour with Ram, engaged in pleasant dialogue. I recall that each such session has usually been followed by an equally pleasant buffet lunch at an Indian curry house. I recall how at lunch, despite my pleas, Ram always pays, and then also discreetly hands me my fee for the day, from a wallet fattened with portraits of long-dead American presidents.

At some point today, assuming Ram and I have got rid of Pat by then, I will have to bring the talk around to my need for an advance. That will perhaps be best done at lunch, with Govind also out of the way. But the need has become pressing, because three days ago my Lakshmi without prior explanation put me in the deep freeze. "What have I done wrong, O Queen of Bulbuls?" I asked on the very first night, and the second, and the third. "If you don't know, I am not going to tell you," she answered on each occasion. Each time this sort of situation has happened in the past it has lasted from one week to ten days. At least four days are yet to go.

"This is stupid!" I shouted angrily, the first time it happened. "Because I don't know what I have done wrong is exactly why you should tell me." She had been scouring a frying pan but as I continued to shout she dropped it in the sink and rushed at me. She pointed at me and mouthed my words and grossly exaggerated my gestures, then pointed at herself and put a finger to her lips and became utterly still. Not one word did she utter, but when she stamped her foot and glared at me I knew her anger was greater than mine. I still just did not know why, or what to do about it.

She has also gone on a kind of musical strike. The food is still being prepared and placed on the table, but already for the past three days during its preparation not one single melodious note has passed the portals of those precious lips. Does a man of my position who has already passed middle age deserve such punishment, is a question I am constrained to ask myself. Perhaps she has done this because she thinks I've forgotten about the necklace? If so, now I must urgently think what reason I can give Ram for asking for such a quick advance; if I tell him I want to buy a gold necklace for my wife, will that make it more likely he will say yes, or would it be better for me to leave her name entirely out of it? How will 'personal emergency' sound? Will he suspect that I'm putting into practice my rarely-to-be-used Principle of Preferable Prevarication? If he says no, then what will I do then? I will have to explain the principle to him in its entirety, and that is usually a six-week course in itself.

While I'm thinking through this quandary, a voice intrudes. "This fellow, Ram," Pat is saying. "Most unusual fellow. Industrious as hell, perhaps, but also very slippery. Doesn't socialize much. Very few people seem to actually know him."

I have to touch Pat's knee to get him to look me in the eye. When he does, I incline my head slightly towards Govind. Pat nods, to let me know he has caught on.

"Wonderful guy, our friend Ram," Pat now says. "But did I call him slippery? Elusive, that's the word I was looking for. That's it, elusive. Hard to fathom, nail down. Very private person. Know what I mean?"

"You've known him long?" I ask.

"Long enough." He tugs at his lower lip. "But only from talking to him over the phone and from hearsay; never had any luck meeting Ram in person. Some three times he has given me appointments and three times he has broken them. Each time I was sure I had a sale. Groundwork had been laid, see? This time I said, 'Ram, Govind is telling me I should be in your office on Thursday, 9.00 a.m. sharp, is that a firm appointment or what?' 'Very firm appointment, most definitely,' is what he tells me. Who am I, not to believe? So here I am. But I ask you—now that I'm here, ready and willing, where the heck is Ram?"

I do not answer. I just wish his own complicating presence had not materialized, more than one hour late at that! My Lakshmi would never let me be even one minute late. Even this morning, although she is not talking to me, when the time came for me to leave for my appointment she quietly opened the front door of our apartment and left it open. If she had not loved me, would she have done that? So as I quietly left, just before closing the door I waved to her over my shoulder; I knew she knew I had done that, even though our backs were turned to each other when I did it. But now I have a question—not about Lakshmi but about Pat. Normally, when I have an appointment and show up, Ram shows up too, and he's always on time; this time around, I'm here, but Pat is also here, and Ram's a no-show. Could this be cause and effect, I ask myself? And this is a very troubling thought: if Ram is deliberately staying away this morning because of Pat, how will I tap him for money?

"Mr. Ram coming shortly, saar, guaranteed," Govind says.

"This much is certain," Pat tells me, ignoring the interruption. "If ever we sit down to a meal face to face, lunch or dinner, I'll surely nail him."

Govind's fingers hit the keys once, twice, and fall silent.

"He's ripe for insurance," Pat says, "but he doesn't know it. You, on the other hand, Dev, when I showed you that you needed coverage, you bought not one policy but three."

"One at a time," I point out hastily.

"One at a time."

"And I've reached my absolute limit."

"Absolutely. But only for the moment."

Oh-oh. I should have known Pat is not one to give up too easily. What if, next time around, instead of approaching me once again, he goes directly to Lakshmi? She will naturally refer him back to me, but what if he persuades her to persuade me? That would be very hard for me to resist.

I become aware again of Pat speaking. "An absolute puzzlement," he says. "A puzzlement to me, and no doubt a puzzlement to you."

"A puzzlement! What puzzlement?" I drag myself back into the present.

"You with me, Dev?" he cries. For such an old codger he seems more than necessarily upset, and his neck veins are beginning to bulge dangerously. "The old mind beginning to wander? Who do you think we've been talking about?"

I remember two—Ram and Govind. To which of them could he be referring now? Or could it even be someone else?

The veins in Pat's head begin to twitch again. "Someone who resists insurance, right?"

Aha! "Right."

"I tell you, old buddy, he won't be able to avoid it for long. He needs coverage, he'll get coverage, and I'm the one he'll get it from. He's my Toby Dick, I'm in relentless pursuit, and I've got the harpoons oiled and ready."

Mental note to my consultees: To minimize unnecessary disagreements, some erroneous statements are best left unchallenged and uncorrected. I could call that my Rule of Restrained Refutation. Learn that, and you can swim with Jaws II *and* with Toby Dick.

You will now begin to see how for an unforewarned individual even a casual conversation with Pat could wind up being, as they say, stress-inducing. The man never stops pushing, in person or on the phone; so Ram may have felt he had to agree to the 9 o'clock meeting, just to get Pat to put the phone down. And now, when he should be here in the office meeting with me, he is probably home, cowering even there in expectation that the phone will ring and Pat will be on the line. I realize with pleasure that this can open up a whole new revenue stream for me: I will teach Ram and others the secret of coping with stress, which I long ago discovered lies not so much in any particular incident but in how one reacts to it. One could reduce this principle to the simplicity of an Einsteinean formula: SS-NR = nS. In plain English: a Stressful Situation minus a Negative Reaction = no Stress. So many times I see white American friends getting red in the face, with veins in their neck and forehead pulsating! Vibrating needlessly, you now realize, since, albeit unbeknownst to them, SS-NR = nS. Think of it; try it yourself. Then you'll agree: If ever I mass-market this formula, the bottom will fall out of the booming tranquilizer bubble.

You will now understand why I can control stress so well, even in Pat's presence. Even his inane and oblique matrimonial allusions slide right by me, like muddy pond water cascading off a noble water buffalo's back. Besides, I don't have to keep listening to him; I've got options. At noon I have a choice; I can either meet Kishorelal on 28th and Lex (he has a collection of Indian postage stamps he wants me to appraise), or I can go down to the East Village, where Amarjit Singh is planning to open a second North-South Indian Fusion restaurant. He's going to call it the Masala Moghul, after a suggestion I made, for which I have been amply rewarded. The cardamom-laced scents of northern mutton biryani and Persian-style pilaf will mingle with heady whiffs of Mysore coffee, rassams, sambars, ("the works", as people here are fond of saying), the rice and the dry spicy curries to be served and eaten on banana leaves. On banana leaves, in Manhattan! So many food choices friend Amarjit gives me, even in his present establishment; so many decisions one has to make, just standing before the buffet tables, with the aromas floating up from the steaming tureens, and the salivary glands overreacting. I am not due to meet with Amarjit this week, but a simple lunch in advance he will surely not deny me. Against that, I must admit that Kishorelal is by far a more entertaining conversationalist. Should the belly then decide, or brain and soul? That depends on where the greater hunger lies, so today Kishorelal would win. No need even to call him in advance—with him, an unexpected visitor is always welcome. Besides, after a quick cup of tea, I'll be able to get back to Ram.

"Mr. Ram says he is not believing in life insurance," Govind says, unexpectedly, without directly addressing either Pat or me. "He says he is only paying for things he can enjoy while he is still alive."

"Pish tosh!" Pat pulls out his wallet. "He'll change his mind once I talk to him." He grabs me by the shoulder. "I have a new business card," he proclaims proudly. "It minces no words—you'll love it." He hands me one, then gives Govind another. "Go on, read the message, Dev. Read it aloud. Read the whole thing."

I put on my glasses. "'Pat, the Pro-Active Planner,'" I read. "'Let the Pro-Active Planner Plan Your Life Insurance Options.' Let me compliment you, Patwardhan—you have encapsulated a whole lot of planning and selling into just two mellifluous lines."

"Glad you think so," he says, reaching for the card.

"Wait a second, there's one more line here," I say. "You have a motto: '*More than insurance—Personal Consultancy too!*'?"

"Just an afterthought," he says. "Something I've been kicking around in the back of my mind for some time now. Of course, I'd never steal your clients, Dev, so there's no need to be alarmed. Certainly, Ram is someone I would never go after. He's your pigeon, has been that for a while! Not that I'd be any threat to you, you're much too suave, you old son-of-a-gun."

I scratch my chin, saying nothing. I see this makes him nervous. I'm nervous, too. If, despite his denials, Pat wants to displace me as Ram's consultant, what resources would I be able to fall back on, and which of my other clients might he also be talking to?

"Insurance is my bag," Pat says. "Surely you know that, Dev. So forget the consultancy bit—I do not want to be the fly that lands in your tamarind curry. Let's look instead at Govind here, he'd be a natural target. How old are you, twenty-five, twenty-six, surely under thirty?"

"Twenty-three, saar."

"For life insurance, an ideal age, though any age would be quite OK. But you don't carry any, I bet. Old Ram doesn't pay you enough, that's your excuse. But if you can scrape together pennies, then you can afford insurance. Begin with a small starter policy, small amount, small premiums—"

The phone rings, and with unexpected speed Govind's right hand snakes out and scoops it off its cradle.

"—very small premiums—"

Govind's eyes grow furtive. "They're here," he says, hunched over the table and speaking low into the mouthpiece. "Huhn. Some few minutes they are here. Fifteen-twenty maybe, maybe more. Yes, he came first. Hunh. Coffee or tea, whatever they want. Okay, saar. Donuts or Danish also. You will reimburse. Them or me? Me. I'll tell them. Hunh. Yes saar."

"Let me talk to him," Pat and I say simultaneously, lunging for the receiver. I grab it first, but Ram has already hung up.

"Mr. Ram just leaving the house," Govind says happily, his faith in his employer plainly vindicated. "He told me he didn't want to delay any more, talking on telephone. He'll be here in one hour latest, depending on train schedule, stopping only for coffee orange juice

204

donut. You want ne to bring you some coffee, or chai? No problem! Coffee shop in same building. Mr. Ram says I should offer; I can surely do the needful and bring everything up in four-five minutes."

"Thank you, but I must go," I say, reaching for my cap. I'm hoping Pat will leave, too. On the other hand, if he says he's staying—

"You staying, Pat?"

"Hell, no, I'll bugger off, too," he says. "Got an appointment with a hot prospect not far from here, and I'm due there in fifteen minutes. You know what they say, a bird in the hand is worth two Rams in the bush. That's a good one, eh Dev? Ram, sheep in the bush?" Then, turning to Govind, he adds, "Tell Ram I'll be here 1.30 sharp, and he should wait for me."

This could be fun: If Ram and I take our time over our lunch, Pat will have some more waiting to do.

"Yes, saar, one-thirty," Govind says, scribbling in his book. "I am writing 'Mr. Pat says please to wait.'"

"Sharp," Pat says, jabbing a finger at the note Govind has made. "Write that in, too. One-thirty p.m., sharp."

"Yes saar, sharp. See here, I have written it."

"And he should wait. You hear me? Wait! Don't let him go anywhere till I come back. Not even to lunch. Most important! Now I must use the men's room. Hand me the key."

"I'll wait for you here," I tell him as he heads for the door.

If Pat is coming back in the afternoon I have to forget about Kishorelal and grab hold of Ram before Pat does. This calls for strategy and timing; not even Govind must suspect what I have in mind.

When Pat's footsteps fade down the corridor, I seize my chance. "Ram's coffee and donut will be cold by the time he gets here," I say.

"No chance, saar, he gets it at coffee shop on main floor," Govind says. "Usually when he gets here he has to pour it into a saucer and blow on it to cool it down."

In a minute Pat is back. "Let's go!" But at the door, he turns. "Nothing must go wrong this time, Govind," he says. "Nothing, you understand? Or your goose I will surely barbecue."

While we wait at the elevator bank he becomes agitated once

again. "Can you beat that?" he says. "Even when I'm an hour-and-a-half late, that bugger was still not there to see me." He's peevish all the way to the main floor. Barely have we stepped out than he lets out a cry. "My briefcase! See how upset I am? I've left it in Ram's office! Wait for me—I'll be right back."

I have to feel sorry for Patwardhan. Stress is something he simply cannot handle. While I wait for him to come back, I use the time to plan my moves. We will leave the building together; if Pat's taking a bus I'll chat with him till he boards it; if he says he's taking the subway at the corner I'll walk him down the stairs right up to the turnstile. That will get him firmly out of the way. But what if he does neither?

While I'm pondering the possibilities, he shows up. "My meeting's at Forty-third and Third," he says. "You going my way?"

He launches into a monologue but interrupts it as we thread our way through crowds outside Grand Central Terminal, then resumes it as we walk one block up Lex and turn right on Forty-third. The sun's rays have been slanting down between the huge buildings and to avoid the scorching heat we hug the shadow on the south side of the street. We're almost at Third Avenue when he breaks off in mid-sentence. "I'm in luck," he cries. "There's the guy I'm going to meet!" And calling out, "Mr. Singh! Singh Sahib! Bikram Singh! Oh Lion of the Punjab!" he leaves me standing there and dashes across the street, dodging the oncoming traffic to pursue a heavily bearded Sikh.

A question now enters my mind. If Bikram Singh is the man Pat has an appointment with, what is he doing out on the street, instead of waiting for Pat in his office? Is he too, as they say in this city, "taking a powder?" But no, the two of them are locked in an animated conversation. I like that, I like that very much, because Pat could not have left me at a better place. Directly behind me a revolving door leads into the lobby of an enormous office complex with a subterranean passage that in turn will take me into the bowels of the old Chrysler building at Lex and Forty-second, then under Lexington Avenue right into Ram's own office tower. The subterranean corridor is also an arcade, and I take my time; with Pat now busy, and Ram not due to arrive at the coffee shop for at least another twenty minutes or so, I can indulge in some window-shopping. I find this to be a particularly rewarding activity that costs absolutely nothing.

When I finally climb up the steps into the lobby of Ram's building, the coffee shop is already crowded. I order a coffee, orange juice, and Danish for myself, and the same for Ram, and tray in hand I head for a table for two with one of the seats facing the door. But to my chagrin someone in the crowd ahead beats me to it and sets his tray down, then with a paper napkin slowly and carefully wipes a table-top that a server has already wiped clean.

When he turns around I see that the man is Pat, and what he takes from his tray and neatly sets on the table are two coffees, two Danishes, and two glasses of orange juice. Is Bikram Singh joining him? But Bikram is nowhere in sight, so the extra coffee, Danish and orange juice tell me that Pat is waiting to ambush Ram. I might have known. Wily jackal Patwardhan, no longer just a potential snake in the grass but now a veritable cobra in a coffee cup.

I can of course go up behind him and, waiting till he has bitten into his overly sugared pastry, be accusatory. "Thought you'd pull one over on me, eh, Pat?" I'll say, wagging a finger in his face. With his mouth full he'll not be able to answer right away, giving me time for another sally. On the other hand he might simply point to my own tray, and what would I say then?

I feel a sharp pain in my chest and I'm having trouble breathing; not a good sign, and it's getting worse. SS-NR = nS, I tell myself, and reinforce that with powerful visualizations: Ram striding into the coffee shop; Ram gathering up his courage and telling Pat to get lost; Pat picking up his briefcase and slinking out the door, a beaten man; Ram, a warm smile on his face, handing me not only the advance I need, but twice the amount I had asked him for; my bulbul overjoyed when I get home.

Still the pressure in my chest increases and as I struggle for breath I keep repeating to myself, SS-NR = nS, SS-NR = nS, over and over again. My mantra should work; my mantra must work. But if by chance it doesn't, if the God of Death still picks his way through this crowd to fetch me, what options will I have then? Since it's going to be my turn today, I'll ask him to please let it not be so early in the afternoon. Not when a treasured necklace still lies nestled in Manganlal's show window, my bulbul's throat is unadorned, and her favorite songs remain unsung.

Uncle Prabhu's Special Y2K Party

Anybody can tell that even at ripe old age of sixty-five Uncle Prabhu is one sporty gent. Of course, with relatives sometimes there are misunderstandings, and with him misunderstandings we were having plenty when we were in India. Yet he has forgiving nature; naturally we also were usually forgiving him. He also is very quiet fellow, that much I can tell you; shy and you might also say retiring. That is not appearance he is giving, however, when he arrives in U.S. of A. in October '99, moving in with Aunty Usha—immediately he's saying he'll throw Y2K party to end all Y2K parties. Imagine how big is commotion!

Here I must tell you both Uncle and Aunty are learned people. Me, somehow I am getting left behind; some even calling me black sheep in family, though not Aunty. That lady I am liking very much. Also liking her is my friend Billy ('Bang Bang') Billimoria. If Billy had said he was throwing big big Y2K party there would have been minimum of upset. Only one raised eyebrow here, maybe another one there, one of them certainly belonging to Aunty Usha. But no real fuss-muss. This Billy after all before retirement was long-time Major-General, Indian Army, commanding critical Western (Pakistan) defensive sector. Responsible old fellow he is, and also funny— Uncle Prabhu and me he calls by name, but Aunty Usha, who is older, he calls Usha Baby. He has many privileges! (Some I am myself supplying, running errands sometimes before he is even asking. He is telling me I would make one excellent ADC.) Such commotion as is happening therefore is strictly because of who Uncle Prabhu is, and also what he is doing. Only because you are my friend I am telling you this about Uncleji; only other fellow who knows is 'Bang Bang' Billy, who after all is living on next block, and also I am knowing him longer than I'm knowing you.

Uncle Prabhu has one big problem. Strictly personal, he kept telling us, but it was surely concerning all of us, all of us extended relatives living in Aunty Usha's two adjoining third floor apartments in Jackson Heights, Queens. What caused it I think is that two days after Uncle is arriving, my three co-inhabitants are saying they are flying back to India to attend wedding. Putting entire matter in coconut shell, to my mind all the wedding talk and preparations make Uncle Prabhu overly excited, so he himself wants to enter state of matrimony.

Aunty Usha, who besides being Uncle's older sister, is also relict and beneficiary of recently departed Uncle Dilip, says matrimony at his age is unwise. Aunty Usha says she did not suspect what was under foot. Not even when she got very first telephone calls was she suspecting. "Is Amul there?" Aunty says voices wanted to know.

"What voices?" I ask.

"*Arre*, voices," she says. "Giggly voices, flirty voices, old voices, young voices, but always soft female voices, except for that nice gentleman—not too old, just seventy-five—who called on behalf of a favorite niece. It was he who told me."

I wait for her to tell me what it is not-too-old nice uncle fellow told her. She waits for me to ask. Sometimes her manner of telling gets in the way of what she is saying.

"Told you what?" I am inquiring.

"His niece is a Gaud Saraswat Brahmin, very fair, and bringing a sizable dowry."

I am very much astounded—for me it could lead to one parlous situation. "Aunty Usha," I am now asking her, "are you perchance entertaining marriage proposals for my humble self? If so, whether girl is Gaud Saraswat Brahmin or not, matters not—I am one confirmed bachelor."

"*Arre, beta*, it was not for you," Aunty Usha says. (Often when I'm upset she calls me 'son'.) "That man and his niece were answering an ad. One Amul has been advertising for a marriage partner, and he has given our telephone number. So the next time a woman called I said to her, describe this Amul person to me; what does his ad say? And she said Amul is mature, fair, tall, independently wealthy, and a double graduate. At once I knew your Uncle Prabhu must have placed the ad himself, because he is all these things, except he is not a double graduate."

"Did you ask him, Aunty Usha?" I am now asking.

"*Arre beta*," she says again, "if I had asked, 'Prabhu, are you Amul?', he would have denied it. So I just went behind him where he sat reading the *New York Post* and said, 'Amul, there's a very nice lady wanting to speak to you on the phone', and he said 'Where? Where?' and jumped up."

Billy laughs when I am telling him this story; I tell him because he has become my adviser in many things. My guru, so to say, even though he is also a funny fellow. But I've told you that. Very good advice he gives. Life is like war, he says, and war is like chess. Three moves ahead you think, then, Move 4, bang! Surprise Billimoria attack. Move 5, feint to the left. Move 6, Boom!!! Checkmate. This idea he has also conveyed to Aunty Usha and Uncle Prabhu, not with success, I think, because they are not listening or talking to him like I am. Once I'm telling him: sooner or later I'll have to checkmate horny Uncle Prabhu. Especially if Aunty asks me to.

"Preferably not before he himself mates," 'Bang Bang' Billy says. Now you know why I am telling you he is one very funny fellow. Also punny.

Aunty Usha says Uncle Prabhu becomes so much embarrassed after being found out that he stops looking for brides.

Day or two after relatives are leaving for India for family wedding, Aunty Usha is springing big surprise. "I am asking Uncle Prabhu to move into your apartment," she is telling me. "I'm putting you in charge. He's new to New York and very trusting. People could simply take advantage of him."

"Without prior consultation with you that is rather an extreme measure," is all 'Bang Bang' Billy will say when I tell him. Even he is afraid of Aunty Usha, I now think. "Still, why didn't you protest?"

I tell him I am too surprised for verbal protestation, but surely Aunty Usha can see my inner feelings?

"You as a retiree can be in charge of Prabhu full-time," Aunty Usha says. "You have nothing much to do all day, anyway. Besides, when you were a child he dandled you on his knee."

Aunty Usha is very good with needle. Always she is reminding me of these things, major minuses they must be in her eyes—that I am junior in age, being only forty plus, and also lead life of leisureliness and contemplation. She does not see how very much effort that is taking. Constantly I have to fight against acquiring New York's impulsive do-it-now behavior. But retiree I am not; although generally relying on Aunty Usha for room and board, and occasional cash money, I am also playing numbers; with modest success I am especially playing opening and closing cotton figures on Bombay Stock Exchange. Better than New York stocks, better even than NASDAQ!

"Distract your Uncle Prabhu," Aunty Usha is now ordering me. "Take him out for a walk locally—or take him to town to visit the Metropolitan Museum. He will certainly enjoy that outing."

What I know about museums?

'Bang Bang' Billy is also against. "Are you kidding?" he is asking Aunty Usha. "The Met is full of naked statues and paintings of nude women." He says that when young he spent many hours in museums, looking at naked Greek statues and Italian paintings especially, because then he also was horny. "Let's not get Prabhu too excited," he says. Just when I am thinking this makes good sense, he winks. "Just kidding, Usha Baby," he says.

If by now you are thinking Billy is nicknamed 'Bang Bang' because he was one naughty fellow in younger days, that is one inaccurate assumption. He was given name for being enthusiastic artillery officer trainee at Royal Military Academy in Sandhurst. Unfortunately during '61 India-China war he was assigned to western front, guarding Pakistan border. That was biggest mistake High Command made, he says, otherwise Chinese invaders would have received hot reception, I am personally telling you. 'Bang Bang' Billy would have

UNCLE PRABHU.

seen to that. Many times he has described battle action to me, always with victorious outcome for our side.

"Go on, beta," Aunty Usha wheedles me. "Take your Uncle Prabhu out. He's truly going through a passing horny phase. But soon his goatishness will subside."

Fortunately Aunty Usha is right. I take Uncle Prabhu for one whole week to Met Museum, which he is liking very much, even without looking at statues; then I am taking him to Modern Art, where after two days he quickly is saying enough is enough.

During that time Uncle Prabhu is being very quiet. But in December he is again talking of having Y2K party. He is talking about it so much, I am thinking Uncle Prabhu and his Y2K party are two bits of very bad news. Very bad bad news. Immediately I am apprizing my adviser.

"You are forgetting about Usha Baby," he says. "When Aunty Usha puts her foot firmly down, it will take a great personal effort on Uncle Prabhu's part to lift it up again. I doubt that he'll have the energy. You'll see, there will be no party."

At once I am hearing Aunty Usha's voice in adjoining room. "Prabhu," Aunty Usha is saying, "listen to me, Prabhu. We'll have a normal, quiet New Year's Eve. No party."

"No Y2K party?"

"There will simply be no party. Are you listening, Prabhu?"

I am expecting big fight, especially since airwaves for weeks are full of talk about ending of century, ending of millennium, ending of whole wide world dot com. But Aunty Usha is enjoying eight years age seniority, and Uncle Prabhu like dutiful younger brother is not disputing further.

Publicly I am glad, but secretly I am little bit disappointed. Even if we had very small party I could have invited Cousin Pramila. Twenty years in this country and still she is wearing elegant sari daily. About my age she is, very buxom, and sporting bright red lipstick. Whenever I can I am kissing her, which usually means twice on each cheek each time we meet, if you are counting coming and going. On New Year's Eve, if lights go out, I'd do some more kissypoo with her myself. Some American customs I am liking very much.

Then just on Friday before Christmas, with millennium countdown becoming imminent, Aunty Usha is getting registered letter. She has won prize in sweepstakes—one round-trip coach flight to San Francisco on 27th, and week's prepaid stay, not at any Patel Motel but in hostelry belonging to one Sir Francis Drake; relative of dowager Queen Mother, no doubt, she is owning so much property in U.S. of A. Still my alert mind is suspecting hoax; where this letter came from? How suddenly it appeared? But Uncle Prabhu says Aunt Usha enters many sweepstakes; one lucky ticket may simply have won. 'Bang Bang' Billy says look, airline ticket is enclosed; hotel voucher is in order, paid in full. "This thing is patently legit," Billy says. Then Uncle Prabhu tells us temperature on West coast is 74° F; in New York winter it is. Who can resist? Tearfully Aunty Usha says bye-bye to us on Monday afternoon; she won't be back one whole week.

"Promise me one thing, *beta*," Aunty Usha says. "Promise me that you will keep one eye on Uncle Prabhu. You are in charge! No parties. He may want to go to Times Square, to watch the ball drop on New Year's Eve. No expeditions, *beta*, especially to Times Square. Too cold, too crowded, too late, and too dangerous. You're in charge while I'm gone, *beta*. Don't let me down."

Meekly I am accepting onus of being the entirely in-charge.

Uncle Prabhu personally escorts Aunty Usha in taxi to La Guardia Airport; he even carries her bag to boarding gate so she won't miss her plane. Only because he is pointing out she is so aged do they allow it. Not every brother would take so much trouble, especially when replay of international cricket test match is on cable TV, and Indian team is winning.

Immediately when he returns Uncle Prabhu is being very jolly and singing melodious raga of sunshine. He is singing this happy raga even though Indian team has suddenly lost three wickets for no extra runs. He is also reviving his party campaign.

"Wonderful," Uncle Prabhu says. "Sad," Uncle Prabhu also says.

"Wonderful, that a new century and new millennium are coming this weekend; sad that we are not celebrating this major, once-in-a-lifetime event. And it's Monday evening—" I see great light is dawning, but it's in my mind, and Uncleji may not like it.

"Did you perchance buy Aunty Usha's airline ticket, Uncle Prabhu?" bluntly I ask. "Is that sweepstakes thing one big fake?" These normally are not questions I would ask respected older relative, but like you I must be remembering that Amul episode—this Uncle Prabhu is one tricky fellow.

Suddenly he is becoming hearing disabled. "Millions will go to Times Square," Uncle Prabhu says.

"I'm not taking you to Times Square," I am telling him. "In Times Square our absence no one will notice. Besides airline ticket, did you also pay for hotel?"

Again Uncle Prabhu still is not hearing. "They'll be running extra subway trains," he says.

"Still we're not going to Times Square."

Finally he backs off. Aunty Usha will be pleased—I have triumphed over Prabhu's Number One Times Square Project. What all foolishness he had planned one can only think, and I can see old Aunty smiling. This does not often happen, let me tell you. Aunty Usha is one formidable person. But also in my mind I see Cousin Pramila. Normally when she sees me she is smiling, even in my dreams, also when being kissed on both cheeks by yours truly. She might be lonesome, with no party. What to do?

At noon on New Year's Eve we have a jolly visitor.

"Uncle Prabhu has pulled off a master-stroke," 'Bang Bang' Billy says. "See what he's accomplished: Move 4, Queen to San Francisco; he has physically removed Aunty Usha from the scene, and has made sure she'll be away one full week. Therefore, move 5—we should improve the shining hour."

My cutting-edge mind is instantly grasping: What this former military fellow may be suggesting, Aunty Usha may not at all be liking. "So, what is move 6?"

"Move 6, we have a small party. Remember, life is a game of

chess," 'Bang Bang' Billy says. "Uncle Prabhu is playing grandmaster's game; Aunty Usha obviously isn't. Who do you think will win? We should play the game, too."

Now I am thinking: To do, or not to do? Purely Shakespearean conflict this is. If Aunty Usha were here, what she would approve, that I must conjecture. Big party? Certainly not. Small party? Maybe. Very small party? Small small private supervised party? I can hear her voice saying, "*Beta*, you're the one in charge, you should supervise!"

Still, Uncle Prabhu is not responding joyfully to my good tidings. "Just we three fellows," Uncle Prabhu says. "That's our party? Two senior citizens, and a middle aged man with a paunch? What sort of party is that sort of party?"

Middle aged man, with paunch? Hurtful words these are, even coming from respected older person who is also revered relative.

"Not to fear, Uncle Prabhu, Cousin Pramila I'm also inviting," I tell him. "Perchance she can also bring two-three good friends. She knows dancers, models, many such artistes."

Cousin Pramila on phone says she and two friends will be delighted to attend. She wants to know from what time to what time? Formal party or informal wear? Uncle Prabhu whispers, "Tell her all night. Tell her harem costumes!" and laughs, and she is hearing him. Her smile is rapidly fading from telephone. Immediately she remembers: both friends have suddenly caught flu. Uncle Prabhu makes a glum face. And then she says, wait a moment, she too has now caught flu. Yes, she says, it is epidemic, very catching it is, and she is hoping Uncle Prabhu catches it too, and catches it bad, that wicked old man.

Uncle Prabhu now makes very glum face, but not so glum as mine, and retires to his room. Not even in sign language he is talking to me, but he has taken Bell Atlantic Yellow Pages with him and some three-four times I hear him talking on phone. One time I hear him say, "No, no, too expensive." Another time he says, "Fantasies definitely. But must be reputable." And "Yes, yes, elegant also. How many? We are only three here." Finally he says, "Okey-dokey, send three; seven p.m. sharp. Yes, yes, hot is good. Hotter is even better."

'Bang Bang' Billy hears last part and says, "What are you ordering? Sicilian pizza? Did you ask for pepperoni?"

And Uncle Prabhu says, "Yes, but not Sicilian, international pizza. Hot and spicy. The best."

"I hope they'll still be hot when they get here," 'Bang Bang' Billy says. "Hot and spicy, I like that very much."

"They'll be very hot," Uncle Prabhu is assuring him. "Piping hot, guaranteed."

"Elegant piping hot international spicy pizza I have never seen," I am confessing, and they both laugh. I am glad Uncle Prabhu again is one happy self. Soon he is sitting cross-legged on sofa singing evening raga and drumming on both knees. He is moving his neck in time to music and at same time swaying side to side. He could have been very fine vocalist or tabla player—I'm thinking only Elvis is having more flexible body parts.

Soon dark it gets. Billy and I have been drinking warm beer — just like in British times in Bombay. Then we follow with Johnny Walker, black label, neat, no soda, no ice. Uncle Prabhu is non-drinker; he is sticking with sweet mango *lassi*. At five p.m. Maj. Gen. Billy 'Bang Bang' Billimoria is volubly again explaining how he would have won Chinese-Indian war. Though he has done this many times before, no escape there is, Chinese Army and Uncle Prabhu and I are trapped. So is Chairman Mao, but he is not knowing it yet.

"War is like chess." Now it is Maj. Gen. Billy 'Bang Bang' Billimoria who is retelling. "Even though your opponent—in this case, the Chinese—may have white, you seize the initiative. Look what happens: Move 1, the Chinese mass forces on our borders. I send out aggressive, probing patrols; the trap is baited. Move 2, the Chinese are provoked, attack too soon in the Himalayas. The bait is taken! I order fierce resistance, blocking their advance. Move 3, the Chinese command, desperate for victory, throw an entire army corps into the battle. Check!

"I order my outnumbered Indian forces to retreat and regroup; the pursuing Chinese army enters the Himalayan mountain passes.

Then I, Maj. Gen. Billy Billimoria, not called 'Bang Bang' for nothing, direct massed artillery barrages at the snow-laden mountain slopes—boom!—burying the enemy in avalanches. Checkmate!"

I think what 'Bang Bang' Billy is seeing right now is one sad Chairman Mao suing for peace, and he himself heading for Beijing to accept Chinese surrender; what I am seeing on TV is only CNN showing us new millennium arriving in Paris. Eiffel Tower is exploding into fireworks. *Arre bap*! Here it is six p.m.

At seven p.m. CNN shows New Year's in London; Thames River absolutely on fire with fireworks. Same time we hear screeching brakes outside building; fearing accident, Billy and I rush to window, Uncle Prabhu slowly walking behind us. He seems little unsteady on two feet; has he perchance suffered minor stroke? Billy whispers that while Uncle was not looking he slipped some little scotch in the *lassi*. Not too much, fortunately, since about this time hot pizza dinner will soon be arriving.

Down on dark sidewalk we see one stout aged Indian lady shuffling into building; must all aged Indian women look like Aunty Usha? Very tired she is, this poor old sari woman dragging airline bag, and taxi driver is not helping. Instead he is complaining loudly about size of tip. He is also cursing while driving away, fortunately in Hindustani, so three bubbly females just stepping out of second cab cannot understand very anti-Indian things this Indian man is saying. Young blondes the three women are, prancing and primping and cracking many jokes at which they themselves are laughing. Where they are going, I wonder? Very jolly party it must be, wherever it is happening.

"Wonderful they look, Billy, even from this height," I tell him. As though he did not know.

"Very busty," Billy says. He has best eyesight, good for observing such details. "Low cut dresses—and did you see those high heels, Prabhu, eh? Like stilts! Damn!"

Uncle Prabhu, not answering, just smiling, busily rubs hands together. Just looking out of window must have made him feel cold, I think. Poor fellow, to be that old, and faced with so much beauty!

Next moment he disappears, rushing for apartment door. What he is hoping to see, standing by peephole, when elevator has solid metal enclosure?

Our elevator is very slow; for four-five minutes Uncle Prabhu is just standing, waiting waiting. Suddenly bell rings. Flinging door open, Uncle Prabhu is loudly yelling, "Surprise!" Then in very small voice I'm hearing him say, "Usha?"

"Don't just stand there, Prabhu" she says. "Take my bag."

"But—but—why back so early? Didn't you enjoy yourself?"

"How, Prabhu?" she says. "Would I be a loving sister, enjoying myself, knowing you'd be spending New Year's Eve alone?"

Alone? Obviously Aunty Usha is forgetting we also are here.

"You look very tired, Usha," Uncle Prabhu says. He is getting very fidgety, holding on to door, looking at departing elevator. "You should have stayed there for the full week."

"Usha Baby," 'Bang Bang' Billy says, "we've been missing you! Welcome home! But you've had a very long flight. Prabhu is right— why don't you go to your own apartment and rest? We can talk in the morning. New Year's Day! New century, new millennium even!"

All the while Uncle Prabhu to me is whispering, "Take her home! Take her home, quickly! *Jaldi, beta! Jaldi karo!*"

Very gently I am taking Aunty Usha by the arm, heeding Uncle Prabhu's urgent request and ushering her to her own doorstep. It is only few feet away, but it is taking long time, very long time, because Aunty is taking small small steps and stopping, then taking deep breaths before moving again. All this while I am listening for elevator door to open. If door opens and three stiletto-heel blondes come dancing out then I am in very big big trouble. It will be coincidence, but will she believe?

Finally we are at Aunty Usha's apartment door. Just before she goes in she says, "*Beta*, a strange thing happens while I am downstairs, waiting for the elevator. Three painted hussies come in and I hear one say they are looking for a mad Y2K party in 3B. 'Dearie,' I say, '3A and 3B both are my apartments, and if I found the three of you at a wild party at either place I would kill myself. Fortunately that won't be necessary, I say, since there's no party being held in 3B. No party at all. You simply have the wrong address and the wrong building.'"

While Aunty Usha stops for breath I am also breathing deeply. Very deeply I am breathing, because now I am asking myself how it is I did not guess that Aunty Usha's hussies were really Uncle Prabhu's hot and spicy international pizza?

"They were quite flustered, *beta*," Aunty Usha continues. "They said they'd been engaged by one Mr. A. F. Pereira in 3B. When I showed them our tenants' directory, that no Pereira at all is listed in this building, they finally went away."

She takes bag from my hands and pats me gently on my cheek. Very trusting she is, thanks be to God. "Happy New Year, *beta*, even though it's five hours too early," she says. "You can stop sweating now. I will see you in the morning. I hope those hussies finally got to the right place on time."

Much relieved I am, that she is still suspecting nothing. She turns away, enters her apartment, then turns back to face me. "About this A. F. Pereira in 3B," Aunty Usha says. "Could the A perhaps stand for 'Amul?' Is that possible, *beta*?"

Again and for long long time she is looking me in both eyes. I must now advise 'Bang Bang' Billy that Usha Baby can surely play grandmaster chess. She will also not be remembering me in her last will and testament any time soon, I don't think.

"Checkmate!" her eyes are saying.

Bonus Story

Dear J.C.

Plotinus, Plotinus, Livy, Umer, Mordecai & Associates
Career Builders and Public Relations Consultants
xvi-ixx via Massima, Caesarea

By special messenger

Januarius I

Dear J.C. (if we may address you so familiarly!),

Congratulations! Even though you are not now, and have never been, one of our clients, we at PPLUM Associates are pleased to inform you that we have, in violation of our own rules, unanimously nominated you to be our Incoming Client of the Incoming Year at the Papryus Invitational Membership level. This signal and unprecedented honor is being bestowed on you after reviewing the hundreds of highly complimentary and enthusiastic reports about your recent activities we have received from our scouts in the field, who, unbeknownst to you, have been following your footsteps first through Galilee, and more recently through Judea.

Enclosed you will find our Complimentary Welcome Package, consisting of three vital documents related to both your present and your future; read them carefully, because, as you well know, ab acto ad posse valet consecutio—*our lives do indeed travel, though not in a straight line, from what has been to what may be:*

I.   *Our recommendations regarding your C.V., as it now stands.*

II.   *Our thoughts on your proposed Mission State-ment*

III.   *Our analysis of your plan of action for the imme-diate future.*

My colleagues and I have reviewed with interest both the curriculum vitae our scouts put together as well as the platform on which they project you will run not just your forthcoming campaign, but, by extension, the rest of your life. Before I go into the details of our recommendations, let me tell you what our first impressions were: Your program, we are delighted to see, is ambitious; your self-confidence, boundless; your means, eheu, are decidedly limited considering the world-impacting goals you have set yourself. One of our associates, in fact, a lone holdout whose name I am not at liberty to reveal for reasons of confidentiality, asked pointedly, "If the world were ready for globalization, wouldn't we have had it already?" and followed it up with, "Who does he think he is?"

We here at PPLUM are aware that you are indeed descended from the Royal House of David, so in reporting his question to you verbatim our intention is not to undermine your confidence in yourself, but rather to prepare you ante factum *for the questions you will inevitably face when you go out into* mondo cane, *the dog-eat-dog world where hecklers abound! It is in a spirit of helpfulness, therefore, that we place before you the following analysis of the materials we have gathered about your program. Note that if our recommendations are carefully followed, they may well make your name a household word for generations to come.*

I.	**YOUR C.V.**	**OUR RECOMMENDATIONS**

Descended from Royal House of David   *Bingo!*

Born in stable, were denied room at inn   *No, no, and no! We suggest you kick it up a notch, and substitute 'log cabin' for stable, as birth in a log cabin provides better opportunities for future advancement. Also, avoid any mention of being turned away from an inn; it can suggest that your parents were mistaken for undocumented vagrants, whom even a mere innkeeper could turn away with impunity.*

We suggest you use this line instead: "Refused accommodations at the palace." Besides elevating the discourse to a higher social level, it can be interpreted to mean that the Tetrarch himself offered your parents lodgings at the palace, but they turned down the offer as being unsuited to their high status. Note how a simple substitution of just a few words can put a far more favorable spin on things!

Serenaded by chorus of Angels *Another nice touch, but consider changing 'chorus' to 'choir', since choirs tend to be better trained. On the other hand, since your claim can be considered rather presumptuous, it would be smart to reduce the number of singing angels to two, or at most three.*

Language Skills: Spoken Hebrew and Aramaic *Not quite enough for our times, when the Empire is expanding. Add Greek and Latin at a minimum, plus whatever language the barbarians speak in Caesar's new westernmost conquest, where he plans to found the city of Londrinium.*

II.   <u>Our Thoughts on Your Proposed Mission Statement</u>

Peace on Earth, Goodwill to All Men

Excellent in its brevity and highmindedness. However, we ran this up the signum polus *and not only would it not fly, it would not even flap. One male staffer, obviously speaking with the Parthian and other invasions in mind, said: "Sounds ultra-pacifist to me; has no stirring call to action." Our women staffers, on the other hand, expressed outrage, because they found the slogan to be too gender-specific, ignoring the need to extend goodwill to all women as well as to all men. We propose you change your slogan to something far more action-oriented, such as "Goodwill to all our friends, death to our enemies."* Mutatis mutandis, *your new slogan will not only meet the aforementioned objections, but will also bring the sword-spear-slingshot-and-shield military-industrial complex heavily down on your side.*

These considerations aside, a basic flaw in your slogan is that it is inherently a 'pro' statement, while experience and our own research has told us that, in public life, a leader must be strongly anti something to attract a strong and fanatical following. Advise us therefore a.s.a.p. as to what issues or public personae or race you wish to be publicly against; may we suggest Assyrians? That would be acceptable to most of our population, who remember the Assyrians coming down on our people like the wolf on the fold. We can also generate a list of other potential targets for you for a very reasonable fee.

III.   <u>**Our Analysis of Your List of Proposed Miracles**</u>

Since acta non verba—*actions rather than words—has long been one of our guiding principles here at PPLUM, we heartily endorse the idea that miracles should be part of your ministry. That said, our enthusiasm is tempered by the fact that we have put some of your proposed initiatives to the test and the results, to say the least, are not propitious.*

*<u>**Water into wine.**</u> Certainly a revolutionary concept, and one that turns on its head our long-standing practice of adding water to wine only when the guests are too soused to notice the difference. May we point out, however, with all due respect, that we tried this idea out in our in-house winery and it did not work? Still, because the potential profits might be astronomical, we intend to keep an open mind on this. If, therefore, you have devised a secret method of pulling this off and are prepared to share it with us, we can interface with Roman venture capitalists, Greek galley owners, and Cypriot vat manufacturers to mass produce your product and ship it eastward to where the sun rises, and westward beyond the Pillars of Hercules, as far as Londrinium. To comply with local regulations we may have to label the contents as "2 per cent" or even "non-grape", depending on the amount of waterization.*

May I insist, however, that you refrain from performing this miracle at any public function, such as a wedding, before our manufacturing and distribution plans are fully operative, to prevent our plans from being stolen by wily Lebanese middlemen.

Walking on Water: *Mind-boggling, if you can pull it off. To test your choice of locale, three weeks ago we sent a batch of interns to the Sea of Galilee to walk on the waters there. We regret to report that they have not yet returned, neither have they gone back to their parents' house, and they must therefore be presumed to have drowned. Naturally you will not be charged for their services unless they resurface within 30 days.*

Not wanting you to suffer a similar fate, we therefore suggest that you forget about that site and try walking on the Dead Sea instead. Absit omen, *nobody has yet died there from drowning.*

In re Walking on Water while Battling a Storm, *our Special Effects Department advises us that this can be done year round, but will be most effective if done during calm weather, when crowds of spectators can gather on the shore with no danger of being swept out to sea. However, the downside is that creating a storm in calm weather will involve the use of large numbers of heavy-duty wind-and-wave making machines, which of course we are prepared to develop on your behalf as soon as we get your AOK. Please advise therefore whether you would prefer to walk on small, medium-sized, or larger waves; equipment and manufacturing costs will vary considerably, as will demands on manpower. For storms above a given size, we may have to consider crowd-funding; for the very largest, we suggest forming a superPac. Please indicate your preference at your earliest.*

Raising the Dead. *We had to give up on the idea of testing this particular project as no member of our staff could be persuaded to become a corpse, even temporarily. Would you consider allowing us to conduct this experiment using either Medes or Persians or some other Gentiles instead? Their* *absence would not be noticed because i) they are here in such large numbers, besides which, ii) being foreigners, they all look alike and will not be missed.*

<u>*Reattaching Ear that has been cut off*</u>: *See comment* *above.*

<u>FINIS: Here ends your Complimentary Welcome Package</u>

Dear J.C.,

You have now come to the end of our introductory membership package, and we have no doubt that you have been impressed by the depth and thought that we have put into our recommendations, even at our Papyrus Invitational Membership Level. Consider, then, how beneficial our program can be to your future if you now upgrade your membership from Papyrus to more distinguished and elegant Premium Leather! You will then receive, not just the excellent type of report you have found in your current package, but also detailed monthly inputs and analyses from our Commercial, Legal, and Social Departments that will increase the profit factors in your favor while reducing all risk of catastrophic losses. More, these life-changing inputs will come to you not on papyrus, which can be easily misplaced or destroyed, but on specially cured leather, ready to be read over and over again, before being filed for future reference. Note that the format will also allow you to make your own detailed notes in the margins.

But that is not all. Would you like to know:

(i) *<u>which action you plan to take, or product you hope to create, is most likely to lead to world commercial success, at minimal cost to you?</u> Consult our **Commerce Specialists**. Hint: Not taming a tempest. It could just be wine! In time people might be drinking JC wine in the far corners of the earth.*

(ii)   *which corrective action you propose to take can in-volve you in escalating legal costs with no guarantee of success?* *Consult our* **Legal Specialists**. *Hint: While applying a whip to bare buttocks is s.o.p., overturning tables and scattering money all over the floor can be considered restraint of trade. There is wisdom in the saying,* Lucri bonus est odor ex re qualibet—*Money smells good no matter what the source. These individuals have the ear of the Pros-ecutor; at trial this could produce a verdict highly unfavorable to you, unless he washes his hands of the whole thing.*

(iii)   *which of your social contacts needs to be closely watched, and possibly even dumped?* *You will need to talk to our* **Director of Social Affairs**. *Hint: Alas, it could be Peter, who calls himself a fisherman, but is also known as Cephas, Symeon, and Simon Barjona. Livy believes he may just be suffering from a multiple personality complex, but Umer, Mordecai, and I take a more sinister view.* Latet anguis in herba—*a snake may be hiding in the grass, and our Social Director agrees. Ask yourself, J. C.: why does a man need three aliases? Either he is hiding from the law in three jurisdictions, or he has shacked up with various women and is hiding from his wife.*

Even with these few examples, you must have become convinced by now that we at PPLUM are accustomed to thinking outside both Pyramid and Colosseum. We urge you therefore to upgrade your membership to the Superior Leather Level right away. The normal rate is 30 denari a month, or 350 per annum, but we are offering you the specially reduced rate of 300 denari p.a., thus giving you five weeks of priceless reports at no charge! And there's more: an immediate positive response will bump you up even higher to Preferred Superior Leather Client Status, entitling you to receive either a Superdeluxe Leather Repository, or a specially designed amphora, inscribed with your initials, large enough to hold several years' worth of our reports. We have prefilled your acceptance form; all you need do is sign on the dotted line. So confident are we of your acceptance, that we have asked our messenger to wait.

Respectfully submitted, etc. etc.

About the Author

Victor Rangel-Ribeiro was born in Goa, India, in 1925, when it was still a Portuguese colony, but he moved to Bombay in British India to complete his university studies, before moving to the United States in 1956 and becoming an American citizen. Having outlived two empires, the Portuguese and the British, at age 91 he now claims to be one of a vanishing breed of pre-postcolonial writers: His earliest stories appeared in print in colonial Bombay in the 1940s; he is still writing today, often far into the night.

Rangel-Ribeiro's short fiction has appeared in such prestigious literary magazines as the *Iowa Review*, the *North American Review*, and *The Literary Review*, and also in his native India. His debut novel, *Tivolem*, set in Goa in 1933, won Milkweed's National Fiction Prize and was declared by Booklist to be one of the twenty best first novels of 1997-98. *Loving Ayesha*, a short story collection, was published by Harper Collins (India) in 2003. Both *Tivolem* and *Loving Ayesha* made that country's best seller list.

Rangel-Ribeiro writes with equal facility of life in colonial times in India, and life in the United States from the immigrant point of view. This explains why half of the stories in this book are based in India, spanning life in the 1930s, 1940s and 1950s, and the other half deal with the immigrant experience in the United States.

To the fourteen stories split equally between India and the United States, we have added a fifteenth. "Dear J. C." is set in a far earlier time, when the Roman Empire was the land of opportunity. In this story, an Israeli-Roman firm of ambitious career counsellors tries to lure a rising young prophet into joining their roster of clients.

Rangel-Ribeiro's interests include a life-long involvement in music. His music criticism appeared in the *New York Times* in the late 1950s. In the 1960s he ran a music antiquariat in New York City specializing in classical music. In 1977 he was appointed Music Director of the Beethoven Society in New York, and in three years steered that young organization to membership in the Lincoln Center for the Performing Arts. He has several books on music to his credit. He is currently working on a second novel, *The Fires of Gangapur*.

About the Artist

Although largely self-taught, the artist Mario de Miranda (1926-2011), quickly developed his own highly individual, quirky style. A social satirist, working solely with pen and ink, he soon became adept at capturing the foibles of both the rich and the poor. He joined the Illustrated Weekly of India in 1953, and his first assign-ments included illustrating stories by Victor that the magazine was publishing. Author and artist came together again in 2002, when Mario illustrated six of Victor's short stories; all six are reproduced here. By then, Mario had long become internationally known. Official recognition came in 2009 from Spain (Order of St. Isabela the Catholic), Portugal (Commander of the Order of Prince Henry the Navigator), France, and Japan; India awarded him the Padma Vibhushan, its second highest civilian award, posthumously in 2012.

Both Victor Rangel-Ribeiro and Mario de Miranda were born in colonial times, in what was then Portuguese India, Victor in Goa in 1925, Mario in Damaon, five hundred miles to the north, a year later; Goa figures strongly in their work. Victor claims they were not just life-long friends but also obliquely related, pointing out that Mario was his first cousin's husband's first cousin once removed, "perhaps forcibly".

Acknowledgments

"The Miscreant" first appeared in the *Iowa Review*; "Angel Wings" in the *North American Review*; earlier versions of both stories, along with "An Object of Singular Desire", formed part of my novel, *Tivolem*, published by Milkweed Editions in the USA in 1998 and in India the same year by Penguin. "Wooing Mr. Ram" appeared in *Dogwood*. The first two stories, along with earlier versions of "Moon Dance", "An Anna's Worth of Kindness", "How I Missed My Chance to Become a Real Porn Star", "Lonely Aging Chinese American New York Neighbor Lady", "Peter and the Ants", "The Specials of the Day", "Night Encounter", "Uncle Prabhu's Special Y2K Party", and "Loving Ayesha" were included in the collection by that name, published by Harper Collins in India in 2003, and now long out of print.

Praise in the US for Victor Rangel-Ribeiro's novel, Tivolem

"In the increasingly chic territory of Indian fiction marked by Arundhati Roy's poetic idiosyncrasy and Salman Rushdie's magic intellectualism, Rangel-Ribeiro anchors his debut novel in old-fashioned realism... *Tivolem* gently evokes the well-made fiction of an earlier age." —*The Philadelphia Inquirer,* Nov. 8, 1998.

"...a tale that luminously evokes life in that former Portuguese colony in India [Goa]... A story to be savored, and winner of the 1998 Milkweed Editions Fiction Prize."—*Kirkus Reviews,* May 15, 1998.

"Rangel-Ribeiro has set a vivid scene, with a colorful cast of characters, addressing personal and societal turmoil with insight and humor. The result, winner of Milkweed's annual prize for fiction, is highly recommended for all libraries." —*The Library Journal,* starred review, April 1, 1998.

"...a novel of perfect nostalgia, in a nicely evoked setting." —*Booklist,* April 15, 1998.

Praise overseas as well

"Humor and verbal virtuosity make *Tivolem* a truly engrossing read." —*Tribune,* Mumbai, Sept. 13, 1998.

"Where the past weaves into the present, the old into the new, a tale of a small village and its villagers, with all the colours of Goa, comes to life. —*The Statesman,* Delhi and Kolkatta, July 8, 1998.

"*Tivolem* comes alive with fine detail.... A nice pleasant read to lull you on a hammock beneath soughing palms and a gentle sea breeze.—*Outlook,* Mumbai, September 21, 1998.